The next morning, they left the van and set off on foot. They went by Tube from Old Street to Bank, and changed on to the Central Line for St Paul's. The concept of the Underground seemed not to worry the King or the wizard, but Brynjolf and Arvarodd didn't like the look of it at all.

'Must be the tombs of kings,' said Arvarodd. 'Look, there's a diagram or something up on the side.'

Brynjolf leant forward and studied the plan.

'I reckon you may be right,' he said, returning to his seat. 'I think there are several dynasties down here. Those coloured lines joining up the names must be family-trees. Funny names they've got, though. Look, there's the House of Kensington all buried together: South Kensington, West Kensington, High Street Kensington—'

'Kensington Olympia,' interrupted Arvarodd. 'They must have been a powerful dynasty.'

'Them and the Parks,' agreed Brynjolf. 'And the Actons away in the west. Hopelessly interbred, of course,' he added, looking at the numerous intersections of the coloured lines at Euston. 'No wonder they got delusions of grandeur.'

TOM HOLT

# Who's Afraid of Beowulf?

Futura

An Orbit Book

First published in Great Britain in 1988 by
Macmillan (London) Limited

This edition published in 1989 by
Futura Publications, a Division of
Macdonald & Co (Publishers) Ltd
London & Sydney

ISBN 0 7088 4258 5

Reproduced, printed and bound in Great Britain by
Hazell Watson & Viney Limited
Member of BPCC Limited
Aylesbury, Bucks, England

Futura Publications
A Division of
Macdonald & Co (Publishers) Ltd
66–73 Shoe Lane
London EC4P 4AB
A member of Maxwell Pergamon Publishing Corporation plc

Acknowledgements. The author would like to thank
Jim Henderson and Iain Carmichael for their kind
assistance.

For K.N.F.

# 1

SOMEONE HAD WRITTEN 'godforsaken' between 'Welcome to' and 'Caithness' on the road sign. When he saw the emendation, the surveyor almost smiled.

'Tourists, I expect,' said the archaeologist disapprovingly. She had decided that the Highlands were authentic and good; therefore, any malice towards them must have proceeded from uncomprehending outsiders.

'I hope not,' yawned the surveyor, lighting a cigarette and changing gear. 'I was taking it as evidence that there's one native of these parts who can read and write.' He paused, waiting for a laugh or an 'I know what you mean'. Neither was forthcoming. 'Though there's no reason why any of them should. After all, you don't need to be able to read if you make your living robbing and killing passing travellers, which has always been the staple industry around here.'

The archaeologist looked away. He was off again. An irritating man, she felt.

'Which explains the ingrained poverty of the region,' the surveyor went on remorselessly, 'because only a few bloody fools ever used to come travelling up here. Until recently, of course. Recently, you've had your coachloads of tourists. Theme holidays for heavy sleepers. Anyway, these days the locals don't even bother killing the travellers; they just sell them tartan key-fobs. And they all take the *FT*, to keep track of currency fluctuations.'

The archaeologist had had enough of her companion's

diatribe, which had started before the car had got clear of Lairg. Rather ostentatiously she fanned away the cigarette smoke and expressed the opinion that it was all lovely. 'I think it's got a sort of—'

The surveyor made a peculiar noise. 'Listen,' he said, 'I was born and bred in bonnie bloody Caithness, and the only thing it's produced in a thousand years is starving people.' He'd read that in a Scottish Nationalist manifesto, but it sounded clever. 'Five years ago, the inhabitants of Rolfsness pleaded with the Water Authority to turn the wretched place into a reservoir so that they could be compensated and move to Glasgow. But it's too remote even for that. The Army won't have it for a firing range, and the CEGB got lost trying to find it.'

He was getting nicely into his stride now, despite the lukewarm response. The archaeologist managed to interrupt him just in time.

'That reminds me,' she said, tearing her eyes away from a breathtakingly lovely prospect of cloud-topped mountains, 'I wanted to ask you, since you were born here. Are there any old traditions or folk-tales about Rolfsness?'

'Folk-tales.' The surveyor frowned, as if deep in thought. 'Well, there's an old superstition among the shepherds and crofters – but you know what they're like.'

'Go on.' The archaeologist felt a tremor of excitement.

'Well, they *say* that every year on the anniversary of the battle of Culloden – you know about the battle of Culloden?'

'Yes, yes, of course.'

'They *say* that every year, at about noon, the bus from Wick to Melvich stops here for three minutes where the old gibbet used to be. But nobody's ever claimed to have seen it for themselves.'

Dead silence. The surveyor shook his head sadly. Americans, he reflected, have no sense of humour.

'Otherwise, apart from Bonnie Prince Charlie hiding from Butcher Cumberland's men in what is now the bus shelter, where Montrose had been betrayed to the Covenanters, no. Totally unremarkable place. Now, if there was a story that Montrose *wasn't* betrayed to the Covenanters here, that would be a bit out of the ordinary.'

'I see.' The archaeologist sniffed. She should have known better than to ask. 'So nothing about giants or fairies or the Wee Folk?'

'Round here,' said the surveyor grimly, 'the Wee Folk means Japanese businessmen looking for sites for computer factories. Not that they ever build any, of course. Have you ever tasted Japanese whisky? All the hotels up here sell it now. Personally, I prefer it to the local stuff.'

The archaeologist gave up in despair, and they drove on in silence for a while. Then, as they turned a sharp corner on the side of a towering hill, the archaeologist suddenly asked the surveyor to stop the car.

'What is it?' said the surveyor, glancing anxiously in his rear-view mirror, but the archaeologist said nothing. She had no words to spare for such an insensitive person at the moment when she caught her first glimpse of the sea that washes the flat top of the British mainland, and, grey and soft-edged as any dream-kingdom should be, the faint outline of Orkney. On an impulse, she opened the car door and scrambled up to the top of a rocky outcrop.

Here, then, was the earldom of her mind, her true habitation. She felt as Orestes must have done when, coming secretly out of exile, he looked for the first time upon Argos, the land he had been born to rule. That was the sea of her Cambridge dreams, those were the islands she had first pictured for herself sitting on the front porch in Setauket, Long Island, with her treasured copy of the *Orkney-men's Saga* open on her knee. As a promised land it had been to her as she trod the weary road of professional scholarship, laying down her harp beside the waters of Cam, marching more than seven times round the bookshops of St Andrews. As she gazed out over the sea, called 'whale-road' and 'world-serpent', she could almost see the blue sails of the Orkney Vikings, the dragon-prows of Ragnar Lothbrok and Erik Bloodaxe, sweeping across their great grey highway to give battle

3

to Bothvar Bjarki or Arvarodd in the *vik* at Tongue.

'On a clear day,' said the surveyor behind her, 'you can just make out the Old Man of Hoy from here. Why you should want to is beyond me entirely.'

'I think it's wonderful,' said the archaeologist softly.

'I think it's perishing cold. Can we get on now?'

They got back into the van.

'Tell me again what it is you've found,' said the archaeologist briskly.

'Well,' said the surveyor, leaning back with one hand on the bottom of the steering-wheel, 'we were taking readings, and I'd just sent the Land-Rover up ahead when it fell clean through this small mound. Right up to its axles, useless bloody thing, we had to use the Transit to pull it out again. Anyway, we got it out and when we looked down the hole it had made we saw this chamber underground, all shored up with pit props. I thought it was an Anderson shelter or something left over from the war, but the lads all said no, ten to one it was a Viking ship-burial.'

'*They* said that?'

'They all work for the Tourist Board over the summer. So we put a tarpaulin over it and sent for your mob.'

'Didn't you want to look for yourselves?'

The surveyor laughed. 'You must be kidding. Roof might collapse or something. Besides, you aren't supposed to touch anything, are you, until the experts arrive. Or is that murders?'

The archaeologist smiled. 'You did right,' she said.

'The lads get paid by the hour,' said the surveyor, 'and I'm on bonus for being in this wilderness. Besides, if it does turn out to be an ancient monument, the project will be cancelled, and we can all go home with money in lieu. Look, there it is.'

He pulled over on to the verge, and they picked their way over the uneven ground to the site. The archaeologist found that she was faced with a long leaf-shaped mound about fifty to sixty yards long, pointing due north. Under her woolly hat her hairs were beginning to rise, and she broke into a trot, her moon-boots squelching in the

4

saturated peat. The sheer size of it made her heart beat faster. If there really was a ship down there, and if anything at all was left of it, this was going to make the *Mary Rose* look like a pedalo.

The survey team were staring at her over their cans of lager, but she took no notice. As she struggled with the obdurate ropes that held the tarpaulin in place, an old man in a raincoat apparently moulded on to his body got up hurriedly and started to wave his arms at her. To her joy, the archaeologist realised that he was a Highlander, and that the gist of his broken English was that she was on no account to open up the mound. She beamed at him (for surely this was some survival of the ancestral terror of waking up the sleepers under the howe) and said, 'Pardon me?' Her pleasure was somewhat diminished when the surveyor explained to her that what the old fool meant was that he'd spent half the morning nailing the tarpaulin down in the teeth of a gale, and that if she insisted on taking it off she could bloody well put it back herself.

The tarpaulin was thrown back, and the archaeologist nerved herself to look inside and seek her destiny. She had always felt that one day she would make a great discovery, something which would join her with Carnavon, Carter, Evans and Schliemann in the gallery of immortals. On the rare occasions when archaeology had lost its grip on her imagination – seemingly endless afternoon spent up to her knees in mud in some miserable Dartmoor hut-circle – she had consoled herself by trying to compose a deathless line, something which would be remembered beside 'I have looked upon the face of Agamemnon'. Although so far in her career she had found, apart from enough potsherds to line the bottom of every flowerpot in the world, nothing more prestigious than a Tudor belt-buckle, she knew that one day she, Hildy Frederiksen, would join that select band of immortals who have been fortunate enough to be the first men and women of the modern age to set eyes upon the heirlooms of the human race. She knelt down and with trembling fingers checked the contents of her organiser bag: camera (with film in it), notebook, pencil,

5

small brush, flashlight (free with ten Esso tokens) and small plastic bags for samples.

In the even, what she actually said when the beam of her flashlight licked over the contents of the mound was 'Jesus!' but in the circumstances nobody could have blamed her for that. What she saw was the prow of a ship – a long clinker-built ship of a unique and unmistakable kind. The timbers were coal-black and glistening with moisture, but the thing actually seemed to be intact. As the blood pounded in her ears she thanked God for the preservative powers of peat-bog tannin, took a deep breath, and plunged into the hole like a small, learned terrier.

The chamber *was* intact; so much so, in fact, that the possibility of its collapsing never entered into her mind. The sides were propped with massive beams – oak, at a guess – which vaulted high overhead, while the chamber had been dug a considerable depth into the ground. Under her feet the earth was hard, as if it had been stamped flat into a floor. The ship itself reclined at ease on a stout trestle, as if it was already taking its rightful place in a purpose-built gallery at the maritime museum at Greenwich. It was an indescribably beautiful thing, with the perfection of line and form that only something designed to be functional can have, lean and graceful and infinitely menacing, like a man-eating swan. Every feature she could have hoped to find in an archetypal Viking longship was present – this in itself was remarkable, since none of the ships so far discovered looked anything like the authoritative reconstructions in the *Journal of Scandinavian Studies* – from the painted shields beside each of the thirty oar-holes on either side of the ship to the great dragon figurehead, carved with a deep confident design of gripping beasts and interwoven snakes. Although it was strictly against the rules, she could not help reaching out, almost but not quite like Adam in the painting, and tracing with the tip of her left forefinger the line of the surrealistic pattern.

Like a child who has woken to find itself inexplicably

6

inside a confectioner's warehouse, she walked slowly round the great ship, noting the various features of it as if with an inventory. Suddenly the light of her flashlight was thrown back by a sparkle of gold: inlaid runes running back from the prow, glowing bright as neon. She spelt them out, like a child learning its alphabet; Naglfar, the ship of nails, the ferry of the dead. It was so utterly perfect that for a moment she could not bear to look, in case her light fell on an outboard motor bolted to the stern, or a slogan draped across the mast advertising Carlsberg lager.

She touched it again, and the damp sticky feel of the tannin reassured her. Turn the Circus Maximus into a carpark, she said to herself, and wrap fish in the First Folio; preserve only this. As if in a dream, she put her foot on the first rung of a richly carved ladder that rested against the side of the ship.

At the top of the ladder was a small platform, with steps leading down into the hold. She stood for a moment unable to move, for the belly of the ship was piled high with the most extraordinary things, jumbled up together as if History was holding a garage sale. Gold and silver, fabrics, armour and weapons, like the aftermath of an earthquake at a museum. She rubbed her eyes and stared. Under the truncated mast, she could see twelve full sets of armour lying wrapped in fur cloaks, perfectly preserved. No, she was wrong. They were human bodies.

Then the flashlight went out.

The human heart is a volatile thing. A second or so before, Hildy I-Have-Looked-Upon-The-Face-Of Frederiksen had been thanking Providence that she alone had been granted the privilege of being the first living person in twelve hundred years to set foot on the planks of the longship Naglfar. Now, however, it occurred to her as she stood motionless in the complete silence and utter darkness that it would have been quite nice to have had someone there to share the moment with her, preferably someone with a reliable flashlight. She reminded herself sternly that archaeology is a science, that scientists are creatures of logic and reason, that she was a scientist, therefore she was not in the least afraid of the dark. However, being afraid seemed at that particular moment the most logical thing in the world, the reason why fear circuits had been planted in the human brain in the first place. So deathly was the silence that for a moment she took the sound of her own breathing for the snoring of the twelve dead Vikings lying just a few yards away from her under the mast. She tried to move, but could not; her muscles received the command from her brain and replied that they had never heard anything so absurd in their lives. She reflected that burglars must feel like this all the time, but the thought was little consolation.

As suddenly as it had gone out, the flashlight came back on again – the ways of petrol-station flashlights pass all understanding – and Hildy decided that, although it was really nice inside the chamber, it was probably even nicer outside it. As she turned away towards the ladder, she felt something under her foot and without thinking stooped and picked it up. It felt very cold in her hand, and was heavy, like a pistol. She stopped for a moment and looked at it. In her hand was a golden brooch inlaid with enamel and garnets, in the shape of a flying dragon. She half-expected it to move suddenly, like an injured bird picked up in the garden. The beam of the flashlight danced on interlocking patterns and spirals, and she felt dizzy. She knew perfectly well that she ought not to touch this thing, let alone thrust it deep into her pocket, and equally well that no power on earth could stop her doing it. Then she imagined another noise in the chamber and, with the brooch in her pocket, she scurried down the ladder and out of the mound like a rabbit with a ferret the size of a Tube train after it.

As the top of her hat emerged into the light, the surveyor put his copy of *Custom Car* back in his pocket and asked: 'Are you all right, then?'

'Of course I am,' Hildy stammered. She was shaking, and sweat had turned her fringe into little black spikes, like the horns of a stag-beetle. 'Why shouldn't I be?'

8

'You were down there an awful long time,' said the surveyor. It had just occurred to him that more portable things than ships are sometimes found in ancient mounds.

'Very interesting,' Hildy said. 'I wish I could be sure it was authentic.'

The surveyor was staring at something sticking out of the pocket of her paddock jacket. She put her hand over it and hitched her lips into a smile.

'So there's nothing like – well, artefacts or anything down there?' asked the surveyor, rather too casually. Hildy tightened her grip round the neck of the brooch.

'Could be,' she mumbled. 'If I'd been brave enough to look. But the roof looks like it might collapse at any minute, so I came out again.'

'The roof?'

'Perilous, if you ask me. I think I heard it moving.'

The surveyor's face seemed to fall. 'Perhaps we should try to shore it up,' he suggested. 'I could go in and have a look. Of course, you needn't go in.'

Hildy nodded vigorously. 'Go ahead,' she said. 'Where's the nearest phone, by the way, in case we have to call for help?'

As she expected, the surveyor didn't like the sound of that. 'On the other hand,' he said, 'it's a job for the experts.'

'True.'

'Best leave well alone.'

Hildy nodded.

It had started to rain, and the survey team were making chorus noises. 'What I'd better do,' the surveyor said, 'since we can't do anything more for the present, is send the lads home and take you back to Lairg. You lot,' he shouted to the survey team, 'get that hole covered up.'

The old man in the raincoat said something authentic, but they ignored him and set about replacing the tarpaulin. 'We'd better wait till they're on their way,' whispered the surveyor. 'Otherwise – well, they might be tempted to see if there was anything of value down there.'

'Surely not?'

Neither Hildy nor the surveyor had much to say on the

way back to Lairg. Hildy was thinking of a passage from *Beowulf* which she had had to do as a prepared translation during her first year at New York State, all about a man who stole a rich treasure from a hoard he found in a burial-mound, and woke a sleeping fire-drake in the process. She could remember it vividly, almost word for word, and it had had a decidedly unhappy ending.

The surveyor bundled her out of the car at Lairg and drove away rather quickly, which made Hildy feel somewhat suspicious. So she telephoned the police at Melvich and explained the situation to them slowly and lucidly. Once they had been made to understand that she was not mad or drunk they sounded very enthusiastic about the prospect of guarding buried treasure and promised to send the patrol car out as soon as it came back from finding Annie Erskine's cat. Feeling easier in her mind, Hildy went into the hotel bar and ordered a double orange juice with ice. As she drank it, she drew out the brooch and looked round to see if anyone was watching. But the barman had gone back to the Australian soaps in the television room, and she was alone.

The brooch was an exquisite example of its kind, the finest that Hildy had ever seen. The form was as simple as the decoration was complex, and it reminded her of something she had seen recently in quite another context. Slowly, the magnitude of her discovery and its attendant excitement began to return to her, and as soon as she had finished her drink she left the bar, reversed the charges to the Department of Archaeology, and demanded to speak to the Director *personally*.

'George?' she said calmly (he had always been Professor Wood to anyone under the rank of senior lecturer, but *he* had never found so much as a row-boat). 'It's Hildy Frederiksen here – yes, that's right – and I'm calling from Lairg. L-A-I-R-G.' He was being vague again, she noticed, an affectation he was much given to, especially after lunch. 'I'm just back from a first inspection of that mound site at Rolfsness. George, you're not going to believe this, but. . . .'

As she spoke, her hand crept of its own accord into her pocket and closed around the flying dragon. Something seemed to tell her that on no account ought she to keep this extraordinarily beautiful and dangerous thing for herself, but that nevertheless that was what she was going to do, fire-drake or no fire-drake.

In the mound, it was dark and silent once again. For the past twelve hundred years, ever since the last turf had been laid over the trellis of oak-trunks and the horsemen had ridden away to the waiting ships, nothing had moved in the chamber, not so much as a mole or a worm. But now there was something missing that should have been there, and just as one tiny stone removed from an arch makes the whole structure unsound, so the peace of the chamber had been disturbed. Something moved in the darkness, and moved again, with the restlessness that attends on the last few moments before waking.

'For crying out loud,' said a voice, faint and drowsy in the darkness, 'there's some of us trying to sleep.'

The silence had been broken, irrecoverably, like a pane of glass. 'You what?' said another voice.

'I said there's people trying to sleep,' said the first voice. 'Shut it, will you?'

'You shut up,' replied the second voice. 'You're the one making all the noise.'

'Do you two mind?' A third voice, deep and powerful, and the structure of beams seemed to vibrate to its resonance. '"Quiet as the grave," they say. Some hope.'

'Sorry,' said the first two voices. The silence tried to return, as the retreating tide tries to claw its way back up the beach.

'I told you, didn't I?' continued the third voice after a while. 'I warned you not to eat that cheese, but would you listen? If you can't sleep, then be quiet.'

There was a sound of movement, metal scraping on metal, as if men in armour were turning in their sleep and groaning. 'It's no good,' said the third voice, 'you've done it now.'

Somewhere in the gloom there was a high-pitched squeaking sound, like a bat high up in the rafters of a barn. It might conceivably have been a human voice, if a man could ever grow so incredibly old. After the sound had died away, like water draining into sand, there was absolute quiet; but an uneasy, tense quiet. The mound was awake.

'The wizard says try counting sheep,' said the second voice.

'I heard him myself,' said the third voice. 'Bugger counting sheep. I've counted enough sheep since I've been down here to clothe the Frankish Empire. Oh, the Hel with it. Somebody open a window.'

There was a grating sound, and a creaking of long-relaxed timber. 'Sod it,' said the first voice, 'some clown's moved the ladder.'

The old man grinned, displaying both his yellow teeth, and cut the final cord of the tarpaulin. Two of his fellows pulled the cover free, while the other members of the survey team, who had come back in the expectation of wealth, stood by with dustbin liners. In about fifteen minutes, they were all going to be rich.

'Can you see anything, Dougal?' someone asked. The old man grunted and wormed his way into the hole. A moment later, he slid out backwards and started to run like a hare. The survey team watched him in amazement, then turned round and stared at the mouth of the hole. A helmeted head had appeared out of the darkness, with a gauntleted hand in front of its eyes to protect them from the light.

'All right,' it said irritably, 'which one of you jokers moved our ladder?'

Hildy waited and waited, but no one came. She tried to pass the time by rereading her favourite sagas, but even their familiar glories failed to hold her attention. For in her mind's eye, as she read, the old images and mental pictures, which had been developed in the distant and unheroic town of Setauket, were all displaced and usurped by new, rather more accurate visions. For example, she had always pictured the lonely hall on the fells where Gunnar of Hlidarend, the archetypal hero of saga literature, had made his last stand as being the disused shed on the vacant lot down by the tracks, so that by implication Mord Valgardsson had led the murderers out of the drugstore on the corner of Constitution Street, where presumably they had stiffened their resolve for their bloody deed with a last ice-cream soda. Sigmund and Sinfjotli had been chained to the log that was the felled apple tree in her own back yard, and there the wolf who was really the shape-changer king had come in the blue night and bitten off Sigmund's hand. Thus was maintained the link between the Elder Days and her own childhood; but the sight of the ship and the heaped gold had broken the link. She had seen with her own eyes a real live dead Viking, who had never been anywhere near Setauket and was therefore rather more exciting and rather less safe. Long Island Vikings were different; they had stopped at the front door, and never dared go into the house. But the Caithness variety seemed rather more pervasive. They were all around her, even under the bed – in the shape of the brooch in her suitcase.

Hildy tried her best not to unpack it from under the shirts and sweatshirts and hold it up to the light, but she was only flesh and blood. It seemed to glow in her hands, to move not with the beatings of her pounding heart but with a movement of its own, as if it were some thing of power. She made an attempt to study it professionally, to see if that would dispel its glamour; undoubted Swedish influences, garnets probably from India but cut in Denmark, yet the main work was in the classical Norwegian style and the runes were those of the futharc of Orkney. She stopped, and frowned. She had not noticed the runes before; but the keen light of the reading-lamp seemed to flow into them, like water into a channel when a dam is opened, so that they stood out tiny but unmistakable on the main curve of the central spiral of the decoration.

Runes. For some reason her heart had stopped beating.

Perhaps it was some magic in those extraordinary letters, first created at a time when any writing was by definition magical, a secret mark on silent metal that could communicate without speech to the eyes of a wise lore-master. Runes cannot help being magical, even if what they spell out is commonplace; a rune cut on the lintel will keep the sleepless ghosts from riding on the roof, or put a curse on the house that curdles milk and makes all the fires suddenly go out. Runes were also spells of attraction; to learn the runes, the god Odin had made himself a human sacrifice at his own altar, and ever since they had had a power to command. For all she knew, it was their command that had drawn her, by way of New York State and Cambridge, across the grey sea all the way from Setauket to be the improbable heroine of some last quest.

The strange wonder of the thing did not altogether fade or wither as it lay in her hands: the runes were still runes, and the brooch was still incredible. A Viking brooch in a museum or under the fluorescent tubes of the laboratory of the Department of Archaeology was resentfully tame, like a caged lion, and its voice was silent. Outside on the cold hill the wild lion roared, fascinating and dangerous, while in the incongruous setting of a hotel bedroom it was like – well, like a wild lion in a hotel bedroom, where no pets or animals of any description are in any circumstances permitted.

Rationalised, what that meant was that she was feeling guilty about having stolen it, which was effectively what she had done, something which no archaeologist, however debased, would ever conceive of doing. So why, she asked her suitcase, had she done it?

'I must put it back,' she said aloud.

The only vehicle for hire in Lairg was a large minibus, by all appearances coeval with the longship Naglfar and about as practical for winding Scottish roads. But Hildy was in no position to be choosy, and she set off with an Ordnance Survey map open on the seat beside her, to drive to Rolfsness and put the brooch back in the mound before the team from St Andrews got there. As the deliberately obstructive road meandered its way through the grey hills, she could feel her resolve crumbling like an ancient parchment; the wild animal commanded her to return it to its natural habitat, not to put it back where middle-aged men with careers would come to find it and make it turn the treadmill of some thesis or scholarly paper.

She stopped the van and took it out once more. The dragon's expression had not changed; his garnet eyes were still red and hot as iron on the anvil; his lips still curved, in accordance with the demands of symmetry and form, in the same half-smile of intolerant mockery. She was suddenly aware that blood had been spilt over the possession of this extraordinary thing, and convinced that blood might well be shed for it again.

A loud hooting behind her, and plainly audible oaths, not in Old High Norse but modern Scots, woke her from her self-induced hypnosis. She rammed the van into first gear and drove on to the verge, letting the council lorry pass. Now she felt extremely foolish, and the voice in the runes fell silent, leaving her to her embarrassment. Listening to dragon brooches, said another, rather more familiar voice in her head, is only one step away from talking to dragons, for which they take you to a place where people are very kind and understanding, and where eventually the dragons start talking back. She bundled the brooch back into her pocket and took off the handbrake.

It was nearly dark when she reached Rolfsness, but the new, sensible Hildy Frederiksen defied nightfall as she defied all the other works of sorcery. She parked the bus under a lonely rowan tree and trotted swiftly over to the mound. There was no tarpaulin over the hole and no sign of the police, and her archaeologist's instinct returned, all the stronger for having been challenged. A terrible fear that the mound had been plundered while her attention was distracted struck her, and she started to blame herself. Why, for a start, had she left the mound in the first place, like a lamb among wolves, unguarded against the return of those unsavoury contractors' men? She fumbled for her flashlight and dropped it; the back came off and all the batteries were spilt into the short wiry grass. Her fingers were unruly as she tried to reassemble it, for clearly everything she tried to do today was fated to come to no good. When the wretched thing was mended, she advanced like an apprentice lion-tamer on the hole in the side of the mound, afraid now not of what she might see but of what she might not. With a deep breath that seemed to fill not only her lungs but also her pockets and the very lining of her jacket she poked one toe into the mouth of the hole, as if it were a hot bath she was testing. Something seemed to move inside.

'Now what is it?' demanded a voice from under the earth.

So she had disturbed the plunderers at their work! Suddenly her small familiar body was filled with cold and unreasonable courage, for here was a chance to redeem herself in the eyes of Archaeology by falling in battle with tomb-robbers and unlicensed dealers in antiquities.

'OK,' she said between clenched teeth, 'you'd better come out now. We have this whole area surrounded.'

There was a clanking noise, as of something very heavy moving, and somebody said: 'Why don't you look where you're putting your great feet?' Then a ray of the setting sun fell suddenly on red gold and blue steel, and a man stood silhouetted against the sky on the edge of the mound.

He was a little over six feet tall, clad in gilded chainmail armour. His face was half-covered by the grotesque mask that formed the visor of his shining helmet, while around his bear-like shoulders was a thick grey fur cloak, fastened at the neck by a brooch in the shape of two gripping beasts. In his right hand was a hand-and-a-half sword whose pommel blazed with garnets, like the lights of distant watch-fires.

'Who the hell are you?' said the man from the mound.

Hildy did not answer, for she could not remember. The man clapped his gauntleted hands, whereupon a procession of twelve men emerged from the mound. Nine of them were similarly armed and masked, and on their arms they carried kite-shaped shields that seemed to burn in the setting sun. Of the other three, one was small and stooping, dressed in a long white robe that blurred the outlines of his body like low cloud over a hillside, but his face was covered by a hood of cat skins and he leant on a staff cut from a single walrus tusk, carved into the shape of a serpent. The second of the three was a huge man, bigger than any human being Hildy had ever seen before, and he was dressed in the pelt of a long-haired bear. On his shoulder he carried a great halberd, whose blade was as long as its tree-like shaft. The third was shorter than the rest of the armed men but still tall, slim and quick-moving like a dancer. He wore no armour, but only a doublet of purple and dark blue hose. Tucked under his arm was a gilded harp, while over his right shoulder was a longbow of ash-wood and a quiver of green-flighted arrows.

They looked around them, shading their eyes even against the red warmth of the setting sun, as if any light was unbearable to them. One of the armed men, who was carrying a spear with a banner of cloth bound to its shaft, turned to the others and pushed his helmet back, revealing a face at once young and old, with soft brown eyes under stern brows.

'Well,' he said. 'Here we are again. So how long do you reckon we've been down there?'

'No idea,' said the man next to him, who carried a silver horn on a woven baldrick. 'Ask the wizard. He'll know.'

The standard-bearer repeated his question, slowly and loudly, to the small stooping man, who made a noise through the cat skins like a rusty hinge.

'He says twelve hundred years, give or take,' said the standard-bearer. No one seemed in the least surprised (except Hildy, of course, and she was not as surprised as she would have expected to be). The horn-bearer cast his eyes slowly round the encircling hills, inexpressibly majestic in the light glow of the sunset.

'Twelve hundred years,' he said thoughtfully. 'Well, if

17

that's true, it hasn't changed a bit, not in the slightest.' He looked round again. 'Pity, really,' he added. 'Miserable place, Caithness.'

Hildy suddenly remembered that she had to breathe sooner or later or else she would die, and it would be a shame to die before she had found out whether the unbelievable explanation for this spectacle, which was nevertheless the only possible explanation, was correct.

'Excuse me,' she said in a tiny voice, 'but are you people for real?' The words seemed to flop out of her mouth, like exhausted salmon who have finally given up on a waterfall.

'Good question,' replied the leader of the men. 'What about you?'

Hildy wanted to say 'I'm not sure', but she realised that the man was being sarcastic, which was the last thing she expected. 'I'm Hildy Frederiksen,' she mumbled, aware that in all this vastness and mystery that one small fact could have little significance. Still, she wanted it put on record before it was wiped out of her mind.

'Well, now,' said the leader, still sarcastic but with a hint of sympathy in his voice, 'you shouldn't have told me that, should you? After all, when strangers meet by night on the fells, they should not disclose their names, nor the names of their fathers, until they have tested each other's heart with shrewd enquiry.' Then his face seemed to relax a little behind the fixed scowl of his visor. 'Don't ask me why, mind. It's just the rule.'

But Hildy said nothing. The other men from the mound were staring at her, and for the first time she felt afraid.

'Damned silly rule if you ask me,' said the leader, as if he sensed her fear. 'The hours I've wasted asking gnomic questions when I could have been doing something else. Is this place still called Rolfsness?'

Hildy nodded.

'Then, allow me to introduce myself. I am Rolf. My name is King Hrolf Ketilsson, called the Earthstar, the son of Ketil Trout, the son of Eyjolf Kjartan's Bane, the son of Killer-Hrapp of Hedeby, the son of the god Odin. I have

18

been asleep in the howe for – how long have I been asleep in the howe, somebody?'

'Twelve hundred years,' said the horn-bearer.

'Thank you. Twelve hundred years, waiting for the day when I must return to save my kingdom of Caithness from danger, from the greatest danger that has ever or will ever threaten it or its people, according to the vow that I made before the great battle of Melvich, when I slew the host of Geirrodsgarth and cast down the power of Nithspél. These are my thanes and housecarls.'

With a sweeping movement of his hand, he lifted his helmet over his head, revealing a magnificent mane of jet-black hair and two startlingly blue eyes. Hildy felt her knees give way, as if someone had kicked them from behind, and she knelt before him, bowing her head to the ground. When she dared to look up, she saw the last ray of the setting sun sparkling triumphantly on the hilt of the King's great sword as, apparently from nowhere, a fully grown golden eagle swooped down out of the sky and perched on his gloved fist, flapping its enormous wings.

# 2

'WILL SOMEONE', said the King, 'get this bird off me?'

The last ray of the sun faded as the standard-bearer made nervous shooing gestures with his hands. The bird shifted from one claw to the other, but made no sign of being prepared to leave. The man in the bear-skin tried prodding it gently with a huge forefinger, but it bit him and he backed away. In a sudden access of daring, Hildy rose to her feet and clapped her hands. At once the eagle flapped its wings, making a sound like a whole theatre full of people applauding at once, and soared off into the sky. It circled slowly three times and disappeared.

'They do that,' said the King, rubbing his wrist vigorously to restore the circulation. 'Comes of me being a king, I suppose.'

'I'm starving,' said the horn-bearer. Several voices told him to be quiet. 'But I am. I haven't had anything to eat for twelve hundred years.'

A babble of voices broke out, and rose quickly in a sustained crescendo. 'Ignore them,' said the King softly to Hildy. 'Sometimes they're like a lot of old women.'

Laying aside his helmet on the grass, he took Hildy's arm, and much to her own surprise she neither winced nor shrank back. He led her aside for a few paces and settled himself comfortably on a small boulder.

'Well, now,' he said, fixing her with his bright eyes. 'So what's been happening in the world while we've been asleep?'

Hildy looked back at the Champions. They seemed to be discussing something of extreme importance, and from what she could make out it was mainly to do with whose job it should have been to pack the food. She sat down beside the King.

'It's a long story,' she said.

'It would be, wouldn't it?' he replied, smiling. There was something about his smile that made her feel safe, as if she was under the protection of some great but homely power. She sat in silence for a while, gathering her thoughts. Then she told him.

When she had finished, she looked up. The men were still arguing; they seemed to have narrowed the responsibility down to either the standard-bearer or the horn-bearer, both of whom were protesting their innocence loudly and simultaneously.

'That's it, basically,' Hildy said.

'That's it, is it? Twelve hundred years of history? The achievements of men? Men die, cattle die, only glorious deeds live for ever?'

'That's it, yes.'

The King shrugged his shoulders, and twelve hundred years of history seemed to slide down his arms and melt into the peat. 'But you're sure you haven't left anything out?'

Hildy shuddered slightly. 'Lots,' she said.

The King nodded. 'Yes, of course,' he said, 'but I mean something really important.'

'Like what?'

'I don't know, do I?' He frowned. 'No, the hell with that. If it was there, you couldn't have left it out.' He stopped frowning, and looked over his shoulder at the bickering champions. 'Among the Viking nations,' he said wistfully, 'the model hero is regarded as being brave, loyal, cheerful and laconic. Three out of four isn't bad, I suppose. So who are you, Hildy Frederik's-daughter?'

'Frederik*sen*,' said Hildy automatically. 'Oh, I forgot. We did away with *-son* and *-daughter* centuries ago.'

'Quite right, too,' said the King. 'Go on.'

21

'I'm an archaeologist,' said Hildy. 'I dig up the past.'

The King raised an eyebrow. 'You mean you refresh old quarrels and keep alive old grievances? Surely not.'

'No, no,' said Hildy, 'I dig up ancient things buried in the earth. Things that belonged to people who lived hundreds of years ago.' As she said this, she began to feel uncomfortable. She had forgotten about the brooch.

'Do you really?' said the King. 'We used to call that grave-robbing.'

Hildy wriggled nervously, and as she did so the brooch slipped out of her pocket and fell on to the ground. 'Oh, I see,' said the King softly. 'Archaeologist. I must remember that one.'

Hildy picked the brooch up, trying unsuccessfully to avoid the King's eye. 'I was going to give it back, honestly,' she said. 'That's why I came back again. I'm sorry.'

The King sighed and took the brooch. It seemed to kick out of her hand, as if it was pleased to be leaving her.

'I was wondering where that had got to,' said the King coldly. 'I went to a lot of trouble. . . . Never mind.'

'What is it?' Hildy asked, but the King only smiled rather scornfully and pinned the brooch on to his cloak. Hildy looked away, feeling utterly miserable, like a child who has done something very wrong and been forgiven.

'You were saying,' said the King.

'I came here to explore the mound,' said Hildy. 'The people laying the pipeline—'

'You, of course, know what a pipeline is,' said the King.

'It's a sort of tube, really. It goes under the sea, and—'

The King frowned again. 'Sorry,' he said, 'I shouldn't have interrupted you. Some men were building a tube, and they broke open the mound. Was it an accident, or done on purpose?'

'Oh, purely accident,' said Hildy. 'Then they sent for the archaeologists, in case it was an ancient burial. And I came and—'

'Yes.' The King smiled again, this time quite kindly. 'You're *sure* it was an accident? It's rather important.'

'Absolutely sure.'

22

Then the King started to laugh, loudly and almost nervously, as if a great fear had been rolled away from his mind. 'That's good,' he said. 'Now, then, a pipeline is a sort of tube, is it? A tube for what?'

So Hildy told him all about oil, and natural gas, and electricity, and even nuclear power and Three-Mile Island, and by the time she had finished the champions had finished quarrelling and come across to listen. But Hildy didn't notice; the King's eye was on her, and she felt absurdly proud that she was the one chosen to tell him, like a child showing off an expensive new toy to a patient uncle. When she had finished with power, she went on with technology; motor-cars and computers and telephones and television. As she did so, she felt that the King's reaction was all wrong; he didn't seem in the least surprised. In fact he appeared to understand everything she was telling him, even about fax machines and the way word-processors swallow whole chapters and refuse to give them back. She tailed off and stared at him.

'I knew you'd left something out,' said the King.

'But how could you have known?' Hildy said. 'I mean, it must all be so strange to you.'

The King raised his eyebrow again. 'What's so strange about magic?' he said. 'Or don't you know anything about the world I lived in?'

'Yes, I do,' said Hildy proudly. 'I've read all the sagas, and the Eddas, and everything.'

The King nodded. 'A wise-woman, evidently,' he said with mock approval. 'A lore-mistress, even. So you should know all about magic, then, shouldn't you?'

'But that's not magic,' Hildy said. 'That's science.'

'And you're not a grave-robber, you're an archaeologist.' The King laughed again, and Hildy blushed, something she had not done for twenty years. 'That is plain ordinary magic, Hildy Frederik's-daughter, only it sounds rather more mundane and there seems to be more of it about than there used to be.' As he said the words, something seemed to trouble him and he fell silent.

'When you've quite finished,' said a voice behind him,

23

'there's some of us starving and freezing to death over here.'

The King closed his eyes and asked some nameless power to give him strength. In the distance Hildy heard the sound of an approaching car. She looked quickly over her shoulder towards the road, and saw headlights. The champions looked round as well; the lights were getting closer but slowing down, and Hildy realised that the car was going to stop. One of the champions had drawn his sword, and the others were muttering something about whose turn it was to fight the dragon, and who had done it the last time, and it wasn't fair that the same person always had to do the lousy jobs. But Hildy suddenly felt that on no account should the King and his men be seen by anybody else; whether it was just a desire to keep them all to herself, for a little longer at least, or whether she had a genuine premonition of danger, she could not tell.

'Please,' she said urgently to the King, 'you mustn't be seen. Come with me.'

The King looked at her, then nodded. The men fell silent and sheathed thir swords. 'This way,' Hildy said, and she made for the minibus, with the King and his champions following her.

'I'm not getting in that,' said the standard-bearer. 'For one thing, it's got no oars.'

'Shut up and get inside,' snapped the King. The standard-bearer climbed in and sat heavily down. His companions followed swiftly, treading on each other's feet in the process.

'Get in here beside me,' Hildy whispered to the King. 'We must be quick.'

She released the handbrake, and without starting the engine or putting on the lights she coasted the van over the bumpy ground down the slope to the road. The police car had pulled up, and she could see the light of the policemen's torches as they climbed up towards the mound. She coasted on down the road until she reckoned that she was out of earshot, then started the engine and drove away.

*

In the deserted mound, nothing stirred and the darkness was absolute. A golden cup, which had been disturbed by a passing foot as the Vikings had climbed out of the ship, finally toppled and slid down into the hold with a bump. But someone with quite exceptional hearing might possibly have made out a slight sound, and then dismissed it as his imagination playing tricks on him; a sound like two voices whispering.

'That's thirty-two above the line, doubled, and six left makes thirty-eight, and two for his nob makes forty, which means another free go, and I'm going to go north this time, so if I make more than sixteen I can pass and make another block.'

'Nuts to you,' said the other voice disagreeably.

There was a tiny tinkling noise. 'Six,' said the first voice, with ill-concealed pleasure. 'Up six, clickety-click, and buckets of blood, down the ruddy snake.'

'Serves you right.'

Then there was silence – real silence, unless you could hear the sound of grass forcing its roots deeper into the earth. But by now, of course, your eyes would have picked out four tiny points of soft white light, deep in the gloom under the keel of the ship.

'This is a rotten game,' said the first voice. 'Why don't we play something else?'

'Just because you're losing.'

'We've been playing this game for twelve hundred years,' said the first voice peevishly. 'I'm bored with it.'

The tinkling sound again. 'Four,' said the second voice. 'Double Rune Score. I think I'll have another longhouse on Uppsala.'

'I've got Uppsala, haven't I?'

'You sold it to me in exchange for a dragon and three hundred below the line.'

'Oh, for pity's sake.' Deep silence again. 'What was all that moving about earlier?'

'What moving about?' said the second voice. 'I didn't notice any moving about.'

'There was a lot of coming and going, and voices,' said

25

the first voice. 'Clanking metal, and people swearing, and even a bit of light.'

'Light,' repeated the second voice thoughtfully. 'That's that stuff that comes out of the sky, isn't it?'

'That or rain. Is that your move, then?'

'Just about.'

'Right, then, I'm taking your castle, and I think that's check. . . . Oh, damn.'

'No, you don't. You took your hand off.'

'Didn't.'

'Did.'

Complete and utter silence. Even the worms seemed to have stopped snuffling in the turf overhead.

'Shall we go and have a look, then?'

'What at?'

'The noise. I'm sure there was something moving about.'

'You're imagining things.'

'No, I'm not. I think it was somebody going out. Or coming in. Anyway, there was something.'

'Look, are we playing this game or aren't we?'

'I'm going to have a look.' Two of the pale lights seemed to move, round the keel of the ship and up the ladder, then down again, and round the inside of the mound. 'Here, come and look at this,' said the first voice excitedly. 'There's a hole here.'

'What sort of hole?'

'Any old hole. I don't know. A hole going out.'

The second pair of lights scrambled up and joined the first pair.

'You're right,' said the second voice. 'It's a hole.'

'So what are we going to do about it?'

'Push.'

A moment or so later, two small forms were lying on the grass outside the mound, dazzled and stupefied by the dim starlight.

'If this is light,' said one to the other, 'you can keep it.'

But the other was cautiously lifting his head and sniffing. 'It smells like light,' he said tentatively. 'Tastes like light. Do you know what this means, Zxerp?'

'It means that by and large I prefer the other one. Rain, wasn't it?'

'It means we're free, Zxerp. After one thousand two hundred and forty-six years, three months and eleven days in that stinking hole we're actually free.'

They were both silent for a moment. 'Bit of an anticlimax, really,' said Zxerp sadly.

'Oh, the hell with you,' said Prexz. Unusually for a chthonic spirit, he was cheerful and optimistic by nature, and ever since he and his brother had got themselves trapped in King Hrolf's mound he had never entirely given up hope of getting out.

'Now what?' said Zxerp. 'You realise, of course, that things will have changed rather since we got stuck in there.'

'And whose fault was that?' asked Prexz automatically – the issue had not been resolved in over twelve hundred years of eager discussion, and minor disagreements over the precise rules of the game of Goblin's Teeth had not helped them to find a solution to it. But Zxerp refused to be drawn.

'I mean,' Zxerp continued, 'things are bound to have changed. Twelve hundred years is a long time.'

'No, it's not,' replied Prexz accurately. Chthonic spirits, like the sources of energy from which they were formed at the beginning of the world, are practically immortal. Like light and electricity, they go on for ever unless they meet some insuperable resistance or negative force; but, having by some freak of nature the same level of consciousness as mortal creatures, they can fall prey to boredom, and Zxerp and Prexz, imprisoned by the staying spell that had frozen the King's company in time, were no exception. It is in the nature of a chthonic spirit to flow imperceptibly through the veins of the earth in search of magnetic fields or feed parasitically on the currents of an electric storm; confinement gnaws at them.

'It is when you're stuck in a mound with nothing to do but play Goblin's Teeth,' said Zxerp. 'I rather think you'll find. . . .'

27

But Prexz wasn't listening. 'Well,' he said, 'only one way to find out.'

The two spirits sat in silence for a while, as if preparing themselves for a great adventure.

'Right,' sighed Zxerp. 'If we're going, we're going. Where *are* we going, by the way?'

'Dunno. The world is our oyster, really.'

'Terrific. Oh, hang on.'

'What?'

'Shall I bring the game, then?'

Prexz scratched his head. On the one hand, the world was full of new, exciting things for a chthonic spirit to do: elements to explore, currents of power coursing through the magma layer to revel in, static to drink and ultrasound to eat. On the other hand, he was winning.

'Go on, then,' he said. 'Might as well.'

'If anybody asks,' Hildy whispered, 'you're the chorus of the Scottish National Opera off to a rehearsal of *Tannhäuser* in Inverness. I'm going to get some food.'

She had parked the van in a backstreet in Thurso, just round the corner from a fish and chip shop. She hated leaving them like this, but the clamour of the King's champions for food was becoming intolerable, and nothing else was open at this time of night, except the off-licence. 'Cod and chips for fourteen and fourteen cans of lager,' she muttered to herself as she trudged up the darkling street. She only hoped she had enough money to pay for all that. And how long was all this going to last, at three meals a day, not to mention finding them all somewhere to sleep?

Back in the van, the standard-bearer was being difficult, as usual.

'But how do we know we can trust her?' he said. 'I mean, you don't know her from Freyja. She's obviously some sort of a witch, or how come this thing moves about without oars?'

The King shook his head. 'We can trust her,' he said. 'But she doesn't seem to know very much. Whether that's good or bad, I don't know.'

'So you think there's still danger?' said the huge man, who was bent nearly double at the back of the van.

'There's danger all right, Starkad Storvirkson,' replied the King thoughtfully. 'That much we can be sure of. I can feel it all around me. And I think the woman Hildy Frederik's-daughter is right that we should not reveal ourselves until we have found out exactly what is going on. I do not doubt that the power of the enemy has grown while we have slept.'

When Hildy returned, exhausted and laden down with two carrier-bags, the King ordered his men to be quiet. 'We had better not stay in this town,' he said. 'Can you take us back into open country?'

Hildy nodded, too tired to speak, and they drove out of Thurso for about half an hour to a bleak and deserted fell under a grey mountain. There the company got out and lit a fire in a small hollow hidden from the road. Hildy handed out paper packages of cod and chips and cans of lager, which the champions eyed with the greatest suspicion.

'I'm afraid it may have got cold,' Hildy said, 'but it's better than nothing.'

'What is it?' asked the horn-bearer. 'I mean, what do you do with it?'

'Try taking the paper off,' said Hildy. The huge man looked up in surprise; he had already eaten the wrapping of his.

'The brown stuff on the outside is called batter,' Hildy said. 'It's made from eggs and flour and things. Inside there's fish.'

'I don't like fish,' said a champion with a silver helmet.

'The small brown things are chips,' Hildy continued. 'They weren't invented in your time. There's beer in the metal tubes.'

The champion in the silver helmet started to ask if there was any mead instead, but the King frowned at him. 'Excellent,' he said. 'We owe you a great debt already, Hildy Frederik's-daughter.'

Hildy nodded; they owed her twenty-two pounds and seventy-five pence, and she could see little chance of her ever getting it back. The authors of all the sagas she had read had been notably reticent about the cost of mass catering.

'You're welcome,' she said wearily. 'My pleasure.'

'In return,' said the King through a mouthful of cod, 'I must explain to you who we are and why we were sleeping in the mound in the first place. But I must ask you to remember that this is a serious business. Wise is he who knows when to speak; wiser still, he who knows when to stay silent.'

'Point taken,' said Hildy, who recognised that as a quotation from the Elder Edda. 'Go on, please.'

The King bent his can of lager into the shape of a drinking-horn and pulled off the ring-pull. 'My father was Ketil Trout,' he said, 'and he ruled over the Orkneys and Caithness. He was a wise and strong king, not loved overmuch by his people but feared by his enemies, and when he fell in battle he was buried in his ship.'

'Where?' Hildy asked, for she still had the instincts of an archaeologist. But the King ignored her.

'I succeeded him as king,' he said. 'I was only fourteen at the time, and my uncle Hakon Claw ruled as regent until I reached the age of sixteen. When I came to the throne, I led my people out to war. I was strong then, tall for my age and burning with the desire to win glory. The people worshipped me, and I foresaw a succession of marvellous victories; my sword never sheathed, my banner never furled, my kingdom growing day by day in size and power.'

The King stopped speaking, and Hildy could see by the light of the fire that there were tears in his bright quick eyes. She waited patiently, and he continued.

'As you can see, Hildy Frederik's-daughter, I was a wicked fool in my youth, blinded with tales and the long names of heroes. That's what comes of paying attention to the stories of long ago; you wish to emulate them, to bring the Elder Days back into the present. But there never was an age of heroes; when Sigurd Fafnir's Bane was digging dragon-traps in the Teutoberger Wald, they were already singing songs about the great heroes and days that would

30

never come again. But I wasted many lives of farmers' sons who could not wait for the barley to ripen, leading armies into unnecessary battles, killing enemies who did not merit killing. What are these songs that they promised me they would make, and sing when I was cold in the howe? You say you have read all the sagas of our people, and studied the glorious deeds of heroes. Is there still a song about the battle of Melvich, or the fight at Tongue, when I struck down Jarl Bjorn in front of his own mainmast?'

Hildy turned away and said nothing.

'They promised me a song,' said the King. 'Perhaps they made one; if they did not, it does not matter very much. I found all those songs very dreary; warflame whistled and wolves feasted when Hrolf the Ring-Giver reddened the whale-road. The arrows always blotted out the sun, I remember, and the poet didn't get paid unless blade battered hard on helmet at least once in the first stanza.'

The King smiled bitterly, and threw more wood on the fire. It crackled and grew brighter, and he continued.

'Then one day I was wounded, quite seriously. Strangely enough, it wasn't a great hero or an earl who did it; it was just a miserable little infantryman whose ship we had boarded. I expected him to hold still and be killed, because I was a hero and he was only a peasant, but I suppose he didn't know the rules, or was too scared to obey them. Anyway, he hit me across the forehead with an axe – not a battle-axe with runes all over the blade, something run up by the local blacksmith. I think it knocked some sense into my thick head, because that was the end of my career as a sea-raider, even though I made a complete recovery. I went back home and tried to take a serious interest in more mundane matters, such as whether the people had enough to eat and were the roads passable in winter. I'm afraid I was a great disappointment to my loyal subjects; they liked their kings bloodthirsty.

'Just when the world was beginning to make a little sense, and nobody bothered to invade us any more because we refused to fight, something started to happen away up north in Finnmark, in the kingdom of Geirrodsgarth,

31

where the sorcerers lived. I think they stopped fighting among themselves and made an alliance. Whatever it was, there was suddenly an army of invulnerable berserks loose in the northern seas; all the fighting men who were too vicious even to be heroes had apparently been making their way there for years, and the sorcerer-king organised them into an army. And that wasn't all. He had trolls, and creatures made out of the bodies of dead men, which he brought back to life, and the spirits of wolves and bears put into human shape. Suddenly the game became rather serious, and the kings and earls settled their differences very quickly, and started to offer high wages to any competent wizard who specialised in military magic. But most of those had joined up with the enemy, and quite soon there were battles about which nobody made up any songs, as the ships from Geirrodsgarth appeared off the coasts of every kingdom in the north.

'There seemed little point in fighting, because the ordinary hacking and slashing techniques didn't seem to work on the sorcerer's army. But I was lucky, I suppose, or my ancestor Odin came to my aid. In a stone hut in Orkney lived a wizard called Kotkel, and he knew a few tricks that the enemy did not. He came to me and told me that I could withstand the enemy, perhaps even overthrow him, if I found a brooch, called the Luck of Caithness; with that in my possession, I could at least fight on equal terms. At that time, all the fugitives from the great kings' armies were pouring into my kingdom, and so I had the pick of the fighters of the age. I chose the very best: Ohtar and Hring, Brynjolf the Shape-Changer and Starkad Storvirksson, Angantyr and Bothvar Bjarki, Helgi and Hroar and Hjort, Arvarodd, who had been to Permia and killed giants, and Egil Kjartansson, called the Dancer. I sent them to find the brooch, and within a month they had found it. Then we went to fight the sorcerer. And we won, at Rolfsness, after a battle that lasted two days and two nights.

'But something went wrong at the last moment. One of us – I can't remember who, and it doesn't matter – had the sorcerer-king on the point of his spear but let him get away, and he escaped, although all his army, berserks and trolls and ghost-warriors, were utterly destroyed. We had failed, in spite of all our efforts, and we knew it. Of course, we did our best to make up. We raised forces in every kingdom in the north and went to Geirrodsgarth, where we razed the sorcerer-king's stronghold to the ground and killed all his creatures in their nests. We searched for him under every rock and in every barn and hay-loft; but he had escaped. Some said he had ridden away on the wind, leaving his body behind, and others assured me that he had sunk into the sea.

'Then the wizard Kotkel came to me and gave me more advice, and I realised that I would have to take it. I ordered my longship Naglfar to be brought up on to the battlefield at Rolfsness and sunk into a mound. While the wizard cast his spells and cut runes into the joists and beams of the chamber, I gathered together my champions and led them into the ship. Then the wizard sang a sleeping spell, and we all fell asleep, and they closed up the mound. That last spell was a strong one; we should not wake until the day had come when the sorcerer-king was once again at the summit of his power and threatening the world. Then we should do battle with him once more, for the last time. And there we have been ever since, Hildy Frederik's-daughter. Quite a story, isn't it? Or aren't there any songs about it? No? I'm not surprised. I think people rather lost interest in stories about heroes after the sorcerer-king appeared; most of them seemed to be in rather bad taste.'

For a while, Hildy sat and stared into the heart of the fire, wondering whether or not she could believe this story, even out on the fells, by night beside a fire. It was not that she suspected the King of lying; and she believed in his existence, and that he had just woken up after twelve hundred years of sleep. But something struggling to stay alive inside her told her that some token show of disbelief was necessary if she was to retain her identity, or at least her sanity. Then it occurred to her, like the obvious solution to some tiresome puzzle, that her belief was not needed, just as the meat need not necessarily consent to being cooked. She had entered the service of a great lord; part of the bargain between lord and subject is that the subject does not have to understand the lord's design; so long as the subject obeys the lord's orders, her part is discharged, and no blame can attach to her.

'So what are you going to do?' she asked.

The King smiled. 'I shall find the sorcerer-king and I shall destroy him, if I can,' he said. 'That sounds simple enough, don't you think? If you keep things simple, and look to the end, not the problems in the way, most things turn out to be possible. That is not in any Edda, but I think it will pass for wisdom.'

The King rose slowly to his feet and beckoned to the wizard, who had been sitting outside the circle of the firelight, apparently trying to find a spell that would make a beer-can magically refill itself. They walked a little way into the night, and spoke together softly for a while.

Hildy began to feel cold, and one of the champions noticed her shivering slightly and took off his cloak and offered it to her.

'My name is Angantyr,' he said, 'son of Asmund son of Geir. My father was earl of—'

'Not you as well,' moaned the horn-bearer. 'Can't we have a song or something instead?'

Hildy wrapped the cloak round her shoulders. It was heavy and seemed to envelop her, like a fall of warm snow.

'Do you mind?' said Angantyr Asmundarson. 'The lady and I—'

'Don't you take any notice of him,' said the standard-bearer. 'He's not called Angantyr the Creep for nothing.'

'Look who's talking,' replied Angantyr.

'Excuse me,' Hildy said. The heroes looked at her. 'Which one of you is Arvarodd?'

'I am,' said a gaunt-looking hero in a black cloak.

Hildy was blushing. 'Are you the Arvarodd who went to Permia?' she asked shyly. For some reason the heroes burst out laughing, and Arvarodd scowled.

'I read your saga,' she said, 'all about the giants and [the] magic shirt of invulnerability. Was it like that?'

'Yes,' said Arvarodd.

'Oh,' Hildy bit her lip nervously. 'Could I have your autograph, please? It's not for me, it's for the Department of Scandinavian Studies at St Andrews University,' she added quickly. Then she hid her face in the cloak.

'What's an autograph?' asked Arvarodd.

'Could you write your name on – well, on that beer-can?'

Arvarodd raised a shaggy eyebrow, then scratched a rune on the empty Skol can with the point of his dagger and handed it to her.

'Everyone's always kidding him about his trip to Permia,' Angantyr whispered in her ear. 'All his great deeds, and the battles and the dragons and so forth – well, you heard the saga, didn't you? – and all anyone ever asks him is "Are you the Arvarodd who went to Permia?" And it was only a trading-voyage, and all he brought back was a few mouldy old furs.'

The King and the wizard came back to the fire and sat down.

'The drinks are on the wizard,' announced the King, and at once the heroes crowded round the wizened old man, who started to pour beer out of his can into theirs.

'Don't worry,' said the King to Hildy, 'the wizard and I have thought of something. But we're going to need a little help.'

There are many tall office-blocks in the City of London, but the tallest of them all is Gerrards Garth House, the home of the Gerrards Garth group of companies. Someone – perhaps it was the architect – thought it would be a good idea to have a black office-block instead of the usual white, and so the City people in their wine bars refer to it as the Dark Tower.

The very top floor is one enormous office, and few people have ever been there. It is full of screens and desk-top terminals, and the telephones are arrayed in battalions, like the tanks at a march-past. On the wall is a large electronic map of the world, with flashing lights marking the Gerrards Garth operations in every country. On a busy day it almost seems as if the entire world is burning.

The building was entirely dark, except for one light in this top office, and in that office there was only one man: a big burly man with red cheeks and large forearms. He was staring into a bank of screens on which there were many columns of figures, and from time to time he would tap in a few symbols. Then the screens would clear and new figures would come up before him. He did not seem to be tired or impatient, or particularly concerned with what he saw; it looked very much as if everything was nicely under control. Thanks, no doubt, to the new technology.

And then the screens all over the office went out, and came on again. All over them, little green figures raced up and down, like snowflakes in a blizzard, while every light that could possibly flash began to flash at once. Unfamiliar symbols which were to be found in no manual moved back and forth with great rapidity, forming themselves into intricate spirals and interweaving curves of flickering light, and all the telephones began to ring at once. The man gripped the arms of his chair and stared. Suddenly all the screens stopped flickering, and one picture appeared on all of them, glowing very brightly, while the overhead lights went out, and the terminals began to spit out miles of printout paper covered in words from a hundred forgotten languages.

The man leant forward and looked at the screen closest to him. The picture was of a golden brooch, in the shape of a flying dragon.

# 3

'ADMIT IT, Zxerp,' said a voice, 'you've never had it so good.' The postman, who had just been about to get on his bicycle for the long ride back to Bettyhill, stopped dead in his tracks and stared at the telegraph wires over his head. He could have sworn that one of them had just spoken. He looked around suspiciously, but nothing stirred in the grey dawn.

'I mean,' said the voice, 'I haven't the faintest idea what this stuff is, but it beats geothermal energy into a cocked hat.'

The postman jumped on his bicycle and pedalled away, very fast.

'It's all right, I suppose,' replied Zxerp. 'A bit on the sweet side for my taste, but it has a certain something.' He wiped his mouth with the back of his hand.

'You're never satisfied, are you?' said Prexz, emerging from the wire and hopping lightly down to the ground. 'You want magnetism on it, you do.'

'Hang on,' said Zxerp. He climbed out of the copper core and dropped rather heavily. 'Ouch,' he said unconvincingly. 'I think I've hurt my ankle.'

They strolled for a while down the empty lane, and paused to gaze out over the misty hills. The cloud was low, so that the peaks were blurred and vague; it was possible to imagine that they rose up for ever to the roof of the sky.

'So whose go was it?' asked Zxerp after a while.

'Mine,' replied Prexz. 'Have you got the dice?'

'I thought you had them.'

They searched their pockets and found the dice: two tiny cubes of diamond that glowed with an inner light.

'So what are we going to do, then?' asked Zxerp after each had had a couple of turns. He was in grave danger of being Rubiconned (again) and wanted to distract his companion's attention.

'Do?' Prexz frowned. 'What we like, I suppose.'

'No, but really. We've had a break; we ought to be getting back to work.'

Prexz shook his head vigorously, causing great interference with Breakfast Television reception all over Bettyhill. 'I've had it up to here with work. At the beck and call of every wizard and sorcerer in Caithness, never a moment to call your own – what sort of a life do you call that? I reckon that if we keep our heads down and play our runes right. . . .'

He stopped, and put his hands to his head. Zxerp stared at him, then suddenly he felt it, too: words of command, coming from not far away.

'Oh, for pity's sake,' muttered Prexz. 'It's that bloody wizard again.'

'I was just thinking', said Zxerp through gritted teeth, 'how nice it would be not to have to see that Kotkel again.'

'He was the worst,' agreed Prexz. 'Definitely the worst.'

The words of command stopped, and the two spirits relaxed.

'Perhaps if we just hid somewhere,' Prexz whispered. 'Pretended to be a bit of static or something. . . .'

'Forget it.' Zxerp was already packing up the game, putting the Community Hoard cards back into their marcasite box. 'I knew it was too good to last.'

They started to trudge back the way they had come.

'Do you suppose he did it on purpose?' asked Prexz. 'Trapped us in the mound deliberately, or something?'

'I wouldn't be surprised,' said Zxerp gloomily. 'He's clever, that wizard.'

Hildy was not used to sleeping out in the open, but at least it hadn't rained, and she had been so tired that sleep came remarkably easily. She had had a strange dream, in which everything had gone back to normal and which ended with her sitting at a table in the University library leafing through the latest edition of the *Journal of Scandinavian Studies*.

When she opened her eyes, she found that the Vikings were all up and sitting round a fire. They were roasting four rabbits on sticks, which reminded Hildy irresistibly of ice-lollies, and passing round a helmet filled with water.

'Why's it always *my* helmet?' grumbled the horn-bearer.

For a moment, the pure simplicity of the scene filled Hildy with a sort of inner peace: food caught by skill in the early morning, and clean water from a mountain stream. Then she discovered that a spider had crawled inside her boot, and that she had a crick in her neck from sleeping with her head on a tree-root. She evicted the spider nervously and tottered over to the fire.

'Have some rabbit,' said Angantyr. 'It's a bit burnt, but a little charcoal never killed anyone.'

Hildy explained that she never ate breakfast. 'Where's the King?' she asked.

'He wandered off with that blasted wizard,' said the horn-bearer, drying out the inside of his helmet with the hem of his cloak. 'I think it's going to rain any minute now,' he added cheerfully.

She found the King sitting beside the bank of a little river that rolled down off the side of the fell just inside the wood. He turned and smiled at her, and put a finger to his lips. On the other side of the stream the wizard was standing on one leg, pointing with his staff to a shallow pool. The King was lighting a small fire with a tinder-box.

'What's he doing?' whispered Hildy.

'Watch,' replied the King.

The wizard had started mumbling something under his breath, and almost immediately two large salmon jumped up out of the water and landed in the King's lap.

'Saves all that mucking about with hooks and bits of string,' explained the King. 'Had any breakfast?'

'No,' said Hildy. 'But I never—'

'Don't blame you,' said the King. 'Rabbit again, I expect. And burnt, too, if I know them. No imagination.'

The wizard had crossed the stream, and the King set about preparing the salmon, while Hildy looked away.

'Kotkel and I have been thinking,' said the King. 'Obviously, it's no good our hanging about out here having a good time and waiting for the enemy to come to us. On the other hand, we aren't exactly suited for going out and looking for him, although I don't suppose he'll be all that hard to find.'

He threw something into the water, and Hildy winced. As a child, she had had to be taken outside when her mother served up fish with their heads still on.

'So I think we should find somewhere where we can get ourselves organised, don't you? And there are things we're going to need. For example, I was never a great follower of fashion, and far be it from me to make personal comments, but does everyone these days wear extraordinary clothes like those you've got on?'

Hildy glanced at the King, in his steel hauberk and wolf-skin leggings. 'Yes,' she said.

'Well,' said the King, 'we don't want to appear conspicuous, do we? So we'll need clothes, and somewhere to stay, and probably other things as well. I'm afraid you'll have to see to that for us.'

Hildy didn't like the sound of that. To the best of her knowledge she had just over two hundred pounds in the bank, and her next grant cheque wasn't due for three weeks.

'The problem is', continued the King, 'what do we have to trade?'

Hildy had a brilliant idea. On the King's tunic was a small brooch of enamelled gold in the shape of a running horse. She pointed to it.

'Could you spare me that?' she asked.

'A present from my aunt, Gudrun Thord's-daughter,' replied the King, looking down at it. 'I never liked it much. Rich is gold, the gift of earls, but richer still the help of friends. So to speak.'

He unpinned the brooch and handed it to her. Hildy looked around at the vast empty hills and the dense wood before her.

'I know a couple of dealers in antiquities down in London. . . . You remember London?'

'Still going, is it?' asked the King, raising an eyebrow. 'You surprise me. I never thought it would last. Go on.'

'They'd pay a lot for this, with no questions asked. Enough to be going on with, anyway.'

'But London is several weeks' journey away,' said the King.

'Not any more,' said Hildy. 'I'd be away two, at the most three days.'

The King nodded. 'I imagine we'll be able to take care of ourselves for three days. It'll give us time to think out what we're going to do. But be careful. For all I know, the enemy is aware of us already.'

For some reason, Hildy felt rather cold, although the King's little fire was burning brightly. She had no notion what this strange enemy was, but when the King spoke his name she was conscious of an inexplicable discomfort, just as, although she did not believe in ghosts, she could never properly get to sleep after reading a ghost story. The King seemed to understand what she was thinking, for he put his hand on her shoulder and said: 'I think you will be able to recognise the enemy when you come across him or his works. I suspect that you know most of them already. It will be like a house or a bend in the road which you have passed many times, until one day someone tells you a story about that place – there was a murder there once, or an old mad woman lived there for many years – and the place is never the same again. Here, in these unchanged mountains, I cannot feel properly afraid of my enemy, even though I fought him here once, and smelt his danger in every fold of the land. But now I think his ships are beached somewhere else, and his army watches other roads. I remember that he used to have birds for spies and messengers, ravens and crows and eagles, so that as we marched we knew that he could see us and assess our

41

strength at every turn. I think he has other spies now; and now it is most important that he does *not* see us. He will look here first, of course, and we are not an army able to do battle; we cannot fight his armies, we can only fight him, hand-to-hand in his own stronghold – if we can find it and get there before he finds us and squashes us under his thumb.'

The King stopped speaking and closed his eyes, but Hildy could not feel afraid, even though fear was all around her, for the King was here with his champions, and he would find a way.

'The salmon's ready,' he said suddenly. 'Help yourself.'

'No, thanks,' said Hildy, 'I never eat breakfast. I'd better get going.'

'Good luck, then,' said the King, not looking up from his salmon. 'Be careful.'

Hildy walked back to the camp, where she had parked the van.

'Going somewhere?' asked Arvarodd, who was sitting by the fire sharpening arrowheads on a stone.

'Yes,' said Hildy. 'I'll be gone for a day or so. The King needs some things before we start out.'

'Going alone?'

'Yes.'

'Risky.' Arvarodd got up and stretched his arms wide. 'Never mind, I expect you'll cope. You know all about everything these days, of course, so I don't suppose you're worried.'

'Yes,' replied Hildy doubtfully, 'I suppose I do.'

'Better safe than sorry, though,' said Arvarodd. He was looking for something in a goat-skin satchel by his side. 'Come over here,' he said softly.

'Well?'

He took out a small bundle of linen cloth and laid it on the grass beside him. 'When I was in Permia,' he whispered, 'I did pick up one or two useful things, although I made sure no one ever found out about them, so you won't have heard of them in any of those perishing sagas. Never saw a penny in royalties out of any of them, by the way. These bits and pieces might come in useful. I'll want them back, mind.'

He unrolled the cloth and picked out three small pebbles and a splinter of bone, with a rune crudely carved on it.

'Not things of beauty, I'll grant you,' he said, 'but still. This pebble here is in fact the gallstone of the dragon Fafnir, whom Sigurd Sigmundarsson slew, as you know better than I. Improbable though it may sound, it enables you to understand any language of men. This remarkably similar pebble comes from the shores of Asgard. If you throw it at something, it turns into a boulder and flattens pretty well anything. Then it turns back into a pebble and returns to your hand. This bone is a splinter of the jaw of Ymir the Sky-Father. Ymir could talk the hind legs off a donkey, and this makes whoever bears it irresistibly persuasive. And this', he said, prodding the third pebble with his forefinger, 'was picked off the roughcast on the walls of Valhalla. I never found out what it does, but I imagine it brings you good luck or something.'

He rolled them back up in the cloth and gave it to her. She tried to find words to thank him, but none came.

'You'd better be going,' he said, and she turned to go. 'Be careful.'

'I will. It's not dangerous, really.'

'Did you really read my saga?'

Hildy nodded.

'Like it?'

'Yes.'

'Wrote it myself,' said Arvarodd gruffly, and he walked away.

Danny Bennett's definition of an optimist was someone who has nothing left except hope, and he felt that the description fitted him well. Ever since he had joined the BBC, straight from university, his career had seemed to drift downhill, albeit in a vaguely upwards direction. True, he had made a reputation for himself with the less intense sort of documentary, the sort that people like to watch rather than the sort that is good for them, but although his work interested the public it was not, he felt sure, in the Public Interest. While all around him his colleagues were exposing scandals in the Health Service and uncovering cover-ups with the enthusiasm of small children unwrapping their Christmas presents, he was traipsing round historic English towns doing series on architecture, or lovingly satirical portraits of charming eccentrics. Better, he thought, to suffer the final indignity of producing 'One Man and His Dog' than to be caught in this limbo of unwanted success.

As he sat in the editing suite with visions of the Cotswolds flickering before him, he had in his briefcase the synopsis of his life's work, a startling piece of investigation that would, if carried through with the proper resources, conclusively prove that the Milk Marketing Board had been somehow connected with the assassination of President Kennedy. He had seen its pages become dog-eared with unresponsive reading, and always it had returned, admired but not accepted, along with a command to go forth and film yet another half-baked half-timbered village green. All around him teemed the modern world, sordid and cynical and infinitely corrupt, but he was seemingly trapped in the Forest of Arden.

He wound his way painfully through the material in front of him, and for only the fifteenth time that hour wished a horrible death on his chief cameraman, who seemed to believe that people looked better with trees apparently growing out of the tops of their heads. He picked up the telephone beside him.

'Angie?' he said. 'Is Bill still in the building?'

'Yes, Mr Bennett.'

'Find him, and personally confiscate that polarising filter. He's used it five times in the last six shots, and it makes everything look like my daughter's holiday snaps. And tell him he's an incompetent idiot.'

'There's been a call for you, Mr Bennett,' said Angie. 'I think somebody wants you to do something.'

Danny Bennett could guess what. There had been a

news report that morning about some fantastic archaeological find up in the north of Scotland, and he had felt the threat of it hanging over him all day, like a bag of flour perched on top of a door he must walk through. Five days on some windswept moor, and all the delights of a hotel bar full of sound-recordists in the evenings. He plodded through the rest of the editing, and went to investigate.

'You want to talk to Professor Wood, Department of Archaeology, St Andrews,' he was told. 'He's on site at the moment with an archaeological team. Apparently, there's gold and a perfectly preserved Viking ship. Sort of like Sutton Hoo only much better.'

'And Professor Wood actually found the ship, did he?'

'No, it was one of his students or something. But Professor Wood is the one who's in charge now.'

'But I'll have to talk to this student,' Danny said wearily. 'What was it like to be the first person in two thousand years, and all that. Can you find out who this person is?'

He went to the bar for a drink before going home to pack. One of his colleagues, a rat-faced woman called Moira, grinned at him as he sat down.

'You drew the short straw, then? That Caithness nonsense with the Viking ship?'

'Yes.'

'I'm just off to do an in-depth investigation into a corrupt planning inquiry in Sunderland. Nuclear dumping. Wicked alderman. Rattle the Mayor's chain.'

'Good for you.'

'It will be, with any luck. Plenty of nice gooey evil in these local-government stories.' She grinned again, but Danny didn't seem to be in the mood.

'There's a rumour that there's a story in this Scottish thing, actually,' she said.

'Don't tell me,' said Danny to his drink. 'The Vikings didn't get planning permission for their mound.'

'The girl who found the thing', said Moira, 'has apparently vanished. Not at her hotel. Hired a van and

45

made herself into air. Can it be that she has looted the mound and absconded with a vanful of Heritage? Or are more sinister forces at work up there among the kilts and heather? You could have fun with that.'

Danny shrugged his shoulders. 'May be something in it,' he said.

'Perhaps' – Moira looked furtively round and whispered – 'perhaps it's the Milk Marketing Board. Again.'

'Oh, very funny,' said Danny.

It took Hildy some time to get used to the idea that she was still in Britain in the twentieth century and that, so far as she could tell, no one was hunting for her or trying to kill her. As she waited for the bus to Inverness, having dumped the hired van outside Lairg, she had the feeling that she ought, at the very least, to be using false papers and a forged driving licence, and in all probability be speaking broken French as well. But she put this down to having seen too many movies about the Resistance, and settled back to endure the long and unpleasant journey.

She made her way uneventfully to the railway station, bought a copy of *Newsweek*, and read it as the train shuffled through northern Britain. It was unlikely, of course, that even in that great rendezvous of conspiracy theories the rising of the sorcerer-king would be reported in so many words, but at the back of her mind she had an inchoate idea of where the enemy might be found. Something the King had said about magic had started her thinking and, although her idea was scarcely distinguishable from healthy American paranoia, that was not in itself a reason for discarding it. God, guts and paranoia made America great.

As she picked her way with difficulty through the various items – for she had been in England a long time now, and found the language of her native land rather tiring in long bursts – she began to feel aware of some unifying theme. There happened to be a long article about a group of companies, a household name throughout the world. Then there was another article about advances in

46

satellite communications, and a discussion of the techniques of electoral advertising. There were several letters about commercial funding of universities, and a great deal about nuclear power, apparently cut from the great bolts of similar material that hang in all editorial offices. The whole thing seemed to make some sort of left-handed sense, and she started again from the beginning. The more she read, the more sense it seemed to make, although what the sense was she could not quite grasp. She told herself that she was probably imagining it, and went to the buffet-car for a coffee.

She had a headache now, and tried to get some sleep, but when she dozed a dream came to her, and she thought she stood on the roof of a very high office-block somewhere in Manhattan or Chicago, from which she could see all the kingdoms of the earth below her. That was curious enough but what was odder still was that large areas of the world were apparently dyed or cross-hatched in a colour she had never been aware of before. Then something rolled out of her pocket, and she stooped to retrieve it. It was the third pebble that Arvarodd had lent her, the one whose use was unknown, and it was the same colour as the cross-hatching.

Then the train went over some points, and she woke up. Once she had recovered her wits sufficiently, she took out the roll of cloth and extracted from it the third pebble. It felt warm in her hand, and something prompted her to put it in her mouth and suck it. It tasted rather bitter, but not unpleasantly so, and she picked up the magazine and started to read it a third time.

By the time the train pulled in to Euston, she was sweating and feeling very frightened. She took the pebble out of her mouth and put it away, then walked briskly to a small and not too horrible hotel she had stayed in before. She did not sleep well that night.

The next morning, promptly at nine-thirty, she walked down to Holborn, where the dealers in antiquities have their lairs. There she converted the golden brooch into seven thousand pounds cash money. It seemed strange to be walking about with so much money in her pocket, but she was in no mood to entrust it to a bank.

Next she went to the London University bookshop, where she bought a number of Old Norse and Anglo-Saxon texts, of such great popularity that the prices on the backs were still in shillings, and then to the British Museum, where she spent several hours in the Reading Room. After a cup of coffee and a hamburger, she caught a train for Inverness. It took even longer than the train down, but the journey passed quickly, for she was used to working on trains.

She stayed the night in a hotel in Inverness, and spent the next morning among the secondhand-car dealers, trying to find a fourteen-seater van. Most of those that were within her price range had no engine or less than the conventional number of wheels, but eventually she found something suitable, which she christened Sleipnir, after the eight-legged warhorse of the god Odin. Then she went to Marks & Spencer and bought fourteen suits; she had to guess at the sizes, but she knew that you can always change things from Marks & Spencer if they don't fit. The woman at the cash-desk gave her a suspicious look, and Hildy could not really blame her; but the worst she could be suspected of doing was organising a cell of Jehovah's Witnesses, which was not a crime, even in Scotland. Shoes were more of a problem, but she decided on something large and simple in black; timeless, she thought to herself. They would need to be, after all.

There were other things, notably food and blankets and camping-stoves, and by the time she had got everything there was not much money left and she was exhausted. She filled the van up with petrol – how do you explain petrol to Viking heroes? This wagon has no horses, it moves by burning dead leaves – and started off on the long drive to Caithness.

'Don't talk daft,' said the horn-bearer, 'that's the Haystack.'

'You're the one who's talking daft, Bothvar Bjarki,' replied Arvarodd. 'That's Vinndalf's Crown. You find Vinndalf's Crown by going left from the Pole Star until you reach the Thistle, then straight down past the Great Goat.'

'If that's all you know about the stars,' replied Bothvar Bjarki, 'it's no wonder you ended up in bloody Permia. Where were you trying to get to – Oslo?'

Arvarodd gathered up his cloak and moved pointedly to the other side of the fire. There the huge man and another champion were sitting playing chess on a portable chess-set made out of walrus ivory.

'Is that checkmate?' asked the huge man.

'Afraid so,' replied his opponent.

'I always lose,' said the huge man.

'You can't help it if you're stupid, Starkad,' replied his opponent kindly. 'A berserk isn't meant to be clever. If he was clever, he wouldn't be a berserk. And you're a very good berserk, isn't he, Arvarodd?'

'Yes,' said Arvarodd. The huge man beamed with pleasure, and his smile seemed to light up the camp.

'Thank you, Brynjolf,' said Starkad Storvirksson. 'And you're a very good shape-changer.'

'Thank you, Starkad,' said Brynjolf, trying to conceal the fact that he had had this conversation before. 'How about another game, then?'

'Don't you want to play, Arvarodd?' Starkad asked, looking at the hero of Permia. Starkad loved chess, even though he invariably lost, although how he managed to do so when everybody cheated to make sure he won was a complete mystery.

'No, not now,' Arvarodd said. 'I'm going to get some sleep in a minute.'

'Can I be black, then?'

'But white always moves first, Starkad,' said Brynjolf gently. 'Don't you want to move first?'

'No, thank you,' said the berserk. 'I've noticed that I always seem to lose when I play first.'

If Brynjolf closed his eyes, it was only for a moment.

They played a couple of moves, and Brynjolf advanced his king straight down the board into a nest of black pieces.

'Tell me something, Brynjolf,' said Starkad softly, marching his rook straight past the place Brynjolf had meant it to go, 'why do Bothvar and the others call me Honey-Starkad?'

Brynjolf stared at the board and scratched his head. Yet again, it was impossible for him to move without checkmating his opponent. 'Because you're sweet and thick, Starkad,' he said.

'Oh,' said the berserk, as if some great mystery had been revealed to him. 'Oh, I *see*. It's your move.'

'Checkmate,' said Brynjolf.

# 4

THE JOB DESCRIPTION had never said anything about this, thought the young man as he scooped up the armfuls of paper that had spilled out of the printers during the night. The Big Bang, yes. The New Technology, certainly. The waste paper, no.

He paused, exhausted by the unaccustomed effort, and cast his eyes over a sheet at random. It said:

ƒØ£⇔¥٪⸨·₥ï℃⸩

And probably meant it, too. It might be BASIC, or it might be FORTRAN, or any other of those computer languages, except that he knew all of them and it wasn't. If he was expected to do a reasoned efficiency breakdown on it and report intelligently in the morning, they were going to be disappointed.

'What are you doing with those?'

The young man jumped, and several yards of continuous stationery fell to the floor and wound themselves round his feet, almost affectionately, like a cat.

'It's last night's printout, Mr. . . .' He never could remember the boss's name. In fact he wasn't sure anyone had ever told him what it was.

'Leave that alone.' The old sod was in a worse mood than usual. 'Have you looked at it?'

'Well, no, not in any great detail *yet*. I was hoping. . . .'

'Put it down and clear off.'

'Yes, Mr. . . .'

No point in even trying to place it tidily on the desk. The young man let it slither from his arms, and fled.

'And find me Mr Olafsen, now.'

The young man stopped. One more stride and he would have been out of the door and clear.

'I'm not positive he's in the building, actually, Mr. . . .'

'I didn't ask you if he was in the building. I asked you to find him.'

This time the young man made it out of the door. There was something about his employer that he didn't like, a sort of air of menace. It was not just the fear of the sack; more like an atmosphere of physical danger. He asked Mr Olafsen's secretary if she knew where he was.

Apparently he was in Tokyo. Where exactly in Tokyo, however, she refused to speculate. He had been sent there on some terribly urgent business with instructions not to fail. In the event of failure, he should carry the firm's principle of conforming to local business methods to its logical conclusion and commit hara-kiri.

'*He* was in a foul mood that day – worse than usual,' went on the secretary. 'You might try phoning the Tokyo office. I don't know what time it is over there, and they might all be out running round the roof or kicking sacks or whatever it is they do, but you might be lucky.'

A series of calls located Mr Olafsen at a golf-course on the slopes of Mount Fuji, and he was put through to his employer.

'Thorgeir, there's trouble,' said the boss. 'Get back here as quick as you like.'

'Won't it wait? If I can get round in less than fifty-two, we'll have more semiconductors than we know what to do with.'

'No, it won't. It's dragon trouble.'

'This is a terrible line. I thought you said—'

'I said dragon trouble, Thorgeir.'

'I'm on my way.'

The boss put down the telephone. The knowledge that he would soon have Thorgeir Storm-shepherd at his side did something to relieve the panic that had afflicted him all day. Thorgeir might not have courage, but he had brains, and his loyalty was beyond question. That at least was certain; any disloyalty, and he knew he would be turned back into the timber-wolf he had originally been, when the sorcerer-king had first found him in the forests of Permia. Timber-wolves cannot wear expensive suits or drive Lagondas with any real enjoyment, and Thorgeir had become rather attached to the good life.

'Why now?' the sorcerer-king asked himself, for the hundredth time that morning. With repetition, the question appeared to be resolving itself. There was the little matter of the Thirteenth Generation, the final coincidence of hardware and software that the sorcerer-king had vaguely dreamt of back at the start of his career under the shade of ancestral fir-trees, when artificial intelligence had been confined to stones with human voices and other party tricks. It had been a long road since then, and he had come a long way along it. No earthly power could prevent him, since no earthly power would for one instant take seriously any accurate description of the threat he posed to the world and its population. But the dragon and the King had never been far from his mind ever since he had abandoned his mortal body on the battlefield at Rolfsness and escaped, rather ignominiously disguised as a Bad Idea.

The sorcerer-king leant his elbows on his desk and tried to picture the Luck of Caithness, that irritatingly elusive piece of Dark Age circuitry. As a work of art, it had never held much attraction for him. As a circuit diagram it had haunted his dreams, and he had racked his memory for the details of its involved twists and curves. For of course the garnets and stones that the unknown craftsman had set in the yellow gold were microchips of unparalleled ingenuity, and in the endless continuum of the interlocking design was vested a system of such strength that no successor could hope to rival or dominate it.

The sorcerer-king shook his head, and struck one broad fist into the other. He had tried everything he knew to avoid this day, and made every possible preparation for it, but now that it had come he felt desperate and hopeless. Yet, if it were to come to the worst, he was still what he had always been, and old ways were probably the best. He rose from his desk and took from his pocket the keys to the heavy oak trunk that seemed so much out of place among the tubular steel of his office. The lock was stiff, but it turned with a little effort, and he pushed up the lid. From inside he lifted a bundle wrapped in purple velvet. He took a deep breath and gently undid the silk threads that held the bundle together, revealing a decorated golden scabbard containing a long beautiful sword. He drew it out and felt the blade with his thumb. Still sharp, after all these years. He made a few slow-motion passes with the blade, and the pull of its weight on the muscles of his forearm reminded him of dangers overcome. With a grunt, he swung the sword round his head and brought it down accurately and with tremendous force on a dark green filing-cabinet, cleaving it from A to J. At that moment, the door opened.

The young man had not wanted to go back into the boss's office. As he turned the handle of the door, he could hear a terrific crash, and he nearly abandoned the mission there and then. But the letters had to be signed.

The sorcerer-king had just lifted his sword clear of the filing-cabinet, feeling rather foolish. He stared at the young man, who stared back. At last the young man, with all the fatuity of youth, found speech.

'Jammed again, did it?'

'Did it?' The sorcerer-king was sweating, despite the air-conditioning.

'The filing-cabinet. I think it's dust getting in the locks.'

The sorcerer-king glanced down at the filing-cabinet, and at the sword in his hands. 'Come in and shut the door,' he said pleasantly.

The young man did as he was told. 'If it's about the luncheon vouchers,' he said nervously, 'I can explain.'

'So can I,' said the sorcerer-king. Of course, there was no need for him to do so, but suddenly he felt that he wanted to. He had kept this secret for more than a thousand years, and he felt like talking to someone. 'Sit down,' he said. 'What can I get you to drink?'

He laid the sword nonchalantly on his desk and produced a bottle from a drawer. 'Try this,' he suggested. 'Mead. Of course, it's nothing like the real thing. . . .' He poured out two glasses and drank one himself, to show his guest that the drink was not poisoned.

The young man struggled to find something to say. 'Nice sword,' he ventured. Then he recollected what Mr Olafsen's secretary had been saying about Japanese business methods.

' "Nice" is rather an understatement,' said the sorcerer-king, and added something about the cut and thrust of modern commerce. The young man smiled awkwardly. 'Tell me, Mr Fortescue,' he continued, 'do you enjoy working for the company?'

'Er,' said Mr Fortescue.

The boss seemed not to have heard him. 'It's an old-established company, of course. Very old-established.' He leant forward suddenly. 'Have you the faintest idea how old-established it is?'

The young man said no, he hadn't. The boss told him. He also told him about the fortress of Geirrodsgarth, the battle of Melvich, and the intervening thousand years. He told him about the dragon-brooch, the King of Caithness, and the wizard Kotkel. He told him about the New Magic and its relationship with the New Technology, and how the Thirteenth Generation would be the culmination of all that had gone before.

'I realised quite early', said the sorcerer-king, 'that magic in the sense that I understood it all those centuries ago had a relatively short future. It wasn't the problem of credibility – that was never a major drawback. But it's basically a question of the fundamental problem at the root of all industrial processes.' The sorcerer-king poured himself another glass of mead and lit a cigar.

'Look at it this way. In all other industries, the quantum

leap from small-scale to large-scale, from workshop to factory, craftsman to mass-production, hand-loom to spinning jenny, is the dividing-line between the ancient and the modern world. Do you follow me?'

'Not really.'

'Magic, I felt, fell into the same category. In my day, you had a small, highly skilled workforce – your sorcerers and their apprentices – turning out high-quality low-volume products for a small, largely high-income-group market. Result: the ordinary bloke, the man on the Uppsala carrier's cart, was excluded from participation in the field. Magic was not reaching the bulk of the population. Given my long-term objective – total world dominance – this was plainly unacceptable. What was the use of a lot of kings and heroes being able to zap each other to Kingdom Come when Bjorn Public could take it or leave it alone? Especially since, as my own experience will testify, a little well-applied brute force and ignorance can put an end to the whole enterprise? You appreciate the problem.'

'Thank you for the drink. I really ought to be getting back. . . .'

'There had to be a breakthrough,' continued the sorcerer-king, 'a moment in the history of the world when magic finally had the potential to get its fingers well and truly round the neck of the human race. There were several key steps along the way, of course. The Industrial Revolution, electricity, the motor-car, and of course television – all these were building-blocks. All my own work, incidentally. They may tell you different down at the Patents Office, but who needs all that? He who keeps a low profile keeps his nose clean, as the sagas say.

'And then I came across an old idea of mine I'd jotted down on the back of a goat-skin hood in the old days – the computer. Originally it was just meant to be an alternative to notches in a stick to tell you how much cheese you needed to see you through the winter, and for all I cared it could stay that way. Except, I got to thinking, how'd it be if everyone had one? I mean everyone. A Home Computer. A little friend with a face like a telly, and its little wires leading into the telephone network. All things to all men, and everything put together. You do everything through it – bank through it, vote through it, work through it, be born, copulate and die through it. Good idea, eight out of ten. But the extra two out of ten is the incredible tolerance the profane masses have towards the evil little monsters. "Computer error," they say, and shake their heads indulgently. Three hours programming the perishing thing, and then it goes *bleep* and swallows the lot.' The sorcerer-king chuckled loudly over his drink and blew out a great cloud of cigar-smoke, for all the world like a story-book dragon. 'Swallows is right. I saw that possibility a mile off. You don't think, do you, that all those malfunctions are genuine? Ever since I got the first rudimentary network established, I've had everything most carefully monitored. Anything I fancy, anything that looks like it might be even remotely useful – *gulp!* and it hums along the fibre-optics to my own personal library.'

Up till then, the young man had been profoundly unconvinced by all this. He had never believed in God or any other sort of conspiracy theory, and he could never summon up enough credulity to be entertained by spy thrillers. But even he had sometimes wondered about the teleology of his own particular field of interest. All computer programmers have at some stage come face to face with the one and only metaphysical question of what happens to all the stuff that gets swallowed by the computer. Here at last was the only possible explanation. He sat open-mouthed and stared.

'Now do you see?' said the sorcerer-king.

'Yes,' said the young man. 'That's clever. That's really clever.'

The sorcerer-king smirked. 'Thank you. Of course,' he continued, 'another fundamental cornerstone of modern commerce is diversification of interests. We may not be the world's biggest multinational, but we hold the most key positions. With an unrivalled position in the Media – don't you like that word, by the way? It gives exactly the right impression. I suppose it's because it sounds so like the Mafia. Anyway, with that and a manufacturing base like ours, we have the establishment to support a truly global concern. So it would be pretty nearly perfect. If it wasn't for the setback.'

'What setback?'

'The dragon. But never mind about all that.' The sorcerer-king was feeling relaxed again. His own narration of his past achievements gave him confidence, for how could such an enterprise, so brilliant in its conception and so long in the preparation, possibly fail? He smiled and offered the young man a cigar. 'Fortescue,' he said, 'I think your face fits around here. I've had my eye on you for some time now, and I think that you could have a future with us after the expansion programme goes through. How would you like to be the Governor of China?'

'What is the point', said Angantyr Asmundarson, 'of having the coat and the trousers the same colour?'

There was no answer to that, Hildy reflected. 'I'm sorry,' she said, 'but I thought. . . .'

'I think they're fine,' said Arvarodd firmly, as if to say that Hildy was not to be blamed for the follies of her generation. 'What are these holes in the side?'

'They're called pockets,' Hildy replied. 'You can keep things in them.'

'That's brilliant,' said the hero Ohtar, who had been familiar to generations of saga audiences as an inveterate loser of penknives and bits of string. 'Why did we never think of that?'

'Gimmicky, I call it,' grumbled Angantyr, but no one paid him any attention. By and large, the heroes seemed pleased with their new clothes – except of course for Brynjolf the Shape-Changer. He had taken one look at his suit and changed himself into an exact facsimile of himself wearing a similar suit, only with slightly narrower lapels and an extra button at the cuffs. The King's suit, of course, fitted perfectly. Even so, like all the others he looked exactly like a Scandinavian hero in a St Michael suit, or a convict who has just been released.

'While you were away,' said the King, taking her aside, 'Kotkel found two old friends.'

'*Old* friends?' Hildy said with a frown. 'Don't you mean. . . ?'

'Kotkel!'

The wizard came out from behind a tree. He had apparently found no difficulty in coming to terms with the concept of pockets; his were already bulging with small bones and bits of rag. He signalled to the King and Hildy to follow him, and led them out of sight behind a small rise in the ground.

'Meet Zxerp and Prexz,' said the King.

At first, Hildy could see nothing. Then she made out two faint pools of light hovering above the grass, like the reflection of one's watch-glass, only rather bigger. 'His familiar spirits,' explained the King. 'It seems they got shut in the mound with us. Probably just as well. They are the servants of the Luck of Caithness.'

'Do you mind?' said one of the pools of light.

'Kotkel has been telling me how the thing actually works,' the King went on, ignoring the interruption, 'and these two have a lot to do with it. The brooch itself is a . . . a what was it?' The wizard made a noise like poultry-shears cutting through a carcass. 'A jamming device, that's right. It interferes with the other side's magic. But in order to do this it requires a tremendous supply of positive energy, which is what these two represent.'

'Glad to know someone appreciates us,' said the pool of light.

'Quarrelsome and unco-operative energy,' continued the King sternly, 'but energy nevertheless. When Kotkel has put together all the right bits and pieces, he can link these two up to the brooch, and all the enemy's magic will be useless. Once that has been achieved, we can get on with the job. He won't be able to use any of his powers to stop us, or even know we're coming, just like the first time. Then it'll just be the straightforward business of knocking

59

him on the head – always supposing that that will be straightforward, of course. But we'll cross that bridge when we come to it.'

'That sounds perfectly marvellous,' said Hildy a little nervously. There was, she suspected, something to follow.

'The problem, apparently,' continued the King, 'lies in getting the right bits and pieces. Kotkel isn't absolutely sure what he'll need. He says he won't know what he wants until he sees it.' The King shook his head.

'What sort of things does he need?'

'That', said the King, 'is a very good question.'

Hildy had been to enough academic seminars to know that a very good question is one to which no one knows the answer – counter-intuitive, to her way of thinking; surely that was the definition of a truly awful question – and her face fell. 'So what now?'

'I think the best plan would be for us to go somewhere where the wizard would be likely to see the sort of thing he might want, don't you? And that would probably have to be some sort of town or city.'

'But wouldn't that be rather dangerous?'

The King smiled. 'I hope so,' he said mischievously. 'I wouldn't like to think that the greatest heroes in the world had been kept hanging around all this time just to do something perfectly safe.'

'What I like least about this country,' Danny Bennett started to say; and then he realised that he had said the same about virtually everything worthy of mention that he had encountered since the aircraft which had brought him there had landed. 'One of the things about this country which really gets up my nose is the way you can rely on all their schedules, timetables and promises.'

'Talk a lot, don't you?' said his senior cameraman. It was raining at Lairg, and the van which was supposed to be meeting them to take them up to Rolfsness had entirely failed to appear. All the shops and the hotel were mysteriously but firmly shut; and the only public building

60

still open, the public lavatory, was filled up with camera and sound equipment, placed there to keep it dry. As a result, the entire crew had been compelled to take what shelter it could, which was not much. There was, of course, a fine view of the loch to keep them entertained; but the presence of ground-level as well as air-to-surface water was no real consolation.

'It's a process of elimination, really,' Danny continued. He believed in making the most of whatever entertainment was available, and since the only entertainment in all this wretchedness was his own coruscating wit he was determined to enjoy it to the full. 'If they say there's rooms booked at such and such or that the van will be there at whenever, you can rely on that. You can be sure that that hotel is definitely closed for renovation, and that that particular time is when all the vans in Scotland are in for their MoT test. Yes,' Danny continued remorselessly, 'I like certainty. It gives a sort of shape to the world.'

The cameraman felt obliged to make some sort of reply. 'I was in Uganda, you know, when they had that coup.'

'Oh, yes?'

'We were stuck waiting for a bus then, an' all.'

'Really.'

'Bloody hot it was. Came eventually, of course.'

That, it seemed, was that. Danny opened his briefcase and, shielding its contents against the weather with his sleeve, began to read through his notes one last time. Not that there was much point. Without any material from the archaeologists, who were up at Rolfsness in nice dry tents, he couldn't hope to start planning anything. The one thing that might make this into television was an interview with this missing female who had been the first into the mound. There was probably a perfectly good reason why she had gone missing, of course, and he felt that if he was now to be reduced to a curse-of-the-pharaohs angle it was probably not going to work in any event; still, there is such a thing as the Nose for a Story. He reminded himself, for about the hundredth time that afternoon, that a routine break-in at a Washington hotel had led to the full glory of

Watergate. As usual when he was totally desperate, he tried to think in children's-story terms, and as he isolated each element he made a note of it in his soggy notebook. Buried treasure. Mysterious disappearance. Remote Scottish hillside. Vikings. A curse on the buried treasure. The fast-breeder reactor twenty miles or so down the coast. Did anyone happen to have a note of the half-life of radioactive gold?

Through the swirling rain, a small man in a cap was approaching. He asked one of the cameramen if Mr Bennett was anywhere.

'I'm Danny Bennett.'

'It's about your van, Mr Bennett. The one you were wanting to go up to Rolfsness,' the small man said. 'I'm afraid there's been a wee mistake.'

'Really?'

'Afraid so, yes.'

That seemed to be all the man was prepared to say. So far as he was concerned, it seemed, that would do.

'What sort of a mistake?'

'Well,' said the man, 'I hired my van out on Tuesday, just for the day, and it hasn't been brought back yet. So it isn't here for you.'

'Oh, that's bloody marvellous, that is. Look, can't you get another one? It'll take forever to get one sent up from the nearest town.'

'There is only the one van.'

Danny wiped the rain out of his eyes. 'Is there any chance of its being returned within the next couple of hours? Who hired it? Is it anyone you know?'

'Not at all,' said the man. 'It was a young woman who hired it. The one who came to look at the diggings up at Rolfsness, the same as yourself.'

Danny looked at him sharply. 'You mean Miss Frederiksen? The American girl?'

'That's right,' said the man. 'And now I'll be getting back indoors. It's raining out here,' he explained. 'Sorry not to be able to help.'

'Hold it,' Danny shouted, but the man had disappeared.

'What was that about our van?' asked the chief sound-recordist.

'It's not coming,' Danny answered shortly.

'Thought so,' said the sound-recordist. The news seemed almost to please him. 'Just like Zaïre.'

'What happened in Zaïre, then?'

'Bleeding van didn't come, that's what.' The sound-recordist wandered away and joined his assistant under the questionable cover of a sodden copy of the *Observer*. Danny walked swiftly across to the telephone-box, with which he had dealt before. When you admitted that the thing did actually take English money and not groats or cowrie shells, you had said pretty much everything there was to say in its favour. However, after a while he managed to get through to a van-hire firm in Wick and arranged for substitute transport. Then he reversed the charges to London.

So cheerful was he when he came out of the phone-box that he almost failed to notice that the rain had got heavier and perceptibly colder. He had – at last – the bones of a story. Of course, none of the researchers had come up with anything new about the Frederiksen woman. But they had called up her supervisor, a certain Professor Wood. Apparently, when she telephoned him from Lairg (God help her, Danny thought, if she was using this phone-box), her manner had been rather strange. Incoherent? No, not quite. Excited, of course, about the discovery. But not as excited as you would expect a career archaeologist to sound after having just made the most remarkable discovery ever on the British mainland. How, then? Pre-occupied, Professor Wood had thought. As if something was up. Something nice or something nasty? Both. Something strange. Strange as in mysterious? Yes. And she had started to say something about a dragon, but then apparently thought better of it.

Danny Bennett sat down and wrote in 'Dragon?' in his list of potential ingredients. Then he stared at it for a while, put down 'Query Loch N. Monster double-query?' and crossed it out again. He then started to draw out the complicated wheel-diagrams and flow-diagrams from which his best work had originated. He felt suddenly relaxed and happy, and soon he was using the red biro that meant 'theme' and the green felt-tip that signified 'potential concept'. A television programme was about to be born.

'That's settled, then,' said the King. 'And if we can't find the bits we want in Wick we'll try somewhere else. And so on, until we do find it.'

The heroes had taken their briefing in virtual silence, since no one could think of any viable alternative, Angantyr's suggestion of declaring war on England having been dismissed unanimously at the outset. After a formal toast and prayer to Odin, the heroes sat down to polish their weapons and pack for the journey.

Hjort and Arvarodd, who had already packed, and Brynjolf the Shape-Changer (who didn't need to pack) lingered beside the fire, playing fivestones.

'I don't know about all this,' grumbled Hjort. 'Complicated. All this stealth and subtlety. I mean, we aren't any good at that sort of thing, are we? What we're good at is belting people about.'

'True,' said Brynjolf wistfully. 'But it doesn't look as if there's much to be gained from belting people about these days.'

'Isn't there, though?' replied Hjort emphatically. 'I reckon there'll be some belting-about to be done before we're finished here. Don't you agree, Hildy Frederik's-daughter?'

Hildy, who was carrying an armful of blankets over to the van, nodded without thinking.

'You see?' said Hjort. 'She's clever, she is.'

'That's right enough,' said Arvarodd briskly. 'There's more to that woman than meets the eye.'

'Just as well,' said Hjort. 'I like them a little thinner myself.'

Arvarodd scowled at him. 'Well, I do,' protested Hjort. 'I remember one time in Trondheim – before they pulled down the old market to make way for that new potter's quarter—'

'That girl has brains,' said Brynjolf hurriedly. 'Brains are what count these days, it seems.'

'Dunno what we'll do, then,' said Hjort. 'Never had much use for brains, personally. Messy. Hard to clean off the axe-blade.'

'I reckon she's an asset to the team,' went on Brynjolf. 'As it is, we're strong on muscle and valour, but a bit short on intellect. There's Himself, of course, and that miserable wizard, but another counsellor on the staff is no bad thing. I reckon we should adopt her.'

'What, give her a name and everything?' Hjort looked doubtful.

'Why not?' said Arvarodd enthusiastically. 'Except that I can't think of one offhand.'

'I can.'

'Shut up, Hjort. Yes, we must think about that.'

Just then, there was a shout from the lookout.

'Hello,' said Hjort, suddenly hopeful. 'Do you think that might be trouble?'

'Who knows?' said Arvarodd, buckling on his sword-belt over his jacket and reaching for his bow. 'Anything's possible, I suppose. Who's moved my helmet?'

The heroes had enthusiastically formed a shield-ring, looking rather curious perhaps in shields, helmets and two-piece grey polyester suits. The King stalked hurriedly past them. 'Not now,' he said shortly.

'But, Chief. . . .'

'I said not now. Get out of sight, all of you.' He crouched down behind a boulder and looked out over the road. Two vans had stopped there. A moment later Hildy and Starkad (who was the lookout) joined him.

'Just drew up, Chief,' whispered Starkad. 'You said to call you if—'

'Quite right,' replied the King. 'Who are they, Hildy Frederik's-daughter?'

Hildy peered hard but could make nothing out. 'I don't know,' she said. 'Probably nobody.'

Out of the first van climbed a man in a blue anorak with a map in his hand. He walked up to the top of a bank, looked around him, and made a despairing gesture.

'What's he looking for, do you think?' muttered the King. 'You stay here. I'm going to have a look.'

Before Hildy could say anything, the King slipped over the boulder and crept down towards the road to where he could hear what the people in the vans were saying. The man in the blue anorak had gone back and was shouting at the driver.

'How was I to know?' replied the driver. 'One godforsaken hillside looks pretty much like another to me.'

'We'll have to go back to that last crossroads, that's all,' said the man in the blue anorak. 'Rolfsness is definitely due north of here.'

'Why don't we just go back to Lairg and see if the pub's open?' growled the driver. 'It's too dark to film anyhow. We're not going to do any good tonight.'

'Because I want to get there as soon as possible and talk to those archaeologists. We've wasted enough time as it is. We've got a schedule to meet, remember.'

'Please yourself, Danny boy. Since we've stopped, though, I'm just going to take a leak.'

'Hurry up, then, will you?'

To the King's horror, the driver jumped out and walked briskly over the rise. The heroes were just over there, hiding. He closed his eyes and waited. A few moments later, he heard a horrified shout, followed by the war-cries of his guard. The driver came scampering back over the rise, pursued by Hjort, Angantyr and Bothvar Bjarki, with the other heroes at their heels and Hildy trotting behind shouting like a small pony following the hunt.

The senior cameraman, who had been about to open a can of lager, dived for his Aaten and started to film through the side-window. The assistant cameraman also kept his head and groped for a light meter, but Danny Bennett was flinging open the van door. 'Not now, for Christ's sake; they're gaining on him,' shouted the senior cameraman, but Danny jumped out and ran to meet the driver. As he did so, one of the maniacs in the grey suits stopped and fitted an arrow to his bowstring.

'*f*8,' hissed the assistant cameraman to his colleague. 'If only there was time to fit the polariser. . . .'

The King jumped up and shouted, and the archer stayed his hand. The heroes stood their ground while the driver leapt into the van, which pulled away with a screech of tyres, closely followed by the second van. A moment later, they were both out of sight. The heroes sheathed their swords and started to trudge back up the rise.

'Who were they?' the King asked Hildy. 'Any idea?'

Hildy had seen the cameras. 'Yes,' she said nervously. 'And I think we're in trouble.'

When they had made sure they were not being followed, the camera crew pulled in to the side of the road and all started to talk at once. Only Danny Bennett was silent, and on his face was the look of a man who has just seen a vision of the risen Christ. At last, he was saying to himself, I have been attacked while making a documentary. There must be a story in it; and not just *a* story but *the* story. Who the men in grey suits had been – CIA, MI5, Special Branch, maybe even the Milk Marketing Board – he could not say, but of one thing he was sure. He was standing on the brink of the greatest documentary ever made. Sweat was running down his face, and in front of his eyes danced the tantalising image of a BAFTA award.

# 5

KEVIN FORTESCUE, Governor of China elect, met Thorgeir Storm-shepherd at the Docklands stolport and drove him back to Gerrards Garth House. On the way, he made it known that he had been let into the secret of the company's history. Thorgeir seemed surprised at this.

'Why?' he said.

'Mr . . . the boss said he thought I had a lot of potential. In fact, he's offered me China.'

'China?'

'I told him I'd give him my decision in the morning, but I'm pretty sure I'm going to take it. I think it would be a good move for me, career-wise. I've got the impression I'm stagnating rather in Accounts.'

Thorgeir made a mental note to water down the sorcerer-king's mead with cold tea before leaving the country next time. He had the feeling that the sorcerer-king was due for a change of direction, career-wise. But it would not be prudent to let the feeling develop into an idea.

The sorcerer-king had come down to the lobby to meet him. 'How was Japan?' he asked.

'Susceptible,' replied Thorgeir, 'highly susceptible. And I did get the semiconductors after all. Just time before the helicopter arrived for a birdie on the last hole.'

'Good,' grunted the sorcerer-king. 'No point in letting things slide just because there's a crisis. You've met our new colleague?'

'Yes,' said Thorgeir. 'What possessed you to do that?'

'Seemed like a good idea at the time.'

'You said that about Copernicus, and look where that got us.'

'Anyway,' the sorcerer-king said, 'he'll come in handy. I've had an idea.'

Thorgeir knew that tone of voice. Sometimes it led to good things, sometimes not. 'Tell me about it.'

'It's like this.' The sorcerer-king reached for the mead-bottle, and poured out two large glasses. 'Our problem is quite simple, when you look at it calmly. Our enemy has reappeared.'

'How do you know that, by the way?'

The sorcerer-king explained about the late-night messages. Thorgeir nodded gravely. 'So King Hrolf is back, and that dratted brooch. We could do one of two things. We could go and look for him, or we could wait for him to come to us.'

'This is meant to be a choice?'

'We could wait for him to come to us.' The sorcerer-king leant back in his chair and put the tips of his fingers together. 'If he tries that, he will be at a certain disadvantage.'

'Namely?'

The sorcerer-king grinned. 'One, he's been asleep for over a thousand years, and things have changed. Two, there's no way he can hope to understand the modern world well enough to endanger us without at the very least a three-year course in business studies and a postgraduate diploma in computers. We are talking about a man who had difficulty adding up on his fingers. Three, he has just crawled out of a mound, in clothes that were the height of fashion a thousand years ago but which would now be a trifle conspicuous. He is likely to be arrested, especially if he strolls into the market-square at Inverness and tries to reclaim his ancient throne. Four, just supposing he makes it and turns up in Reception brandishing a sword, his chances of making it as far as the lift are slim. Very slim. I don't know if you've dropped into Vouchers lately, but I didn't hire them for their mathematical ability.'

'Fair enough,' said Thorgeir patiently. 'So?'

'So, since he's not a complete moron, he's not likely to come to us. So we have to go to him. But on whose terms?'

The sorcerer-king leant forward suddenly and fixed Thorgeir with his bright eyes. This had been a disconcerting conversational gambit a thousand years ago, but Thorgeir was used to it by now. After over a millennium of working with the sorcerer-king, he was getting rather tired of some of his more obvious mannerisms.

'Ours, preferably,' Thorgeir said calmly. 'Explain.'

'His best chance', said the sorcerer-king, 'is to use the brooch again. He jams up our systems, blacks out our networks, and fuses all the lights across the entire world. Then he sends us a message – probably, knowing him, by carrier-pigeon – to meet him, alone, on the beach at Melvich for a rematch. Personally, I am out of condition for a trial by combat.'

Thorgeir nodded. He, too, had grown soft since his timber-wolf days. Apart from retaining a taste for uncooked mutton and having to shave at least three times a day, he had become entirely anthropomorphous. 'We can rule that out, then,' he said. 'I never did like all that running about and shouting.'

'Me neither. So we have one course of action left to us. We find him before he's ready, and we kill him. That ought not to be difficult.'

'Agreed.'

The sorcerer-king poured out more mead. 'In that case, where is he likely to be? He's just risen from the grave, right? And he's on foot. All we need to know is where he was buried, and we've got him. Simple.'

Thorgeir smiled, and drank some of his mead. Now it was his turn.

'Over the last thousand years,' he said, in a slow measured voice, 'I, too, have been turning this problem over in my mind, and the big question is this. Given that King Hrolf was the greatest of the Vikings, and his companions the most glorious heroes of the northern world, how come there is no King Hrolf Earthstar's Saga?'

He paused, for greater dramatic effect, and took a cigar from the box on the desk. Having lit it, he resumed.

'And, for that matter, why are the sagas of all the other heroes of northern Europe so reticent about the greatest event of the heroic age, namely our defeat and overthrow? You'd have thought one of them might have seen fit to mention it.'

The sorcerer-king frowned. With the exception of the latest Dick Francis or Jeffrey Archer, he rarely opened a book these days, and he had never been a great reader at the best of times.

'There is no record of the final resting-place of King Hrolf Earthstar,' said Thorgeir. 'If there had been, I'd have bought the place up and built something heavy and substantial over it five hundred years ago. There is no trace or scrap of folk tradition in Caithness about King Hrolf or the Great Battle or anything else; just a lot of drivel about Bonnie Prince Charlie. The only clue is a single place-name, Rolfsness, which happens to be the site of a certain battle.'

'There you are, then,' said the sorcerer-king.

'There you aren't. I've been back hundreds of times. If there had been anything there, I'd have felt it. And there is no record whatsoever of what became of Hrolf Earthstar while we were floating around as disembodied spirits. He just vanished off the face of the earth. For all I know, he could have sailed west and discovered America.'

'You think he's in America?'

Thorgeir closed his eyes and counted up to ten. 'No, I think he's probably somewhere in Europe. But where in Europe I couldn't begin to say.'

The sorcerer-king smiled. 'You'd better start looking, then, hadn't you?' he said, and poured himself another drink.

'Those people', said Hildy, 'were from television.'

'What's that?' asked one of the heroes.

Hildy racked her brains for a concise reply. 'Like a saga, only with lights and pictures. By this time tomorrow, everyone in the country will know we're here.'

The King frowned. 'That could be serious,' he said. 'We can't have that.'

'But how can we stop it?'

'That's easy.' The King stood up suddenly. 'Where do you think they've gone?'

'Back the way they came, probably to Lairg. They'll want to get the film off to London as quickly as possible. But—'

'We can't make any mistake about this. Kotkel!'

From a small pouch in his pocket, the wizard took a couple of small bones and threw them in the air. As they landed, he stooped down and peered at them intently. Then he pointed towards the south and made a noise like a buzz-saw.

'They went that way,' the King translated.

Hildy had never been fond of driving, and at speeds over thirty miles an hour her skill matched her enthusiasm. But somehow the van stayed on or at least close to the road as they pursued the camera crew along the narrow road to Lairg, and caught up with them in a deserted valley beside a river.

'What do we do now?' Hildy asked as the van bumped alarmingly over a cattle-grid.

'Board them,' suggested Angantyr. 'Or ram them. Who cares?'

'Certainly not,' Hildy shouted.

'Stop here,' the King said. 'Brynjolf!'

'Not again,' pleaded the shape-changer. 'Last time I sprained my ankle.'

No sooner had Danny Bennett realised that the second van had suddenly stopped for no reason than he became aware of a huge eagle, apparently trying to smash the windscreen. The driver swore, and braked fiercely, but the bird merely attacked again, this time cracking the glass. The senior sound-recordist, who had done countless nature programmes in his time, was thoroughly frightened and tried to hide under his seat. The eagle attacked a third time, and the windscreen shattered. The driver put up both his hands to protect his eyes, and the van veered off the road into a ditch.

When Danny had recovered from the shock of impact, he tried to open his door, but a man in a grey suit with a helmet covering his face opened it for him and showed him the blade of a large axe. If this was the Milk Marketing Board, they were probably exceeding their statutory authority.

'Who are you?' Danny said.

'Bothvar Bjarki,' said the man with the axe. 'Are you going to surrender, or shall we fight for a bit?'

'I'd rather surrender, if it's all the same to you.'

'Be like that,' said Bothvar Bjarki.

The camera crew were rounded up, while Starkad, apparently without effort, pushed the two vans into a small clump of trees and covered them with branches. The King had found a hollow in the hillside which was out of sight of the road, and the prisoners were led there and tied up securely. Meanwhile, at Hildy's direction, Starkad and Hjort found the cans of film and smashed them to pieces. When Hildy was satisfied that all the film was destroyed, the heroes got back into their vans and drove away.

As the sound of the engine receded in the distance, the assistant cameraman broke the silence in the hollow.

'Reminds me of the time I was in Afghanistan,' he said.

Danny Bennett asked what had happened that time in Afghanistan.

'We got tied up,' said the assistant cameraman.

'And what happened?'

'Someone came and untied us,' replied the assistant cameraman. 'Mind you, that time we were doing a report for "Newsnight".'

Danny had never worked for 'Newsnight', and people had been known to die of exposure on Scottish hillsides. He pulled on the rope around his wrists, but there was no

73

slack in it. A posthumous BAFTA award, he reflected, was probably better than no BAFTA award at all, but awards are not everything.

'If I can raise my wrists,' he said to the assistant cameraman, 'you could chew through the ropes and I could untie you.'

'I've got a better idea,' said the cameraman. 'You could shut your bloody row and we could get some sleep while we're waiting to be untied.'

'But perhaps', Danny hissed, 'nobody's going to come and untie us.'

'Listen,' said the assistant cameraman fiercely, 'I dunno what union you belong to, but my union is going to get me a great deal of money from the Beeb for being tied up like this, and the longer I'm tied up, the more I'll get. So just shut your noise and let's get on with it, all right?'

Danny's head was beginning to hurt. He closed his eyes, leant back against the assistant cameraman (who was starting to snore) and tried to make some sense of what was happening to him.

The men had been partially disguised as Vikings, with helmets and shields and swords; but they had been wearing grey suits, which tended to spoil the illusion. They had, as he had expected, destroyed the film; but that was all. Not even an attempt to warn him off. Only the barest minimum of physical violence. And then there was that girl – Hildy Frederiksen, beyond doubt. Who was she working for, and what lay behind it all? And where in God's name had they got that incredible bird from?

The obvious clues pointed at the CIA. Whatever they do in whichever part of the world, they always wear grey suits. They buy them by the hundred from J. C. Penney or Man at CIA. That would tie in with the Kennedy connection – at last, after all these years, they were trying to silence him – but the Viking motif was beyond him, unless it was something to do with that tiresome ship. Or perhaps they were in fact wearing protective clothing (the nuclear power station angle) *made to look like* Viking helmets. In which case, why? Unless they were all going on to a fancy-dress party afterwards. The more he thought about it, the more inexplicable it seemed; and the more baffled he became, the more convinced he was that something major was going on. All the great conspiracies of history have been bizarre, usually because of the incompetence of the leading conspirators. As the long hours passed, he traced each convoluted possibility to its illogical conclusion, but for once no pattern emerged in his mind. At last he fell asleep and began to dream. He seemed to hear voices coming from a small pool of light hovering overhead.

'Seventy-five to me, then,' said one voice, 'plus the repique on your declaration, doubled. Your throw.'

Danny sat up. He wasn't dreaming.

'Six and a four. I take your dragon, and that's forty-five to me. Four, five, six, – oh, sod it, go to gaol.'

The rest of the crew were asleep. Danny sat absolutely still. The hair on the back of his neck was beginning to curl, and he found it hard to breathe.

'Trade you Hlidarend for Oslo Fjord and seventy points,' said the first voice. 'That way you'll have the set.'

'No chance,' said the second voice. 'Up three, down the serpent four five six, and that's check.'

'No, it isn't.'

'Yes, it is.'

The voices were silent for a while, and Danny swallowed hard. Perhaps it was just the bump he had suffered when the van crashed.

'Good idea, that,' said the first voice.

'Brilliant,' replied the second voice sarcastically. 'You don't imagine we're going to get away with it, do you?'

'Why not?'

'Because he'll notice we're not there, that's why. And he's not going to be pleased.'

The first voice sniggered. 'He'll be miles away by now. And the rest of them. They're going to Inverness. He won't be able to reach us from there.'

'Where's Inverness?'

'I haven't the faintest idea. But it sounds a very long way away to me.'

The second voice sighed audibly. 'You and your ideas,' it said.

'Well, what choice did we have?' replied the first voice irritably. 'I don't know about you, but I didn't fancy having copper wire twisted round my neck and being linked up to that perishing brooch. Last time, my ears buzzed for a week.'

'He'll be back. Just you wait and see.'

Another silence, during which Danny thought he could hear a rattling sound, like dice being thrown.

'Well,' said the second voice, 'we'd better make ourselves scarce anyhow. No good sitting about here.'

'Just because I'm winning. . . .'

'Who says you're winning?'

The voices subsided into a muted squabbling, so that Danny could not make out the words. He longed for the voices to stop, and suddenly they did.

The reason for this was that Prexz had just caught the vibrations from an underground cable a mile or so away to the south. He had no idea what it might be, but he was hungry, and it seemed irresistible.

'Put the game away, Zxerp,' he said suddenly. 'I can feel food.'

But Zxerp didn't answer. 'I said I can feel food,' Prexz repeated, but Zxerp glowed warningly at him.

'There's a man over there listening to us,' he whispered.

'Why didn't you say?'

'I've only just noticed him, haven't I?'

Prexz cleared his throat and turned his glow up a little. 'Excuse me,' he said.

'Yes?' replied Danny.

'Would you happen to know anything about a cable running under the ground about a mile from here and going due north?'

'I would imagine', Danny replied, his heart pounding, 'that it has something to do with the nuclear power station on the coast.'

'*Nuclear* Power?' Prexz said. 'Stone me. Did you hear that, Zxerp? Nouvelle cuisine.'

The two pools of light rose up into the air and seemed to dance there for a moment.

'By the way,' said Prexz, 'if the wizard comes looking for us. . . .'

'The wizard?'

'That's right, the wizard. If he comes looking for us, you haven't seem us.'

'Before you go,' whispered Danny faintly, 'do you think you might possibly untie these ropes?'

'Certainly,' said Prexz. As he did so, Danny was aware of a terrible burning sensation in his hands and arms. 'Is that all right?'

'That's fine, thank you,' Danny gasped. Then he fainted.

'What a strange man,' Prexz said. 'Right, off we go.'

The Dow up three – that won't last – early coffee down, tin's still a shambles, and soon they'll be giving copper away with breakfast cereal. Who needs to buy a newspaper to learn that?

Thorgeir had adapted splendidly to most things in the course of his extremely long life, but the knack of reading the *Financial Times* on a train still eluded him. How one was supposed to control the huge unruly pages was a complete mystery. He was sorely tempted to get the boss to buy up the damned paper, just to make them print it in a smaller format. With a grunt, he retrieved the news headlines. Earthquake in Senegal, elections in New Zealand, massive archaeological find in Scotland. . . .

Massive archaeological find in Scotland. Like a raindrop trickling down a window, his gaze slid down the pink surface and locked on to the small paragraph. At Rolfsness, in Caithness; archaeologists claim to have unearthed a ninth-century Viking royal ship-burial. Unprecedented quantities of artefacts including treasure, armour and weapons. Gold prices, however, are unlikely to be affected.

His fellow-passengers saw the small thin-faced man go suddenly white as he read his *FT*, and assumed that he had failed to get out of cocoa before the automatic doors closed. Thorgeir tossed the paper down on the seat beside him, and fumbled in his briefcase for his radiophone.

'Have you seen it?' he said. 'In the paper?'

'What are you going on about, Thorgeir?' said the sorcerer-king, his voice faint and crackly at the other end.

'Front page of the *FT*.'

'Hang on, I've got that here.' Thorgeir could picture the sorcerer-king retrieving the paper from the early-morning mess on his desk.

'The news section, about a third of the way down.'

'You've called me up to tell me about the Chancellor?'

'Stick the Chancellor; it's the bit below that.'

When the sorcerer-king panicked, he tended to do so in Old Norse, which is a language admirably suited to the purpose, if you are not in any hurry. Thorgeir listened impatiently for a while, then interrupted.

'Who have we got in archaeology?'

There was silence at the other end of the line. Twelve hundred years he's managed without a Filofax, reflected Thorgeir. The moment he gets one, nobody knows where they are any more. Marvellous.

'In Scotland?'

'Preferably.'

'There's a Professor Wood at St Andrews. What do you want an archaeologist for, anyway? I'm going over to Vouchers.'

Thorgeir frowned. 'No, don't do that,' he said quietly. 'Get Professor Wood. It says in the paper he's in charge of this dig at Rolfsness. Tell him I'll meet him there.'

'I'm still going over to Vouchers.'

'You do whatever you like. By the way, where's this train I'm on going to? I've forgotten.'

'Manchester.'

'Thanks.' Thorgeir switched off the phone and consulted his train timetable. He was feeling excited now that the enemy had been contacted, although he still could not imagine how he had overlooked something as obvious as a ship-burial on his many visits to that dreary place. Then it occurred to him that any wizard with Grade III or above would have been able to conceal the traces of life in such a mountainous and isolated spot from any but the most perceptive observer, and King Hrolf's wizard had been a top man. Pity they hadn't headhunted him back in the 870s. What was that wizard's name? Something about the pot and the kettle.

In the age of the supersonic airliner, a man can have breakfast in London and lunch in New York (if his digestion can stand it); but to get from Manchester to the north coast of Scotland between the waxing and the waning of the moon still requires not only dedication and cunning but also a modicum of good luck, just as it did in the Dark Ages. By the time Thorgeir had worked out an itinerary, the view from the train window had that tell-tale hint of First World War battlefield about it that informs the experienced traveller that he's passing through Stockport. Thorgeir closed his briefcase and leant his head back against the cushions. Kotkel. Hrolf's wizard was called Kotkel, and he had had quite a reputation around Orkney in the seventies. Winner for three years in succession of the Osca (Orkney Sorcerers' Craft Association) for Best Hallucination. No slouch with a rune, either.

'That's all I needed,' groaned Thorgeir.

Telephone wires were humming all over Britain, for they had just had to shut down the nuclear reactor on the north coast of Scotland. There was, it had been decided, no need to evacuate the area; there was no danger. It was just that someone had contrived to mislay the entire output of electricity from the plant for just over half an hour. Even the lights had gone out all over the building.

'Has anyone', the controller kept asking, 'got a fifty pence for the meter?' The senior engineers led him away and got him an aspirin, while his deputy made another attempt to get through to Downing Street.

No one had yet got around to checking the underground cable that ran due south from the plant, which was where the fault actually lay. It lay on its back, its eyes closed, and it was singing softly to itself.

'For ye defeated', it sang,
'King Hrothgar's army,
And sent them home,'
To think again.'

The fault's companion was scarcely in a better state. He had never even claimed to be able to hold his electricity, and he had very nearly been sick. It was just as well that he had not, or the entire National Grid would have been thrown into confusion. He gurgled, and went to sleep.

'Prexz,' said the fault, 'I just thought of something.'

Prexz moaned, and rolled on to his face, vowing never to touch another volt so long as he lived.

'How would it be,' Zxerp said, 'how would it be if. . . . '

'Don't want any more,' mumbled Prexz. 'Had too much already. Drunk. Totally drunk. Going to join Electronics Anonymous soon as I feel a little better.'

'Don't be like that,' whined Zxerp.

'Think they put something in it at the generator,' continued Prexz. 'Going to sleep it off. Shut up. Go away.'

'Wimp,' snarled Zxerp. 'You're no fun, Prexz. Don't like you any more.'

Prexz had started to snore, sending clouds of undecipherable radio signals to jam up the airwaves of Europe.

'I don't like it here,' said Zxerp. 'I want to go home.'

No reply. Zxerp shook his head, which made him feel worse, and he fell heavily against the cable. There was nothing in it, and he was feeling terribly thirsty. He was also feeling guilty.

'Poor old wizard,' he said. 'Always been good to us. Never a cross word in twelve hundred years. Prexz, shouldn't we go and find the wizard? Shouldn't have run away from the wizard like that. Not right.'

Zxerp started to cry, and negative ions trickled down the side of his nose, electrolysing it. At the government listening post in Cheltenham, a codes expert picked up his tears on the short-wave band and rushed off to tell his chief that the Russians had developed a new cipher.

*

Thorgeir heard about the closedown of the power station over the radio as he drove his hired car past Loch Loyal. The shock made him swerve, and he nearly ended up in the water.

He pulled over and examined an Ordnance Survey map, but that told him nothing he did not already know, and his own personal map, which was traced in blood on soft goat skin and was somewhat out of date. But a call to London on his radiophone told him all he needed to know, and he asked that a helicopter should be laid on to meet him at Tongue. He also enquired whether there was an equivalent to the Vouchers department at the company's Glasgow office.

'Yes? Then, send a couple of them up. Tell them to bring plenty of vouchers.'

He pushed down the aerial so violently that he nearly snapped it off, and drove on towards the coast. As he turned a bend in the road beside a small clump of trees, he noticed and just managed to avoid a patch of broken glass in the middle of the carriageway. In doing so he stalled the engine, and while he was persuading it to start again his eye fell on the windscreen of a van among the trees. Someone had apparently been to the trouble of covering this van up with tree-branches. For some reason this seemed terribly significant, and Thorgeir went to investigate.

What he found was two vans with broken windscreens and a good deal of smashed camera gear. As he stood scratching his head, the wind carried back to him what sounded like an argument from the hill on the other side of the road. Something about due north having been over those hills there ten minutes ago, and it reminded someone of that time in Iraq.

Thorgeir looked at his watch. He had plenty of time before he was due to meet the helicopter, and he was starting to get a tingling sensation all down the side of his nose, where his whiskers had once been.

'Told you someone would come and find us,' croaked th assistant cameraman. 'Just like that time in Cambodia

'That wasn't Cambodia,' said the assistant sound-recordist, 'that was Kurdestan.'

'We *started* in Iraq,' replied the senior cameraman. 'That's the bloody point.'

'Thank you,' gasped Danny Bennett to the stranger. He was hoarse from arguing. For a long time, he had thought that he had imagined the sound of a car engine. 'We've been wandering round in circles all day. That fool of a cameraman's got one of those compasses you buy at filling stations, and we'd been walking for hours before we realised that it was being attracted by his solar calculator.'

'Are those your vans up there?' said the stranger.

'Yes.' Suddenly, Danny seemed to notice something about his rescuer and recoiled violently.

'What's up?' said the stranger.

'Sorry,' Danny said. 'It's just that suit you're wearing.'

'My suit?' The stranger looked affronted.

'It's a very nice suit,' Danny said. 'It's just that it's grey. But it's not from Marks and Spencer.'

'I should think not,' said the stranger irritably. 'Brooks Brothers, this is. OK, the lapels are a bit on the narrow side, but—'

'It's a long story,' Danny said. 'And you'd probably think I was mad.'

'I already think you're mad,' said the stranger, smoothing out the creases on his sleeve, 'so what have you got to lose?'

So Danny told him. He explained about the ship-burial, the first attack, the second attack, the eagle and the men in the grey suits. The stranger seemed entirely unsurprised and utterly convinced by it all; in fact he seemed so interested that Danny was on the point of telling him about his President Kennedy theory when the stranger interrupted him.

'Was there an old man with them, by any chance? Very old indeed, with a horrible squeaky voice?'

'Yes,' Danny said, 'I think so.'

'And what about the others?' The stranger described the men in grey suits. Danny nodded feebly.

'Do you know them, then?' he asked.

'Oh, yes. They and I go way back.'

Danny dug his fingernails into the palms of his hands. 'Who are they, then?'

The stranger grinned in a way that reminded Danny of an Alsatian he had been particularly afraid of as a boy. 'I don't really think you want to know,' he said. 'Not in your present state of mind.'

'Yes, I do,' Danny said urgently. 'And what has Hildy Frederiksen got to do with it?'

The stranger raised an eyebrow. 'Who's Hildy Frederiksen?'

'The archaeologist. The one who found the burial. She's with them.'

'You don't say.' The stranger had stopped grinning. 'Listen,' he said, taking hold of Danny's sleeve.

'Yes?'

'Who do *you* think those men are?'

Danny blinked twice. 'Are they from the CIA?'

'In a sense. You're a TV producer, Mr. . . .'

'Bennett, Danny Bennett.'

'I envy you, Mr Bennett. You've stumbled on to something big here. Really big.'

'Have I?'

The stranger nodded. 'This is once-in-a-career stuff. If I were you, I'd forget all about that ship-burial and get after the men in the grey suits.'

'Really?' The roof of Danny's mouth felt like sandpaper.

'Just don't quote me, that's all. The road's over there. It was good meeting you.' The stranger started to walk away.

'So you don't think I've gone crazy, then?' Danny called after him.

'No,' replied the stranger.

'I didn't tell you about the little blue lights, did I?'

The stranger stopped and turned round. Strange-shaped ears that man has, Danny thought. Almost pointed.

'Tell me about the little blue lights,' said the stranger.


'If you must hum,' said Prexz, 'hum quietly.'

'I'm not humming,' Zxerp replied, 'you are.'

'No, I'm not. And do you mind not shouting? I feel like I've got a short just above my left eye.'

'It must be that cable, then,' replied his companion. 'Humming.'

'Will you shut up about that cable?'

Prexz closed his eyes and resolved to keep perfectly still for at least half an hour. If that didn't work, he could try a brief electric storm.

'Prexz.'

'Now what?'

'It's not the cable. It's coming from up there.'

Prexz opened his eyes. 'You're right,' he said. 'And it isn't a humming. More like a buzzing, really.'

'I don't like it, Prexz. Shouldn't we take a look?'

'Please yourself,' grunted Prexz. He lay back against the cable and dozed off. Zxerp tried to follow his example, but the buzzing grew louder. Then it stopped. After a moment, another sound took its place. Prexz sat upright with a jerk.

'It's that perishing wizard,' he groaned.

'It's not, you know,' whispered Zxerp. 'Do you know who I think that is?'

The two chthonic spirits stared at each other in horror as the summons grew louder and louder, until they could resist it no longer. Something seemed to be dragging them up to the surface. As they emerged into the violent light of the sun, they were seized by strong hands and copper wire was twisted around their necks. They were trapped.

# 6

AFTER BREAKFASTING on barbecued rabbit and lager (from the wizard's now perpetually refilling can) in the ruined broch just south of the Loch of Killimster, King Hrolf Earthstar and his heroes – and heroine – drove into Wick in search of thin copper wire, resistors, crocodile clips and other assorted bits and pieces needed by the wizard for connecting the two chthonic spirits up to the Luck of Caithness. Of course, it had not occurred to any of them to check that the two spirits were still in the small sandalwood box into which the wizard had sealed them with a powerful but imperfectly remembered spell; but even a wizard cannot be expected to think of everything.

The fog and low cloud, which had been hovering over the tops of the mountains for the last few days, had come down thickly during the night, and Hildy, who was not used to driving under such conditions, made slow progress along the road to Wick. The town itself seemed, as usual, deserted, and Hildy felt little trepidation about leading her unlikely looking party through the streets. As it happened, such of the local people as were out and about did stop for a moment and speculate who these curious men in grey suits might be; but after a little subdued discussion they decided that they were a party of Norwegians off one of the rigs, which would account for their uniform dress and long shaggy beards.

There is an electrical-goods shop in Wick, and if you have the determination of a hero used to long and apparently impossible quests you can eventually find it, although it will of course be closed for lunch when you do.

'I remember there used to be a mead-hall just along from here,' said Angantyr Asmundarson. His shoes were hurting, and he liked the town even less than he had the last time he had visited it, about twelve hundred years previously. 'They used to do those little round shellfish that look like large pink woodlice.'

'I thought you hated them,' said the King. 'You always used to make a fuss when we had them back at the castle.'

'I never said I did like them,' Angantyr replied. 'And, anyway, I don't expect the mead-hall's there any more.'

Oddly enough it was, or at least there was a building set aside for roughly the same purpose standing on the site of it. Hildy was most unwilling that the company should go in, but the King overruled her; if Angantyr didn't get something to eat other than rabbit pretty soon, he suggested, he would start to whine, and that he could do without.

'All right, then,' Hildy said, 'but be careful.'

'In what way?' asked the King.

Hildy could not for the moment think of anything that the heroes should or should not do. She tried to imagine a roughly similar situation, but all she could think of was Allied airmen evading the Germans in occupied France, and she had never been keen on war films. 'Don't draw attention to yourselves,' she said, 'and keep your voices down.' As she said this, something that had been nagging away at the back of her mind resolved itself into a query.

'By the way,' she asked the King, as she brought back a tray laden with twelve pints of Tennants lager and twelve packets of scampi fries, 'how is it that I can understand everything you say? It's almost as if you were speaking modern English. You should be talking in Old Norse or something, shouldn't you?'

'We are,' said the King, wiping froth from the edges of his moustache. 'I thought you were, too. And what's English?'

At this point, the wizard made a sound like a slate-saw.

The King raised an eyebrow, then translated for Hildy's benefit.

'He says it's a language-spell he put on us all. He says it would save a great deal of trouble. Unfortunately,' the King went on, 'he couldn't put one on himself. He tried, using a mirror, but it didn't work. He's now got a mirror that can speak all living and dead languages, but even we can't understand most of what he says because he's got this speech impediment and he mumbles.'

Not for the first time, Hildy wondered whether the King was having a joke at her expense, or whether her new friends were just extremely different from anyone she had ever met before. However, the King's explanation seemed to be as good as any, and so she let it go. The thirteen helpings of grilled salmon and chips she had ordered (and pair for; the money wasn't going to last much longer at this rate) arrived and were soon disposed of, despite the heroes' lack of familiarity with the concept of the fork. However, even though they did not know what to use them for, they displayed considerable unwillingness to give them back, and Hildy had to insist. All in all, she was glad to get them all out of the hotel before they made a scene.

'And who do you suppose they were?' asked the waitress as she cleared away the plates.

'English, probably,' said the barman.

'Ah,' replied the waitress, 'that would account for it.'

By now the keeper of the electrical shop had returned from lunch, and Hildy, the wizard and the King went in while the heroes waited outside. After a great deal of confusion, they got what they wanted, and Hildy led them back to where the van was parked. She considered stopping and buying some postcards to send to her family back in America, but decided not to; 'Having a wonderful time saving the world from a twelve-hundred-year-old sorcerer' would be both baffling and, just for the moment, untrue. She did, however, nip into a camping shop and buy herself a new anorak. Her paddock-jacket was getting decidedly grubby and it smelt rather too much of boiled rabbit for her liking.

'Where to now?' she asked, as they all climbed into the van.

'Home,' said the King.

Hildy frowned. 'You mean Rolfsness?' she asked. 'The ship? I don't think—'

'No, no,' said the King, 'I said Home.'

'Where's that?'

The King, who had already grasped the principle of Ordnance Survey maps, pointed to a spot just to the north-east of Bettyhill. 'There,' he said.

'Why?' Hildy asked.

'I live there,' replied the King simply. 'I haven't been home for a long time.'

Hildy looked again at the map. It was a long way away, and she was tired of driving. But the King insisted. They filled up with petrol (Hildy now had enough Esso tokens for a new flashlight, but she couldn't be bothered) and set off. Their road lay first through Thurso and then past the now functioning nuclear power station, and the turning for Rolfsness; but the area seemed deserted. Hildy wondered why.

Eventually they crossed the Swordly Burn and took the turning the King had indicated. There were quite a few houses along the narrow road, but Hildy found a small knot of trees where the van could be hidden, and they packed all their goods into the rucksacks she had bought and the heroes wrapped blankets over their shields and weapons. The company looked, Hildy thought, like a cross between an attempt on Everest and a party of racegoers with a picnic lunch.

They had walked about a mile from the road when they came to a small narrow-necked promontory overlooking the Bay of Swordly. Below them the cliffs fell away to the grey and unfriendly sea, and Hildy began to feel distinctly unwell since she suffered from attacks of vertigo. There was only a rudimentary track heading north, over a broad arch of rock, apparently leading nowhere. Hildy hoped that the King knew where he was going.

Suddenly the King scrambled off the path and seemed to disappear into the rock. The heroes and the wizard followed, leaving Hildy all alone on the top of the cliff. She was feeling thoroughly ill and not at all heroic. This was rather like going for walks with her father when she was a child.

'Are you coming, then?' she heard the King's voice shouting, but could not tell where it came from.

'Where are you?' she shouted.

'Down here.' The sound seemed to be coming from directly below. She tried to look down, but her legs started to give way under her and she stopped. After what seemed a very long time, the King reappeared and beckoned to her.

'There's a passage just here leading down to the castle,' he said. 'Mind where you put your feet. I never did get around to having those steps cut.'

This time Hildy summoned all her courage and followed him. A door in the rock, like a small porthole, stood open before her, and she dived through it.

'That's the back door,' said the King, pulling it shut. It closed with a soft click, and the tunnel was suddenly pitch-dark. The passage was not long, and it came out in a sort of rocky amphitheatre perched on the edge of the cliff. Just below them were the ruins of ancient masonry; but all of a much later period, medieval or perhaps sixteenth-century. The amphitheatre itself, with a deep natural cave behind, was little more than a slight modification of the original rock.

'I see they've mucked up the front door,' said the King with a sigh. 'Still, that's no great loss.' He looked out over the sea, and then turned back to Hildy. 'Unless you know what to look for,' he said, 'this place is invisible except from the sea, and now the front gate's been taken out the only way down here is that door we came through, which is also impossible to find unless you know about it. Someone's been building down there, but this part is exactly as it was. Let's see if the hall's been got at.'

He led the way into the cave. The heroes had evidently

had the same idea, for another small door had been thrown open, and the sound of voices came out of it. Hildy followed the King into a wide natural chamber.

In the middle of the chamber was a long stone table, on which Starkad and Arvarodd were standing, poking at the ceiling with their spears. 'Just getting the windows open,' Arvarodd grunted, 'only the wretched thing seems to have got stuck,' and he pushed open a stone trapdoor, flooding the chamber with light. Hildy looked about her in amazement. The walls were covered in rich figured tapestries, looking as if they had just been made but recognisable as typical products of the ninth century. The table was laid with gold and silver plates and drinking-horns, with places for about a hundred. Beside the table was a hearth running the length of the chamber, and the rest of the floor was covered in dry heather that crackled under Hildy's feet. Against the wall stood a dozen huge chests with massive iron locks, and in the corners of the room were stacks of spears and weapons. Everything appeared to be perfectly preserved, but the air in the chamber was decidedy musty.

'The doors and shutters on the windows are airtight,' explained the King. 'We knew a thing or two about building in my day.'

'What is this place?' Hildy asked.

'This', said the King with a hint of pride in his voice, 'is the Castle of Borve, one of my two strongholds. The other is at Tongue, but I never did like it much. The Castle of Borve is totally impregnable, and the view is rather better, if you like seascapes. On a clear day you can see Orkney.'

The heroes had got the chests open, and were busily rummaging about in them for long-lost treasures; favourite cloaks and comfortable shoes. Someone came up with a cask of mead on which a preserving spell had been laid, while Arvarodd, who had lit a small fire at one end of the hearth, was roasting the last of the sausages Hildy had bought in Marks & Spencer at Inverness. The heroes had discovered that they liked sausages.

'The Castle of Borve', said the King, 'was built for my father, Ketil Trout, by Thorkel the Builder. My father was a bit of a miser, I'm afraid, and, since he was forever going to war with all and sundry, usually very hard up. So when he commissioned the castle from Thorkel, the finest builder of his day, he stipulated that if there was anything wrong with the castle on delivery Thorkel's life should be forfeit and all his property should pass to the King. Actually, that was standard practice in the building industry then.'

Hildy, who had had bad experiences with builders in her time, nodded approvingly.

'The trouble was that there was nothing at all wrong with the castle,' the King continued, 'and Ketil was faced with the horrible prospect of having to pay for the place, which he could not afford to do. So he persuaded the builder to go out into the bay with him by ship, on the pretext of inspecting the front gate. Meanwhile my mother hung a rope over the front ramparts, which, seen from the sea, looked like a crack in the masonry. Ketil pointed this out to Thorkel as a fault in the work, and poor old Thorkel was left with no alternative but to tie the anchor to his leg and jump in the sea. This was really rather fortuitous, since apart from my father he was the only other person to know the secret of the back door, which we came in by. Oddly enough, ever after my father had terrible trouble getting anyone to do any work on the place, which was a profound nuisance in winter when the guttering tended to get blocked.'

The heroes had drunk half of the enchanted mead and were beginning to sing. The King frowned. 'Anyway,' he said briskly, 'that's the Castle of Borve for you. Back to business.'

He clapped his hands, and the heroes cleared a space on the table. The wizard laid out the various items he had obtained in Wick, and the King laid the dragon-brooch beside them. The wizard set to work with some tools he had retrieved from one of the chests, and soon the brooch was festooned with short lengths of wire, knitted into an intricate pattern. Then he made a sign with his hand, and Ohtar brought over the sandalwood box. The wizard picked it up, shook it and held it to his ear.

'Now what?' demanded the King impatiently. The wizard made a subdued noise, like a very small lathe.

'You haven't!' shouted the King.

The wizard nodded, made a sound like a distant dentist's drill, and hid his face in his hands.

'I don't believe it,' said the King in fury. 'You stupid. . . . Oh, get out of my sight.' The wizard promptly vanished, turning himself into a tiny spider hanging from the ceiling.

'What's the matter?' Hildy asked.

'He's only gone and lost them, that's all,' growled the King. 'Here, give me that box.'

He threw open the lid, but there was nothing inside except the chewed-up remains of a couple of torch-batteries Hildy had put in for the two spirits to eat. For a moment there was total silence in the chamber; then the King threw the box on the ground and jumped on it.

'Now look what you've made me do,' he roared at the spider swinging unhappily from the roof.

'But what's happened?' Hildy wailed. She felt that she was in grave danger of being forgotten about.

'I'll tell you what's ruddy well happened,' said the King. 'This idiotic wizard has let those two spirits escape, that's what. He was supposed to have sealed them in his magic elf-box. . . .' The King stepped out of the smashed fragments of the magic elf-box, which would henceforth be incapable of holding so much as a bad dream. 'Now we've got nothing to work the brooch with. Without them it's useless.'

The heroes all started to complain at once, and even the spider began cheeping sadly. The King banged his fist on the table and shouted for quiet.

'Let's all stay calm, shall we?' he muttered. 'Let's all sit down, like reasonable human beings, and discuss this sensibly.' He followed his own suggestion, and the rest of the heroes, still murmuring restlessly like the sea below them, did likewise. The spider scuttled down his gossamer thread and perched on the lip of the King's great drinking-horn.

'All right, Kotkel,' snapped the King to the spider, 'you've made your point. You can come back now.'

The wizard reappeared, hanging his grizzled head in shame, and took his place at the King's left hand. The company that had, a few moments ago, resembled nothing so much as a football team stranded in the middle of nowhere with no beer had become, as if by some subtler magic, the King's Household, his council in peace and war. A shaft of sunlight broke through the stone-framed skylight into the chamber, highlighting the King's face like a spotlight – Thorkel the Builder had planned the effect deliberately, calculating where the sun would be in relation to the surrounding mountains at the time when the Master of Borve would be likely to be seated in his high place. Hildy found herself sitting, by accident or design, in the Counsellor's place at his right hand, so that such of the sunlight as the King could spare fell on her commonplace features. A feeling of profound awe and responsibility came over her, and she resolved, come what may, to acquit herself as well as she could in the King's service.

Arvarodd of Permia, who carried the King's harp, and Angantyr Asmundarson, who was his standard-bearer, rose to their feet and pronounced in unison that Hrolf Ketilsson Earthstar, absolute in Caithness and Sutherland, Lord of the Isles, held court for policy in the fastness of his House; let those who could speak wisely do so. There was total silence, as befitted such an august moment. Then there was more silence, and Hildy realised that this was because nobody could think of anything to say.

'Well, come on, then,' said the King. 'You were all so damned chatty a moment ago. Let's be having you.'

To his feet rose Bothvar Bjarki, and Hildy suddenly remembered that he had been the adviser of the great king Kraki, devising for him stratagems without number, which generations of skalds had kept evergreen in memory.

'We could go back and look for them,' suggested Bothvar Bjarki.

'Oh, sit down and shut up,' said the King impatiently. 'Has anyone got any *sensible* suggestions?'

Bothvar sat down and started to mutter to himself. Angantyr was sniggering, and Bothvar gave him a look. Hildy, thoroughly bewildered, realised that she was on her feet and speaking.

'Perhaps', she stammered, 'the wizard can find them. Wasn't there that bit in *Arvarodd's Saga* where someone put a seer-stone to his eye. . .?'

'Have you got a seer-stone, Kotkel?' demanded the King, turning to the wizard. Arvarodd, sitting opposite Hildy, seemed to be blushing slightly. He leant across the table and whispered: 'Actually, I made that bit up. I wanted a sort of mystical scene to counterpoint all the starkly realistic bits. You see, the structure seemed to demand. . . .' Hildy found herself nodding, as she so often had at Cambridge parties.

The wizard was turning out his pockets. From the resulting pile of unsightly junk, he picked out a small blue pebble, heart-shaped, with a hole through the middle. He breathed on it, grunted some obscure spell, and set it in his eye like a watchmaker's lens.

'Well?' said the King impatiently.

There was a sound like a carborundum wheel from the wizard. 'Interference,' whispered Arvarodd. 'Ever since they privatised it—'

But the wizard shook his head and took out the stone. Then he leant across the King and offered it to Hildy.

'Go on,' the King said. 'It doesn't hurt.'

Hildy closed her mouth, which had fallen open, and took the stone from the wizard's hand. It felt strangely warm, like a seat on a train that someone has just left, and Hildy felt very reluctant to touch it. But she held it up to her eye, squinting through the hole. To her amazement, and horror, she found that she could see a picture through it, as if it were a keyhole in a closed door.

She saw a tower of grey stone and glass, completely

unfamiliar at first; then she recognised it as an office-block. Pressing the stone hard against her eye, she found that she could see in through one of the windows, and beyond that through the open door of an office. Inside the office was a glass case, like a fish-tank, and inside that were two pools of light. There were wires leading from the tank into the back of a large square box-like trunk, which she could not identify for a moment. Then, with a flash of insight, she realised that the box was a computer, and that whoever it was that had control of the two spirits was using them to cut down on his electricity bills.

She thought she could hear voices; but the voices were very far away – they were coming from the picture behind the stone.

'And two for his nob makes seven, redoubled,' said the voice. 'Proceed to Valhalla, do not pass Go, do not collect two hundred crowns.' The other voice sniggered.

It's them, Hildy thought. She felt utterly exhausted, as if she had been lifting heavy weights with the muscles of her eyes, and her head was splitting.

'I give up,' said the first voice. 'I never did like this game.'

'Let's play something else, then,' said the other voice equably.

'I don't want to play anything,' retorted the first voice. 'I want to get out of here, before they plug us in to something else. I don't mind being kidnapped, but I do resent being used to heat water.'

'Impossible,' said the second voice. 'We're stuck. I suggest we make the most of it.' The first light flickered irritably, but the second light ignored it. 'My throw. Oh, good, that's an X and a Y. I can make "oxycephalous", and it's on a triple rune score—'

'There's no such word as "oxycephalous",' said the first voice, 'not in Old Norse.'

'There is now,' replied the second voice cheerfully. 'Up the tree, six, and I think I'll see you.'

Hildy's eyes were hurting, but she struggled to keep them open, as she had so often struggled at lectures and seminars. With a tremendous effort of will, she forced herself to zoom backwards, widening her angle of view. She saw the office-block again, standing in a familiar landscape, but one which she could not put a name to. Then she made out what could only be a Tube station, stunningly prosaic in the midst of all the magic. With a final spurt of effort she read the name, 'St Paul's'. Then the stone fell from her eye, and she slumped forward on to the table.

When she came round, she found the heroes gathered about her. She told them what she had seen, and what she deduced from it. The King sat down again, and put his face in his hands.

'We must take a great risk,' he said at last. 'I shall have to go to this place and recover the two spirits. Otherwise, there is no hope.'

'You mustn't,' Hildy protested. 'They'll catch you, and then there really won't be any hope.' She dug her fingers into the material of her organiser bag until they started to ache. 'Let me go instead.'

The King suddenly lifted his head and smiled at her. 'We'll both go,' he said cheerfully, almost lightheartedly. 'And you, Kotkel. Only this time you'll do it properly, understand? And you, Brynjolf,' he said to the shape-changer, who was trying unsuccessfully to hide behind the massive shoulders of Starkad Storvirksson, 'we'll need you as well. And two others. Any volunteers?'

Everyone froze, not daring to move. But after a moment Arvarodd stood up, looked around the table, and nodded. 'I'll come,' he said quietly. 'After all, it can't be worse than Permia.' He laughed weakly at his own joke, but all the others were silent. The King looked scornfully about him, and sighed. 'Chicken,' he said, 'the whole lot of you.'

Starkad Storvirksson rose to his feet. 'Can I come?' he asked mildly. If no one else was prepared to go, he might at last get his chance to do something other than fighting. Fighting was all right in its way, but he was sure there was more to being a hero than just hitting people.

'No, Starkad,' said the King kindly. 'I know *you're* not afraid. But not this time. I'll explain later.'

Starkad sat down, looking dejected, and Brynjolf patted him comfortingly on the shoulder. 'It's because you're so stupid, Starkad,' he said gently. 'You'd only be in the way.'

'Oh,' said Starkad happily. 'If that's the reason, I don't mind.'

'I'll go,' said Bothvar Bjarki suddenly, and all the heroes turned and stared at him. 'What this job needs is brains, not muscle.' The King muttered something inaudible under his breath, and said that, on second thoughts, five would be plenty. Bothvar scowled, but the heroes cheered loudly, and raised the toast; first to Odin, giver of victory; then to the six adventurers; then to their Lord, King Hrolf Earthstar. Then Ohtar remembered that there had been another cask of enchanted mead in the back storeroom, and they all went to look for it.

'The others had better not stay here,' said the King to Hildy, while they were gone. 'They'll have to hunt for food and find water, and I saw too many houses on the road back there. I'll send them up into the mountains.' From the back storeroom came sounds of cursing; someone, back in the ninth century, had left the top off the barrel. The King grinned. 'It'll give them something else to complain about until we get back.'

'Will they be all right?' Hildy asked doubtfully. 'They don't seem terribly practical to me.'

The King nodded. 'I should think so,' he said. 'Take Angantyr Asmundarson, for instance. To join the muster at Melvich, he marched all night from Brough Head to Burwick – that's right across the two main islands of Orkney – and since there was no boat available he swam over from Burwick to the mainland, in the middle of a storm. Then he ran all the way from Duncansby Head to Melvich, on the morning before the battle, and still fought in the front rank against the stone-trolls of Finnmark. Complaining bitterly about his wet clothes and how he was going to catch his death of pneumonia, of course, but

97

that's just his way.' He paused, and contemplated his fingernails for a moment. 'Put like that, I suppose, it rather proves your point. Only a complete idiot would have gone to so much trouble to get involved in a battle. Come on,' he said briskly, 'it's time we were going.'

Thorgeir Storm-Shepherd was feeling his age, and since he was nearing his thirteen-hundredth birthday this was no small problem. He could not, he reflected, take the long journeys like he used to, when a flight from Oslo to Thingvellir, perched uncomfortably between the shoulderblades of the huge mutant seagull that his employer had bred specially for him, had just been part of a normal day's work.

He had not been idle. What with dashing about by train, car and helicopter, interviewing Danny Bennett and capturing the two chthonic spirits, then hurrying back to Rolfsness to clear the area of Professor Wood and his archaeologists, he felt he had earned a rest. But now he was back in London, and the sorcerer-king was in the bad mood that usually attended the tricky part of any enterprise.

The two spirits were safely locked up in a spellproof perspex tank, and the Professor had been shunted off to the British Museum to ferret about among the Old Norse manuscripts one more time, just in case anything had been overlooked. Still, the Professor was a useful man. Another practical benefit of commercial sponsorship of archaeology. It had, of course, been fortuitous that a freak and entirely localised storm had threatened to flood the site at Rolfsness, forcing the excavation team to close up the mound and go away, but Thorgeir was not called Storm-Shepherd for nothing. He was glad that he had kept his hand in at that particular field of Old Magic, useful over the past thousand years only for betting on draws in cricket matches and then washing them out. He leant back in his chair and ruffled the papers on his desk. As well as being a Dark Age sorcerer, he was also one of the key executives in the world's largest multinational, and work had been piling up while he was away. As he flicked through a sheaf of 'while-you-were-out' notes, he reflected that it was a pity that he had never mastered the art of delegation.

The intercom buzzed, and his secretary told him that his boss was on the scrambler. Thorgeir disliked the machine, but it was better than telepathy, which had until recently been the main method of in-office communication between himself and the sorcerer-king, and which invariably gave him a headache.

'Now what?' said the sorcerer-king.

'That's that,' replied Thorgeir, 'at least for the moment. Without those two whatsits, the brooch is useless.'

'Why can't they just plug it into the mains?'

'Even if they could, they couldn't get enough power from the ordinary mains,' Thorgeir explained patiently. 'But they can't. They need direct current, and you'd need a transformer the size of Liverpool to convert it. The only power source in the world big enough to power that brooch is sitting in a perspex tank in Vouchers. You have my word on it.'

'So now what?'

'With the brooch out of action, they're up the fjord without a paddle.' Thorgeir grinned into the receiver. 'Lucky, wasn't I?'

'Yes,' said the sorcerer-king, 'very.'

Thorgeir stopped grinning. 'So we have all the time in the world to find them and dispose of them. They can't do us any harm.'

'You said that the last time, before Melvich.'

'That was different.'

'So is this different. How do you know they can't modify it?'

'Trust me. Let me rephrase that,' Thorgeir added hurriedly, for that was a sore point at all times. 'Rely on it. They can't. All they can do is try breaking in here and springing the two gnomes.'

'Just let them try.'

'Exactly. So relax, won't you? Enjoy yourself. Set up a

new newspaper or something. The situation is under control.'

'I hope so.' The sorcerer-king rang off.

Thorgeir shook his head and returned to his work. The papers from the Japanese deal were starting to come through, and he didn't like the look of them at all. Come the glorious day, he said to himself, I'll turn that whole poxy country into a golf-course, and we'll see how they like that. But before he could settle to it the telephone went again. This time it was Professor Wood, ringing from the call-box outside the British Museum. Thorgeir sat up and reached for a pen and some paper.

After a few minutes, he put the phone down carefully and read back his notes. Things were starting to take shape. In a nineteenth-century collection of Gaelic folk-tales, the Professor had found a most interesting story, all about a chieftain called Rolf McKettle and his battle with the Fairies. Allowing for the distortions inevitably occurring over a millennium of the oral tradition and home-made whisky, it was a fair and accurate report of the battle of Melvich, and it went on to tell the rest of the story, including where the King had been buried and who was buried with him.

The Professor would be round in about half an hour. Thorgeir dumped a half-hundredweight of unread contracts in his out-tray and went to tell his boss. 'Not', he reflected as he got into the lift, 'that he'll take kindly to being called a fairy. But there we go.'

How long he had been there, or where exactly there was, Danny had no idea, but he was beginning to wonder whether the senior cameraman might not have been right after all. It had been the senior cameraman, armed with the map, who had insisted that the big cloudy thing over to their right was Ben Stumanadh, and that the road was just the other side of it. Danny had been a Boy Scout (although he had taken endless pains to make sure that no one in the Corporation knew about it) and he knew that the assertion was patently ridiculous, and that the cameraman was determined to lead the crew into the bleak and inhospitable interior, where death from exposure was a very real possibility. He had reasoned with him, ordered him, and finally shouted at him; but the fool had taken no notice, and neither had the rest of the crew. Finally, Danny had washed his hands of the lot of them and set out to walk the few miles to the road, which he knew was just over to the left.

Of course the mist hadn't helped, but the further he had gone, the more Danny had become convinced that either the map had been wrong or that someone had moved the road. As exhaustion and hunger, and the loss of both his shoes in a bog had taken their toll, he had inclined more and more to the latter explanation, especially after his short but illuminating chat with the two brown sheep which had been the only living things he had seen since meeting the strange man who had pointed them all in the wrong direction. Shortly after he had arrived at that conclusion, his eyes started playing tricks on him, and he had spent the night in what appeared at the time to be a fully equipped editing suite, complete with facilities for transposing film on to video-tape. In the cold (very cold) light of morning it had turned out to be a ruined shieling, and he had somehow acquired a rather disconcertingly high fever. But at least it kept him warm, which was something.

Rather optimistically, he tried out his arms and his legs, but of course they wouldn't work, just as his car never used to start when he had a particularly urgent meeting. He felt surprisingly calm, and reflected that that was probably one of the fringe benefits of going completely mad. If he wasn't deeply into the final stage of hallucination that came just before death by exposure, he wouldn't be imagining that the men in the grey suits were coming over the hill towards him.

'Just like old times,' one of them was saying. 'Out on the fells with no shelter and nothing to eat but rabbit and perishing salmon. If I have to eat any more salmon, I'll start looking like one.'

Since over his suit he was wearing a coat of silvery scale armour he already did; but of course, Danny reflected, since the man was not really there he was not to know that. He groaned softly, and slumped a little further behind the stones. If he had to see visions in his madness, he would have preferred something a little less eccentric.

'If you hadn't been so damned fussy,' said another of the men, 'we could have had one of those sheep.'

'He said not to get into any trouble,' said the salmon-man. 'Stealing sheep counts as trouble. Always did.'

'There might be deer in that forest we passed,' said a third man.

'Then, again, there might not,' replied the salmon-man, who seemed a miserable sort of person. Danny decided he didn't like him much and tried to replace him with a beautiful girl, but apparently the system didn't work like that. 'And if you think I'm going to go rushing about some wood in the hope that it's full of deer you can think again,' the salmon-man said. The others didn't bother to reply. Danny approved.

'That'll do,' said one of them. He was pointing at the shieling, and Danny realised that they intended to make their camp there. That was a pity, since he had wanted to spend his last hours on earth in quiet meditation, not making conversation with a bunch of phantasms from the Milk Marketing Board. In fact, Danny said to himself, I won't have it. An Englishman's fallen-down old shed is his castle, even in Scotland. 'Go away,' he shouted, and turned his face to the stone wall. The words just managed to clear his lips, but they fell away into the wind and were dispersed.

'There's someone in there,' said Starkad Storvirksson.

'So there is,' said Ohtar. 'I wonder if he wants a fight.'

'Better ask him first,' said Angantyr. 'It's very bad manners to fight people without asking.'

'I thought we weren't supposed to fight anyone,' Starkad said.

'We can if we have to defend ourselves,' said Ohtar, but his heart wasn't in it. The man hardly looked worth

102

fighting anyway. In fact he looked decidedly unwell. Ohtar turned him over gently with his foot.

'Ask him if he's got anything to eat,' Angantyr whispered. 'Tell him we'll trade him two rabbits and a salmon for anything in the way of cheese.'

'Hold it, will you?' said Ohtar. 'It's that sorcerer from the van, the one who wouldn't fight with Bothvar.' He turned to his companions and smiled. 'Things are looking up,' he said. 'We've got ourselves a prisoner.'

# 7

'HAVE SOME more rabbit,' said Ohtar kindly. Although Danny had done nothing but eat all night, he felt it would be rude to refuse. Obviously the strange men prided themselves on their hospitality.

'Are you sure you'll have enough for yourselves?' he asked desperately, as Ohtar produced two more burnt drumsticks, still mottled with little flecks of singed fur. The man they called Angantyr made a curious snorting noise.

'Don't you mind him,' said Ohtar. 'Plenty more where that came from.'

'Well, in that case. . . .' Danny sank his teeth into the carbonised flesh and tried not to remember that he had been very fond of his pet rabbit, Dimbleby, when he was a boy. 'This is very good,' he said, forcing his weary jaws to chew.

'Really?' Ohtar beamed. He had been field-cook to King Hrolf for most of his service, and this was the first time anyone had paid him a compliment. 'You wait there,' he said and, gathering up his sling and a handful of pebbles, walked away.

'You've made his day,' said Angantyr, sitting down beside Danny and absentmindedly picking up the second drumstick. 'Personally,' he said with his mouth full, 'I hate rabbit, but it's a sight better than seagull. You ever had seagull?'

'No,' Danny said.

'Very wise,' said Angantyr, and he spat out a number of small bones. 'Not that you can't make something of it with a white sauce and some fennel. Don't get me wrong,' he added, 'I'm not obsessive about food, like some I could mention. Five square meals a day is all I ask, and a jug or so of something wet to see it on its way. But I draw the line at seaweed,' he asserted firmly. 'Except in a mousse, of course.'

'Of course,' Danny agreed.

Having looked to make sure that there was no more rabbit lying about, Angantyr lay back against the wall of the ruined bothy and pulled his helmet down over his eyes. 'Ah, well,' he said, 'this is better than work. What do you do with yourself, by the way? I know you're a sorcerer of sorts, but that could mean anything, couldn't it?'

'I'm a producer,' Danny said.

'Good for you,' Angantyr said. 'Me, I'm strictly a consumer.' The early-morning sun was shining weakly through a window in the cloud, and the hero was in a good mood. 'That was always the trouble with this country,' he went on. 'Too few producers and too many consumers. I admire you people, honestly I do. Out behind the plough in all weathers, or driving the sheep home through the snow. Rotten job, always said so.'

'No, no,' Danny said, 'I'm not a farmer, I'm a producer. A television producer.'

Angantyr sat up, a caterpillar-like eyebrow raised. 'What's that, then?'

'You know . . .,' Danny said weakly. 'I work out the schedules, supervise the crews, that sort of thing.'

'You mean a forecastle-man?' Angantyr suspected that his leg was being pulled. 'Get out, you're not, are you?'

'Not that sort of crew,' Danny said, wishing he had never mentioned it. 'Camera crews. Keys, grips, gaffers, that sort of thing. I make television programmes.'

'Don't mind me,' said Angantyr after a long pause. 'I've been asleep for a thousand-odd years.'

'No, but really.' Danny nerved himself to ask the question that was eating away at the lining of his mind. 'Who are you people?'

Angantyr looked at him sternly, remembering that he was a sorcerer. But he looked harmless enough, and they had smashed up all his magical instruments in the Battle of the Vans.

'If I tell you,' he said, lowering his voice, 'you won't turn into a bird or something and fly away? Give me your word of honour.'

'On my word of honour,' said Danny. Obviously, he reflected, the man really didn't know what a television producer was, or he would have demanded a different oath.

'We're King Hrolf's men,' whispered Angantyr. 'We went to sleep in the ship, and now we've been woken up for the final battle.'

'You mean the ship at Rolfsness?' Danny asked. Something at the back of his mind was making sense of this, although he wished it wouldn't. By and large, he preferred it when he thought he was going mad.

'That's right,' said Angantyr patiently. 'We were asleep in the ship for twelve hundred years, and now we've woken up.'

Danny closed his eyes. 'Then, what about the grey suits?'

'You mean the clothes? That Hildy got them for us. She said we'd be less conspicuous dressed like this.'

'Hildy Frederiksen?'

'Hildy Frederik's-*daughter*. Can't be Frederik*sen*, she's a woman. Stands to reason.' Angantyr shook his head. 'Funny creature. But bright, I'll say that for her. It was lucky we met her, really, what with her knowing the sagas and all. Between you and me,' he whispered into Danny's ear, 'I think old Arvarodd's gone a bit soft on her. No accounting for taste, I suppose, and there was that time at Hlidarend—'

'Could we go through this one more time?' Danny said. 'You were actually *in* the ship when Frederiksen went into the mound?'

106

'Course we were.' It suddenly occurred to Angantyr that the prisoner might find this hard to believe, if he didn't know the story. So he told him the story. Even when he had done this, the prisoner seemed unconvinced.

'I'm sorry,' Danny said, when Angantyr put this to him. 'I'm not calling you a liar, really. But it's all the magic stuff. You see. . . .'

Angantyr remembered something he had overheard the King saying to Hildy, or it might have been the other way around. 'Just a moment,' he said. 'You call it something else now, don't you? Technology or something.'

'No, that's quite different,' Danny interrupted. He had a terrible feeling that there was something wrong with his line of argument. 'Technology is healing the sick, and doing things automatically. Magic is—'

'Watch this,' Angantyr said, and from his pocket he pulled a small doe-skin pouch. 'Here's a bit of technology I picked up in Lapland when I went raiding there.' He emptied the contents of the pouch on to the ground, and picked up two small bones and a pebble. Then he drew his knife, and with a single blow cut off his left hand just above the wrist. Danny tried to scream, but before the muscles of his larynx had relaxed from the first shock of what he had seen Angantyr picked up his severed left hand with his right hand and put it on Danny's knee.

'Hold that for me, will you?' he said cheerfully. Then he popped the pebble into his mouth, took back the severed hand and drew it back on to his wrist like a glove. Then, with his *left* hand, he took the pebble out of his mouth, wiped it on his trouser-leg and put it back in the pouch. 'How's that for technology?' he said. 'Or do you want to try it for yourself?'

Danny assured him that he did not.

'It's a bit like grafting apples,' said Angantyr, 'only quicker. What was the other thing you said? Doing things automatically. Right.'

He threw the two small bones up in the air and blew on them as they fell. One started to glow with a bright orange light, and the other burst into a tall roaring flame.

Angantyr blew on it again, and it grew smaller, like a gas jet being turned down. Then he whistled, and the flame stopped.

'That's just a portable one,' he said, putting the bones and the pouch away. 'You can get them bigger for lighting a house and cooking large meals. And they're more controllable than an open fire for gentle simmering and light frying. Cookability, you might say.'

Just then, Ohtar came back, throwing down a large sack. Angantyr turned and looked at him cautiously.

'Couldn't find any rabbits,' said Ohtar, sitting down beside them and opening the sack. 'Will seagull be all right?'

According to the road signs at Melvich, they had finished digging up the A9 at Berriedale, and the main road along the coast was fully open again. Hildy was relieved; she had not been looking forward to going back down the Lairg road, for she felt sure that if their enemy had heard about them he would be watching it, and probably the Helmsdale road as well. The main road would be much safer, as well as quicker.

She still had her doubts about leaving the rest of the heroes to their own devices, even in the wilds of Strathnaver; but she consoled herself with the thought that it would have been even more dangerous to take them to London, not to mention the expense of food, accommodation and Tube tickets for them all. As she turned these questions over in her mind, she realised, with no little pride, that she had become the effective leader of the company, and as she drove she found herself composing the first lines of her own saga. 'There was a woman called Hildy Frederiksen. . . .'

'Mind out,' said the King suddenly, 'you're going out into the middle of the road.'

'Sorry,' Hildy mumbled. It was like having driving lessons with her father. Even now, seven years after she had passed her test, he still tended to give her helpful advice, such as 'Why aren't you in third?' and 'For Christ's sake, slow down,' when she was doing about thirty-five along the freeway. She hurriedly put *Hildar Saga Frederiksdottur* back on the bookshelf of her mind, and concentrated on keeping closer in to the side of the road.

The King, she felt, was adapting remarkably quickly to the twentieth century, asking perceptive questions and making highly intelligent guesses about the various things he saw as they drove along. Even when they had passed through Inverness, the King's first sight of a major town had not seemed to throw him in any way. When she asked him about this, he simply said that he had seen many stranger things than that in his life, especially in Finnmark, and he expected to see many things stranger still. That, Hildy reckoned, she could personally guarantee. Large container-lorries seemed to intrigue him, but aircraft he regarded as inefficient and somehow rather old-fashioned. The one thing he did find fault with was what he called the 'decline of civilisation'. Coming from a Viking, Hildy thought, that was a bit much, but the King refused to be drawn on the subject, and Hildy guessed that he meant all that noble-savage stuff that you got in Victorian academic writing.

Rather than risk staying the night in a hotel, they left the motorway at Penrith and found a deserted corner of Martindale Common, near where, disconcertingly enough, the King had fought a battle with the Saxons.

'A race of men I never did take to,' the King added, as they roasted the inevitable rabbit. 'What became of them, by the way?'

Hildy told him, and he said that he wasn't in the least surprised. 'A nation of shopkeepers,' he muttered, 'bound to do well in the end.'

Hildy had written a paper on early Saxon trade, and would have discussed the matter further, but the King seemed not to be in the right mood. In fact, she thought to herself, he's been strange all day. Preoccupied.

The next day, after filling up with petrol at a service station (enough tokens now for a cut-glass decanter, only she didn't want one), they pressed on towards London. In the back, Arvarodd and the wizard were playing the same complicated game of chess that had kept them occupied all the way from Caithness, and the journey seemed not to trouble them at all. It was only when they stopped outside Birmingham for more petrol and a sandwich that Hildy noticed that the shape-changer was nowhere to be seen. 'Not again,' she muttered to herself, and asked where he'd got to.

'Down here,' said one of the chess-pieces.

'We left the black rook behind,' Arvarodd explained.

'But don't you mind?' Hildy asked the black rook. The rook shrugged its rigid shoulders.

'It passes the time,' he said. 'And chess-pieces don't get travel-sick.'

'It's just that black always seems to win,' Arvarodd said. They had drawn for colours before setting off, and he was playing white. 'Not that I mind that much, of course. I generally lose to Kotkel anyway.'

'Do chess-pieces get hungry?' Hildy asked. She had only bought enough sandwiches for four.

'This one does,' said the rook firmly. Then the wizard grabbed him by the head and used him to take Arvarodd's queen.

They arrived in London late in the evening, and Hildy realised that she had made no plans for their stay there.

'That's all right,' said the King absently. 'We can sleep in this thing.'

Hildy started to explain about yellow lines, traffic wardens and loitering with intent, but the King wasn't listening. He was looking about him and frowning deeply.

'Of course,' Hildy said, 'this must be all totally strange to you.'

'Not at all,' said the King. 'It's most depressingly familiar.'

'It can't be,' said Hildy.

'I assure you it is. Isn't it, lads?'

Arvarodd looked up from the chessboard. 'Hello,' he said, 'I've been here before. It's just like—'

'It's just like Geirrodsgarth,' explained the King, 'where

the sorcerer-king had his first stronghold, and which we erased from the face of the earth, so that not even its foundations remained.'

Hildy shook her head. 'Surely not,' she said.

'I started to worry when we went to Wick, but it might just have been coincidence. At Inverness I felt sure. All the other cities we have passed confirmed my suspicions. The enemy has built his new city as a replica of the old one, except that it's much bigger and rather more primitive.'

'Primitive?'

'Oh, decidedly so. For a start, the whole of Geirrodsgarth was covered over with a transparent roof. But I suppose it's because he could only influence its design, not order it entirely according to his wishes. All the buildings in Geirrodsgarth were square towers like those over there.' He waved his hands at a grove of tower-blocks in the distance. 'I suppose he found the Saxons rather more stubborn than the Finns. That's shopkeepers for you.'

In the end, Hildy parked in a side-street in Hoxton, beside the Regent's Canal; it would somehow not be safe to go any further. She was aware of some vague but localised menace, and something of the sort was clearly affecting the King and the wizard, who huddled together in the back of the van and talked in low voices. Hildy realised that the wizard had put aside the language-spell, so that she could not understand what was being said. She felt betrayed and rejected. In a strained voice she said something about going and getting some food, and opened the door. The King looked up and said something, but of course she could not understand it. Arvarodd, however, translated for her.

'He says you shouldn't go,' he said.

'But I'm hungry,' Hildy replied. 'And I'm sure it'll be all right.'

The King said something else. 'He says go if you must, but take the shape-changer with you.'

'Don't I get any say in the matter?' asked the black rook. 'Two more moves and it'll be check.'

Arvarodd picked up the rook and offered it to Hildy. 'Just slip him in your pocket,' he said.

'No, thanks,' said Hildy stiffly. 'I don't want to spoil your game.'

'Just to please me,' said Arvarodd. Startled, Hildy took it and put it in her pocket. Then she opened the door and slipped out.

It took a long time for her to find a chip-shop, and she had a good mind not to buy anything for the King or the wizard. In the end, however, she bought five cod and chips, five chicken and ham pies, and a saveloy for herself, as a treat. She failed to notice that the two youths in leather jackets who had been playing the fruit machine had followed her out.

Halfway back to the van they made their move. One stepped out in front of her, waving a short knife, while the other made a grab for her bag. Hildy froze, clutching the parcels of food to her breast, and made a squeaking noise.

'Come on, lady, give us the bag,' said the youth with the knife, ''cos if you don't you'll get cut, right?'

He took a step forward. At that moment, something fell from Hildy's pocket and rolled into the gutter. The knife-man looked round, and suddenly dropped his knife. Apparently from nowhere, a terrifying figure had appeared. At first it looked like a gigantic bear; then it was a wolf, with red eyes and a lolling tongue. Finally, it was a huge grim man brandishing a broad-bladed axe. The two youths stared for a moment, then started to run. For a few moments, they thought that they were being pursued by a vast black eagle. They quickened their pace and disappeared round the corner.

'I knew that stuff you sold me was no good,' said one to the other.

'Are you all right?' said Brynjolf, returning and perching on a wing-mirror. He ruffled his feathers with his beak, and then turned back into a chess-piece. 'Sorry to be so long,' he said. 'I couldn't make up my mind what to be. The bear usually does the trick, but the wolf is more comfy.'

'That was fine,' Hildy mumbled. She was breathing

heavily, and there was vinegar all over her new anorak.
'Thank you.'

'Not at all,' said a voice from her pocket. 'Who were they,
by the way?'

'Just muggers, I think,' Hildy replied. 'That's sort of
thieves.'

'I don't know,' said her pocket. 'Young people nowadays.'

'Don't say anything to the King,' said Hildy. 'He'd only
worry.'

'Please yourself.'

Hildy didn't tell the King when she got back, but she
gave Brynjolf the saveloy. It was, she felt, the least she
could do.

The next morning, they left the van and set off on foot.
They went by Tube from Old Street to Bank, and changed
on to the Central Line for St Paul's. The concept of the
Underground seemed not to worry the King or the wizard,
but Brynjolf and Arvarodd didn't like the look of it at all.

'You know what I reckon this is?' Arvarodd whispered to
the shape-changer.

'What?'

'Burial-chambers,' replied the hero of Permia, 'like
those shaft-graves on Orkney only bigger. They must go
on for miles.'

'And what are we in, then – a coffin?' Brynjolf looked
around the compartment. 'Can't see any bodies.'

'Must be the tombs of kings,' replied Arvarodd. 'Look,
there's a diagram or something up on the side.'

Brynjolf leant forward and studied the plan.

'I reckon you may be right,' he said, returning to his
seat. 'I think there are several dynasties down here. Those
coloured lines joining up the names must be the family-
trees. Funny names they've got, though. Look, there's the
House of Kensington all buried together: South Kensington, West Kensington, High Street Kensington—'

'Kensington Olympia,' interrupted Arvarodd. 'They
must have been a powerful dynasty.'

'Them and the Parks,' agreed Brynjolf. 'And the Actons
away in the west. Hopelessly interbred, of course,' he

113

added, looking at the numerous intersections of the coloured lines at Euston. 'No wonder they got delusions of grandeur.'

Hildy overheard the end of this conversation but decided not to interrupt. It would be too complicated to explain; and, besides, as a trained archaeologist she felt that their explanation was rather better than the conventional one.

They got off at St Paul's and were faced by the escalator. This Hildy felt she would have to explain, but the heroes seemed to recognise it at once – they must have had them in Geirrodsgarth. At the foot of it, Arvarodd stopped and studied the notice.

'Dogs must be carried on the escalator,' he read aloud. 'I knew we should have brought a dog. I suppose we'll have to flog up all those stairs now.'

'All right,' said Brynjolf wearily, 'leave it to me.' He sighed heavily and turned himself into a small terrier, which Arvarodd picked up and tucked under his arm. 'Only, if you've lost your ticket', said the dog, 'you're on your own.'

Once they reached street-level, the object of their quest was obvious. Before Hildy could point to it and identify it as the building she had seen through the stone, her companions were staring at the soaring black tower that dominated the rest of Cheapside.

'That's him all over,' said the King. 'No originality.'

'Well,' said Arvarodd, 'do we go in, or what?' His hand was tightening around the grip of the sports-bag in which he was carrying his mail shirt and short sword.

'No,' said the King.

'Why not, for crying out loud?' Hildy could see that Arvarodd was sweating heavily; but he was not afraid. There was something uncanny about him, and Hildy edged away.

'Because we wouldn't get past the front gate,' replied the King quietly. For his part, he was as cold as ice. He stood motionless, but his eyes were flicking backwards and forwards as he considered every scrap of evidence that the view of the building had to offer. 'Or, rather, we would, which would be all the worse for us. I don't think physical force is the answer.'

'I don't see that we have that many options,' muttered Brynjolf. 'Unless you'd like me—'

'Certainly not,' snapped the King. 'Your magic wouldn't work in there.' He turned sharply on his heel and walked away.

'Now what?' Hildy whispered to Arvarodd. 'He's not going to give up now, is he?' Arvarodd shook his head.

'He is the King,' was all he would say.

The King was talking with the wizard, and they seemed to have agreed on something, for the King turned back and approached Hildy.

'Tell me,' he said, 'how would the power to work all the machines get into that building?'

Hildy told him about the mains and the underground cables. He nodded, and suddenly smiled.

'And all the houses and buildings in the city are connected to the same source of power?' he asked.

'I think so,' Hildy said. 'I can't be certain, of course.'

'What we need, then,' said the King, 'is a building.'


'Down the tree, four spaces over, and that's check*mate*.'

The power-level in the computer wavered suddenly. The grim-faced man got up from his desk and banged on the side of the tank.

'Any more of that,' he said savagely, 'and I'll take that game off you.'

'Sorry,' chorused the pale glow inside the tank.

'Well, all right, then,' said the grim-faced man, 'only let's have less of it.' He scowled and returned to his desk.

'For two pins,' said Prexz, 'I'd run straight up his arm and electrocute him.'

'You wouldn't dare,' replied Zxerp scornfully. 'And, besides, he might have rubber soles on his shoes, and then where would you be?'

'As I was saying,' said Prexz through clenched teeth, 'checkmate.'

'Who cares?' Zxerp stretched out his hand and knocked

115

over his goblin to signify surrender. 'What does that make the score?'

Prexz consulted the card. 'That's ninety-nine thousand, nine hundred and ninety-nine sets and eight games to me, and four games to you.'

'Inclusive?'

'Exclusive,' replied Prexz, making a mark on the card. 'So I now need only one more game for one match point. You still have some work to do.'

'I might as well concede, then,' said Zxerp. He pressed his feet against the side of the tank and put his arms behind his head. 'Then we can start again from scratch.'

'Don't be so damned pessimistic,' replied Prexz. 'A good match to win, I'll grant you, but it's still wide open.'

'We should have brought draughts instead,' yawned Zxerp. 'I'm hungry.'

'You're always hungry. Is there any of that static left, or have you guzzled it all?'

'Help yourself.' There was a faint crackling noise and a few blue sparks. 'That box of tricks over there fair takes it out of you,' Zxerp went on. 'I'll need more than static to keep electron and neutron together if I've got to keep that thing going much longer.'

Prexz turned and glowered at the computer. It winked a green light at him, and started to print something out. Just then, Prexz felt a vibration in the wire running into his left ear. Zxerp could feel the same thing. He started to protest, but Prexz hissed at him to be quiet.

'It's coming in over the mains,' he whispered.

'Tastes all right,' said Zxerp. 'A bit salty perhaps. . . .'

'Don't eat it, you fool, it's a message.'

'The old file-in-a-cake trick, huh?'

'Something like.' Prexz closed his eyes and tried to concentrate. 'I think it's the wizard.'

'Kotkel?' Zxerp leant forward.

'He's talking through the mains running into that machine we're linked up to. Honestly, the things he thinks of.'

The two spirits lay absolutely still. 'We're going to try to get you out,' they heard, 'so be ready. But it won't be easy. Don't try to reply or you'll blow the circuit. Bon appétit.'

'Very tastefully put,' said Zxerp, and he burped loudly.

The proprietor of the hotel gave Hildy a very strange look as she went past, and she could not blame him. After all, she had come in just under an hour ago with four strange-looking men and hired a room; and now they were all going away again. Still, it had been worth the embarrassment, for the wizard had managed to talk to the two captives via the shaver socket – how he had managed it she could not imagine – and they seemed to have received the message. The thing to do now was get away fast, just in case their message had been intercepted and traced.

The van was still where she had left it (why was she surprised by that? It was just an ordinary van parked in an ordinary street) and they all climbed in and drove off, entirely uncertain as to where they were going and why. The King was sitting in the back with the wizard and the shape-changer, and they were all deep in mystical discussion. But Arvarodd sat in the front, and he seemed to be in unusually good spirits.

'Don't you fret,' he said, as they drove through Highgate. 'We've been in worse fixes than this, believe you me.'

'Such as?' Hildy cast her mind back through the heroic legends of Scandinavia in search of some parallel, but the search was in vain. Usually, the old heroes had overcome their improbable trials with brute force or puerile trickery.

'Offhand,' said Arvarodd, remorselessly cheerful, 'I can't think. But it looks to me like a straightforward impregnable-fortress problem. Let's not worry about it now.'

'What's gotten into you?' Hildy asked gloomily. She found the words 'straightforward' and 'impregnable fortress' hard to reconcile.

'You worry too much,' Arvarodd replied, to Hildy's profound irritation. 'That's what comes of not having faith in the King. That's what kings are for, so people like you and me don't have to worry.'

117

Hildy, who had been brought up to vote Democrat, objected to this.

'The King doesn't seem to realise—' she started to say.

'The King realises everything,' said Arvarodd. 'And, even if he doesn't, who wants to know?' The hero of Permia yawned and folded his arms. 'If the King says, "Charge that army over there," and you say, "Which one?" and he says, "The one that outnumbers us twentyfold in that superb natural defensive position just under that hill with the sheep," then you do it. And if it works you say, "What a brilliant general the King is," and if it doesn't you go to Valhalla. Everyone's a winner, really.'

'That's what you mean by a straightforward impregnable-fortress problem?'

'Exactly. You have two options. You can work out a subtle stratagem to trick your way in, with an equally subtle stratagem to get you out again afterwards, or you can grab an axe and smash the door down. We call that the certain-death option. On the whole, it's easier and safer than all the fooling about, but you have to go through the motions.'

'So you think it'll come to that?' Hildy asked.

'No idea,' Arvarodd said. 'Not my problem.'

After more petrol – if she collected enough tokens, Hildy wondered, could she get a Challenger tank, which really would be useful in the circumstances? – they parked in a side-road on the edge of Hampstead Heath and held a council of war.

'The situation as I see it is this,' said the King. 'The tower, which would be unassailable even if we were in a position to attack it, which we aren't, is guarded night and day. Our enemy has control of the two spirits, who are essential to us if we are to have any hope of survival, let alone success. Because of the risk of detection, and because detection would mean certain defeat at this stage, we cannot make a more detailed survey of the ground, so to all intents and purposes we know absolutely nothing about the tower, how to get into it or out of it. Again, because of the risk of detection, if we are going to do anything we must do it now. I am in the market for any sensible suggestions.'

'Why not attack?' Brynjolf said. 'Then we could all go to Valhalla and have a good time.'

The wizard made a noise like worn-out disc brakes, and the King nodded. 'The wizard says', translated the King, 'that the case is not yet hopeless, that courage and wisdom together can break stone and turn steel, and that we have a duty that is not yet discharged. Also, Valhalla is looking pretty run-down these days what with nobody going there any more, the towels in the bathrooms are positively threadbare, and he's in no hurry. He says he has this on the authority of Odin's ravens, Hugin and Munin, who bring him tidings every morning, and they should know. Anyone else?'

Before anyone could speak, the van was filled with a shrill whistling, and Hildy realised that it was coming from her bag. At first she thought it was her personal security alarm, but that went *beep-beep* and, besides, she had left it in St Andrews.

'It's the seer-stone,' said Brynjolf, shouting to make himself heard.

'You mean like a sort of bleeper?' Hildy rummaged about and found the small blue pebble. It was warm again, and the noise was definitely coming from it. With great trepidation, she put it to her eye, and saw. . . .


'Really,' Danny said, 'we'll come quietly.'

The police sergeant raised himself painfully on one elbow. 'Oh, no, you don't,' he groaned. 'You said that the last time.'

'You shouldn't have tried to handcuff him,' Danny said. 'He didn't like it.'

'I gathered that,' said the police sergeant, spitting out a tooth. 'If it's all the same to you, I'm going to go and call for reinforcements.'

'Are you refusing to accept our surrender?' said Ohtar angrily.

'Yes,' said the police sergeant. 'I wouldn't take it as a gift.'

'Please yourself,' Ohtar said, fingering a large stone. 'The last person who refused to accept my surrender made a full recovery. Eventually.'

The police sergeant looked round at his battered and bleeding constables, and at the eight grim-faced salmon-poachers standing over them. It seemed that he had very little choice.

'If you're sure,' he said.

'We're sure,' said Ohtar impatiently. 'We've got orders not to get into any trouble.'

'It's the others,' Hildy said. 'They've gotten into trouble.'

# 8

IT IS 520 miles from London to Bettyhill as the crow flies, but if the crow in question is a fully trained shape-changer in a hurry the journey takes just over two and a half hours.

Brynjolf perched on the window-sill of the police station and preened his ruffled feathers. Apart from turbulence over Derby and a nasty moment with a buzzard passing over Dornoch it had been an uneventful flight, and he knew that the tricky part of his mission still lay ahead of him. Cautiously he peered in through the window, and listened.

'No, I don't know who they are,' the man in blue was saying, 'but they beat the hell out of us. Maybe you should send up some water-cannon or something.'

The reply to this request was clearly not the one the man in blue was expecting, for he said, 'Oh, very funny,' and slammed the phone down. Brynjolf hopped away from the window-sill, spread his wings and floated away to consider what to do next.

Very tricky, he said to himself, and to assist thought he started to sharpen his beak on a flat stone. Shape-transformation is, however, only skin-deep, and he gave it up quickly. Getting the heroes out would be no problem in itself; it was one that they could handle easily by themselves. But getting them out inconspicuously, so as not to cause any further disturbance, would be difficult. He went through his mental library of relevant heroic precedent – heroes rescued by sudden storms, conveniently passing dragons, or divine intervention – but something told him that such effects might be counter-productive. The obvious alternative was the false-messenger routine, but that required a fair amount of local knowledge to be successful. He had no idea who the men in blue took their orders from, what they looked like or what identification would be needed. He had almost decided to turn himself into the key of the cell door and have done with it when he thought of what should have been the obvious solution: the duplex confusion routine or Three-Troll Trick.

First he turned himself into a fly and crawled into the building through a keyhole in the back door. Once inside, he buzzed tentatively round until he had located the cells where the prisoners were being held. It was a small cell, and they all looked profoundly uncomfortable. Then he made a second trip and counted up the number of men in blue. There were only three of them; just the right number.

The Three-Troll Trick, so called because trolls fall for it every time, is essentially very simple. The shape-changer simply waits until only one of the gaolers is supervising the prisoners; then he turns himself into an exact facsimile of one of the other gaolers and, claiming to have received instructions from a higher authority, releases the prisoners, who get away as best they can. He then disappears, and leaves the other gaolers to discover the error and beat the pulp out of the one they believe has betrayed his trust. In a more robust age, the presumed traitor would not survive to clarify the misunderstanding; even if things had changed drastically over the years, Brynjolf reckoned, the mistake would still be put down to administrative confusion and quietly covered up. He set to work, and as usual the system worked flawlessly. The real gaoler lent him his key to the cell, the door swung open, and the heroes, looking rather sullen, trooped out.

What Brynjolf had overlooked was the fact that nearly three hours' confinement in a cramped cell, with Angantyr keeping up a constant stream of funny remarks, had not improved Bothvar Bjarki's temper, which was at the best of times chronically in need of all the improvement it could

get. Also, Brynjolf had inadvertently chosen to imper-
sonate the policeman who had been foolish enough to aim
a blow at Bothvar's head just before the fight started. So
when Brynjolf, acting out his part to the full, shoved
Bothvar Bjarki in the back and said, 'Move it, you,' in his
best gaoler's snarl it was inevitable that Bothvar should
wheel round and thump him very hard on the chin. It was
also inevitable that Brynjolf, who had never really liked
Bothvar because of his habit of paring his toenails with an
axe-blade when everyone else was eating, should forget
that he was playing a part, revert to his own shape, and
return the blow with interest. The fact that he
rematerialised with three extra arms was pure reflex.

Brynjolf realised in a moment what he had done, but by
then it was too late. The other two men in blue had come
rushing up when they heard the commotion, and they
were standing open-mouthed and staring.

'That', Bothvar said as he picked himself up from the
ground, 'is what comes of trying to be clever.'

'I'll deal with you later,' Brynjolf replied. The three
policemen, guessing who he meant to deal with first, made
a run for the door, but the massive bulk of Starkad
Storvirksson was in the way. After a one-sided scuffle, the
policemen landed in a heap on the ground, and Starkad,
remembering his manners, shut the door.

'Here,' said a voice from the back of the room, 'let me
deal with this.'

Brynjolf turned and looked for the source. 'Is he one of
them?' he asked, pointing to Danny Bennett.

'No,' said Ohtar, 'he's that sorcerer from the van, when
you turned into an eagle.'

'Him,' Brynjolf exclaimed. 'What's he doing here?'

'We found him on the fells,' said Angantyr, putting a
tree-like arm round his new friend's shoulders. 'Strange
bloke. Eats a lot, very fond of seagull. But he's on our
side now. You'll sort it all out for us, won't you?' And he
slapped Danny warmly on the back, nearly breaking his
spine.

Danny stepped forward and bent over the policemen.

'I'm afraid', he said, 'there's been a slight misunderstanding.'

'You don't say,' said the sergeant.

'You see,' Danny continued, 'my – my friends here weren't poaching salmon. Like me, I'm sure they're firmly opposed to bloodsports of every sort.' The sergeant laughed faintly, but Danny ignored him. 'In fact they're part of a team investigating a massive conspiracy to undermine democracy. Really, we need your help.'

The sergeant was curiously unmoved by this appeal. He groaned and rolled over on to his face. Danny sighed; he was used to this obstructive attitude from policemen.

'If it's all right by you,' he said, 'I'll just go through and use your phone.' He stepped over them and left the room.

'Is that all sorted out, then?' said Angantyr. 'No hard feelings?' One of the policemen raised his head and nodded. 'Good,' said Angantyr. 'We'll just tie you up and then we'll get out from under your feet.'

Meanwhile, Danny had got through to his boss in London.

'What the hell are you doing up there?' said his boss. 'I've just had a very strange call from a film crew who claim to have been beaten up by lunatics and stranded on a deserted hillside. They also said you'd wandered off and died of exposure. I think they're claiming compensation for bereavement because of it.'

'Listen,' Danny said, 'I haven't much time.'

'Oh, no,' said his boss. 'You're not being followed by the Wet Fish Board again, are you? I thought we'd been through all that.'

'It's not the Wet Fish Board, it's—' Danny checked himself. The important thing was to stay calm. 'I'm on to something really big this time.'

'Whatever you're on,' said his boss, 'it can't be legal.'

'This story's got everything,' Danny continued. 'Multinationals, nuclear power, spiritualism, ley lines, the lot.'

'Animals?'

Danny thought of the eagle that had wrecked his van.

'Yes,' he said, 'there's a definite wildlife angle. Also ecology and police brutality.'

The boss was silent for a moment. 'This has nothing at all to do with milk?'

'This is bigger than milk,' Danny said. 'This is global.'

Something told Danny that his lord and master wasn't convinced. Desperately, he played his ace.

'You don't want to miss out on this one,' he said. 'Like when you didn't run the thing about that little girl's pet hamster getting lost inside Porton Down, and the opposition got it. Got her own series in the end, didn't she?'

'All right,' said Danny's boss. 'Tell me about it.'

'What took you so long?'

The crow flopped wearily off the roof of the van, and perched on the King's wrist.

'Lost my way, didn't I?' it muttered, folding its rain-drenched wings. 'My own silly fault. Next time I go as a pigeon.' The crow disappeared and was replaced by an exhausted shape-changer.

'Well?' said the King, offering him the enchanted lager-can. Brynjolf swallowed a couple of mouthfuls and wiped his mouth with the end of his beard.

'Not so good, I'm afraid,' he said. 'Everyone safely rescued, but there were complications.' He told the King what had happened.

'And', he continued, 'there's more. You remember those sorcerers in the vans that Hildy told us we should stop?'

'What about them?'

'One of them, the chief sorcerer, has turned up again. Apparently, the lads captured him wandering about in the hills. Angantyr thinks he's on our side now.' He paused to allow the King to draw his own conclusions.

'And is he?'

'Who can tell? After the scuffle, he went off to use one of those telephone things. Could be he really is on our side, but I wouldn't bet on it.'

'We'll soon know,' Hildy said, and looked at her watch. 'We must find somewhere with a TV set.'

There was a set in the third pub they tried, but it was showing 'Dynasty'. There were several protests when Hildy switched the channels, including one from Brynjolf, but when the King stood up and looked around the bar nobody seemed inclined to make too much of it. The nine o'clock news came on. Hildy gripped the stem of her glass and waited.

First there was a Middle East story, then something about the Health Service and an interview with the minister ('I know him from somewhere,' Arvarodd said, leaning forward. 'Didn't he use to farm outside Brattahlid?'), followed by a long piece on rate-capping and a minor spy scandal. Then there was a beached whale near Plymouth – the Vikings licked their lips instinctively – and the sports news. Hildy started to relax.

'And reports are just coming in', said the presenter, marble-faced, 'of a major manhunt in the north of Scotland, which is somehow connected with the recent discovery of a Viking ship-burial and the disappearance of an American archaeologist, Hildegard Frederiksen.'

Panoramic shot of an unidentifiable mountain.

'Ten men, believed to be violent, escaped from police custody today at Bettyhill. They have with them a BBC producer, who they are believed to be holding hostage. Police with tracker dogs are searching for the men, who are thought to be armed with swords, axes and spears. Reports that the men are members of an extremist anti-nuclear group opposed to the Caithness fast-breeder reactor project are as yet unconfirmed. The connection with the burial-mound containing a rich hoard of Viking treasure discovered at nearby Rolfsness is also uncertain. A spokesman for the War Graves Commission refused to comment. The man held hostage, Danny Bennett, is best known for his evocative depictions of Cotswold life, including "The Countryside on Thursday" and "One Man and His Tractor", which was nominated for the Golden Iris award for best documentary.'

'I didn't know you could disappear, Hildy,' said Brynjolf admiringly. 'Do you use a talisman, or just runes?'

126

Back at the van, the King and his company debated what to do for the best.

'I still say we should make an attack and get it over with,' said Arvarodd. 'Stick to what we know, and don't go getting involved with all these strange people. If we stick around now, and the enemy does come looking for us, we're done for.'

'I'm not so sure.' The King's eyes were shining, as they had not done since they left the Castle of Borve. 'I think our enemy may have got quite the wrong idea from that little exhibition.'

'How do you mean?'

'Think,' said the King, smiling. 'Doesn't it give the impression that we're all still up there, being chased across the hills by those soldiers, or whatever they are? He won't be able to resist the temptation to go up there and see if he can't find us and finish us off. After all, he has nothing to fear from us, so long as he has the spirits safe here.'

'He might take them with him,' Hildy suggested.

'He wouldn't do that. He wouldn't risk them falling into our hands. But if he thinks we're on the run up there – more important, if he thinks we're so weak that we can be chased around by those idiots Brynjolf was telling us about' – the King grinned disconcertingly – 'then he's not going to be too worried about what we can do to him. He'll be concentrating more on what he can do to us. And that'll give us a chance, especially at this end.'

If that was the King's definition of a chance, Hildy said to herself, she didn't like the sound of it. 'But what about the others?' she said. 'What if he catches them?'

'They'll have to look after themselves,' said the King shortly, and Hildy could see he was worried. 'If the worst comes to the worst, Valhalla. That doesn't really matter at this stage.'

'But surely,' Hildy started to say; but Arvarodd trod on her toe meaningfully. The pain, even through her moon-boot, was agonising. 'Maybe you're right,' she mumbled.

'And meanwhile', said the King suddenly, 'we have work to do.'

Half-past three in the morning. There were still lights in the windows of Gerrards Garth House; like a crocodile, it slept with its eyes open. Two of the lights, having failed to draw the telex machine into conversation, were playing Goblin's Teeth.

'Are you sure about that?' said Prexz.

Zxerp smiled. 'Yes,' he said. 'Checkmate.'

'But what if . . .?' Prexz lifted the piece warily, then put it back. He was worried.

'Ninety-nine thousand, nine hundred and ninety-nine sets and nine games to you,' said Zxerp, 'and *five* games to me.' Could it be that his luck was about to change?

Prexz knocked over his goblin petulantly. 'All right, then,' he said, as casually as he could, 'I'll accept your resignation.'

'Who's resigning?' Zxerp was setting out the pieces.

'You offered to resign after the last game. I'm accepting.'

'I've withdrawn,' said Zxerp, shuffling the Spell cards.

'Can't do that,' replied Prexz. 'Rule fifty-seven.'

'Yes, I can,' said Zxerp. 'Rule seventy-two. Mugs away.'

Sullenly, Prexz threw the dice and made his opening gambit. ChuChullainn's Leap; defensive, but absolutely safe. There was no known way to break service on ChuChullainn's Leap.

'Checkmate,' said Zxerp.

In the street below, a van had drawn up outside the heavy steel doors. The King loosened his short sword in its scabbard and pulled his jacket on over it.

'Remember,' he said. 'You two wait down here, keep quiet, and do nothing. Just be ready for us when we come out.'

Hildy nodded, but Arvarodd made one last effort. 'Remember Thruthvangir,' he said.

The King stiffened. 'That was different,' he said. 'The lifts weren't working.'

'They might not be working now,' Arvarodd wheedled,

'and then where would you be?'

'For the last time,' said the King, 'you stay in the van and keep quiet. If we need help, we'll signal.'

He opened the back doors and jumped lightly out, followed by the wizard and the shape-changer. They ran silently across to the doors – Hildy was amazed to see how nimbly the wizard moved – and crouched down beside them. The wizard had taken something out of his pocket and was inserting it into the lock.

'Is that an opening spell?' Hildy whispered.

'No,' replied Arvarodd, 'it's a hairpin.'

The great door suddenly opened, and Hildy braced herself for the shrill noise of the alarm. But there was silence, and the door closed behind them.

'Well,' said Arvarodd, 'they're on their own now.' He shrugged his shoulders and ate the last digestive.

'I still don't understand,' Hildy said. 'Why tonight?'

'Obvious,' said Arvarodd with his mouth full. 'The Enemy, we hope, has gone off to Scotland. Tomorrow he'll probably be back, having guessed that we aren't there. So now's our only chance.'

'But that's not what the King said earlier.'

'Him,' Arvarodd grunted. 'Changes his mind every five minutes, he does.'

'The King said', Hildy insisted, 'that it was too dangerous to try it now. That's why he was so glad that the others had won us some time.'

Arvarodd sighed. 'If you must know,' he said, 'he's worried about the others. He doesn't think they'll be able to cope on their own. Probably right. He knows he ought to leave them to it but, then, he's the King. His first duty is to them. It's going to be Thruthvangir all over again.'

'What happened at Thruthvangir?'

'The lifts didn't work.' Arvarodd scowled at the steel doors. 'That's why he left me out. My orders are, if he doesn't make it, to go back to Scotland and try to save the others. I should be flattered, really.'

So that was what they had all been whispering about while she was getting petrol. 'Arvarodd,' she said quietly,

129

'just how dangerous do you think it is?'

'Very,' said Arvarodd, grimly. 'Like my mother used to say:

> "Fear a bear's paw, a prince's children,
> A grassy heath, embers still glowing,
> A man's sword, the smile of a maiden."

There's a lot more of that,' he continued. 'Scared me half to death when I was a kid.'

Hildy, who had, from force of habit, taken out her notebook, put it away again. The verses suggested several fascinating insights into various textual problems in the Elder Edda, but this was neither the time nor the place. 'If it's that dangerous,' she said firmly, 'we must go and help him.'

'But . . .' Arvarodd waved his hand impatiently.

'He is the King,' said Hildy cleverly. 'Our duty is to protect him.'

'Don't you start,' Arvarodd grumbled. He rolled the biscuit-wrapper up into a ball and threw it at the windscreen.

Hildy sat still for a moment, then took the seer-stone from her bag and put it in her eye. She saw the King and his companions crossing a carpeted office. They had not seen the door open behind them, and two men in blue boiler-suits with rifles. Hildy wanted to shout and warn them. The door at the other end of the office opened, and the King shouted and drew his sword. There was a shot and Hildy cried out, but the King was still standing; the man had shot the sword out of his hand. The wizard was shrieking something, some spell or other, but it wasn't working; and Brynjolf was staring in horror at his feet, which hadn't turned into a bear's paws or the wings of an eagle. The guards were laughing. Slowly, the King and his companions raised their hands and put them on their heads.

'Can you see them?' Arvarodd was muttering. There was sweat pouring down his face.

'Yes,' Hildy said. 'It's no good; they've been captured. Their magic isn't working.' She looked round, but

Arvarodd wasn't there. He had snatched up his bow and quiver, and was running towards the steel doors. Wailing 'Wait for me', Hildy ran after him.

The door was still open. Hildy tried to keep pace with Arvarodd as he bounded up the stairs but she could not. She stopped, panting, at the first landing, and then looked across and saw the lift. Against all her hopes, it was working. She pressed 4 – how she knew it would be the fourth floor she had no idea – and leant back to catch her breath. The doors slid open, and she hopped out.

What on earth did she think she was doing?

She turned back, but the lift doors had shut. Down the corridor she could hear the sound of running feet. She opened the door of the nearest office and slipped inside.

It was a small room, and the walls were covered with steel boxes, like gas-meters or fuseboxes. She had a sudden idea. If she could switch off the lights, perhaps the King could escape in the darkness. She pulled out her flashlight and started to read the labels. Down in a corner she saw a little glass box.

'MAGIC SUPPLY', read the label. 'DO NOT TOUCH'. And underneath, in smaller letters: 'In the event of power supply failure, break glass and press button. This will deactivate the mains-fed spell. The emergency spell will automatically take effect within seven minutes.'

With the butt of her torch Hildy smashed the glass and leant hard on the button. A moment later, the guards' rifles inexplicably turned into bunches of daffodils.

'Daffodils?' asked the King, as he banged two heads together. The wizard shrugged and made a noise like hotel plumbing.

'Fair enough,' said the King. 'Let's get out of here.'

They sprinted back the way they had come, nearly colliding with Arvarodd, who was coming up the stairs towards them.

'What happened?' he said.

'Our magic failed,' replied the King. 'Then theirs did. No idea why.'

'Have you seen Hildy?' At that moment, Hildy appeared,

running towards them. 'Quick,' she gasped, 'we've only got three minutes.'

A shot from an ex-daffodil bounced off the tarmac as they drove off.

'Far be it for me to criticise,' said Thorgeir, gripping his seat-belt with both hands, 'but aren't you driving rather fast?'

The sorcerer-king grinned. 'Yes,' he said. He drove even faster. Childish, Thorgeir said to himself, but, then, he's like that. Mental age of seventeen. Only a permanent adolescent would devote hours of his valuable time to laying a spell on a Morris Minor so as to enable it to burn off Porsches at traffic lights. 'I want to get back to London as quickly as possible,' he explained.

'Then, why didn't we fly?' asked Thorgeir.

'We can do that if you like,' said the sorcerer-king mischievously. 'No problem.'

'Stop showing off,' Thorgeir said. A land-locked Morris Minor was bad enough. 'You don't seem to appreciate the situation we're in.'

'On the contrary,' said the sorcerer-king, putting his foot down hard. 'That's why I'm in such a good mood.'

'You seem to have overlooked the fact that they got away,' Thorgeir shouted above the scream of the tortured engine. He shut his eyes and muttered an ancient Finnish suspension-improving spell.

'Only by a fluke,' replied the King. 'Next time they won't be so lucky. Next time we'll be there.'

'You think there'll be a next time?'

'Has to be.' The sorcerer-king removed the suspension-improving spell and deliberately drove over the cat's eyes. 'What else can he do?'

Thorgeir, whose head had just made sharp contact with the roof, did not reply. The sorcerer-king chuckled and changed up into fourth.

'The trouble with you', he said, 'is that you can't feel comfortable unless you're worried about something.' Thorgeir, who was both worried and profoundly uncomfortable, shook his head, but for once the sorcerer-king had his eyes on the road. 'You don't believe in happy endings. Look at it this way,' he said, overtaking a blaspheming Ferrari. 'If they had anything left in reserve, why did they try to pull that stunt last night? They're finished and they know it. That was pure Gunnar-in-the-snake-pit stuff, a one-way ticket to Valhalla. Not that I begrudge them that, of course,' said the sorcerer-king magnanimously. 'If they want to go to Valhalla, let them. Nice enough place, I suppose, except that the food all comes out of a microwave these days and the wish-maidens are definitely past their prime. A bit like one of those run-down gentlemen's clubs in Pall Mall, if you ask me.'

Thorgeir gave up and diverted his energies to worrying about the traffic police. Last time, he remembered, the sorcerer-king had let them chase him all the way from Coalville to Watford Gap, and then turned them all into horseflies. Turning them back had not been easy, especially the one who'd been eaten by a swallow.

'Now you're sulking,' said the sorcerer-king cheerfully.

'I'm not sulking,' said Thorgeir, 'I'm taking it seriously. Who did you leave in charge, by the way?'

'That young Fortescue,' said the sorcerer-king. 'Since he's in on the whole thing, we might as well make him useful. Or a frog. Whichever.'

Thorgeir shuddered. Much as he deplored unnecessary sorcery, he felt that the frog option would have been safer.

In fact, the Governor of China elect was doing a perfectly adequate job back at Gerrards Garth House. He had seen to the removal and replacement of the anti-magic circuit, debriefed the guards and written a report, all in one morning. At this rate, he felt, he might soon count as indispensable.

After putting his head round the door at Vouchers to make sure that the prisoners were still there, he sent for the chief clerk of the department and asked him about the arrangements for tracking the getaway van the burglars had used. All that was needed was a simple tap into the police computer at Hendon, he was told, to get the registered owner's name and address. Then it would be perfectly simple to slip the registration number on to the computer's list of stolen vehicles and monitor the police band until some eagle-eyed copper noticed it.

'But what if they get arrested?' Kevin asked.

'Then we'll know where they are,' replied the Chief Clerk. 'Easy.'

'No, it's not,' Kevin objected. 'They won't get bail without having plausible identities or anything, and they'll probably resist arrest and be kept in for that. And we can't go bursting into a police station to get them; it'd be too risky.'

The Chief Clerk's smile was a horrible sight. 'No sweat,' he said. 'Lots of things can happen to them. In the police cells, on remand, being transferred, on their way to the magistrates' court, anywhere you like. Easiest thing would be to wait till they're convicted and put away. We can get to them inside with no trouble at all. But I don't suppose the Third Floor will want to wait that long. Best thing is if they do resist arrest. Dead meat,' he said graphically. 'I think our police are wonderful.'

Kevin Fortescue was relieved to get back to his office, for the Chief Clerk gave him the creeps. Still, he reflected, you have to be hard to get on in Business. He dismissed the thought from his mind and took his well-thumbed *Oxford School Atlas* from his desk drawer.

'Winter Palace in Chungking,' he said to himself. 'Not too cold and a good view of the mountains.'

Danny Bennett was being shown round the Castle of Borve.

'Mind you,' said Angantyr Asmundarson, as Danny expressed polite admiration, 'it's perishing cold in winter and one hell of a way to go to get a pint of milk. Or was,' he reflected. 'We used to have our own house-cows, of course. Enchanted cows, naturally. But they were enchanted to yield mead, honey and ale, which is all very well but indigestible on porridge. Couple of Jerseys.'

Danny ducked his head under a rock lintel. The one

thing he wanted was access to a television set, for his story, if it was going to break at all, would be doing so at this very minute, and it was too much to hope that anyone would tape it for him.

'That's the mead-hall through there,' said Angantyr, 'and the King's table. The main arsenals and the still-room are round the back.'

This man would make a good estate agent, Danny reflected. He nodded appreciatively and smiled. Why hadn't he bought one of those portable wrist-watch tele-visions, like he'd seen them wearing at the Stock Exchange?

'So how long do you think we can stay here for?' he asked.

'Indefinitely,' said Angantyr. 'You see, this place is totally hidden. Unless you know how to find it. . . .'

'Yes,' said Danny, 'but you'll have to go out occasionally, to get water and food and things.'

'No need,' said Angantyr proudly. 'There's a natural spring – still there, we checked – and as for food there's any amount of seagulls. You like seagull,' Angantyr reminded him. 'You're lucky.'

Danny repressed a shudder. 'Actually—' he started to say.

'Last time we were besieged in here,' Angantyr went on, 'we stuck it out for nine months, until the enemy got bored out of their minds and went away. We were all right, though,' said Angantyr smugly. 'We remembered to bring a couple of chess sets.'

'I can't play chess.'

'I'll teach you. It's pretty easy once you've got it into your head that the knight can go over the top of the other pieces. And there's other things to do, of course. I used to make collages with the seagull feathers. Anyway,' Angantyr said, 'we probably won't be here too long this time. It'll all be over soon, one way or another. That reminds me.' He dashed off, and Danny sat down on a stone seat and took off his shoes. His feet were killing him after the forced march from Bettyhill. The Vikings walked very quickly.

Angantyr came back. He was holding a helmet and a suit of chain armour, and under his arm was tucked a sword and a spear.

'Try these,' he said. 'They should be small enough. Made for the King when he was twelve.'

Danny tried them on. They were much too big, and so heavy he could hardly move in them. 'Thanks,' he said, as he struggled out of the mail shirt, 'but I won't be needing them anyway, will I?'

'Don't be so pessimistic,' Angantyr said. 'There's always a bit of fighting at a siege. I remember when we were stuck in Tongue for six months—'

'You don't understand,' said Danny, 'I'm a non-combatant. Press,' he explained. 'And anyway, if there is any violence, these wouldn't help.'

'What do you mean?' said Angantyr, puzzled. Danny explained; he told him about CS gas and stun-grenades, machine-pistols and birdshot.

'You mean Special Effects,' said Angantyr. 'Don't you worry about that. All our armour is spellproof.'

'Spellproof?'

'Guaranteed. All that stuff', he said, dismissing all human endeavour from Barthold Schwartz to napalm with a wave of his hand, 'is obsolete now.'

'No, it's not.'

'Well, it *was*. Don't say you people still believe in the white-hot heat of magic and so on. Very old-fashioned. No, all our gear's totally magic-resistant. Unless, of course, the other side's got counter-spells.'

'Counter-spells?' All this reminded Danny of something.

'Counter-spells. Of course, most of those were done away with after the MALT talks. It was only when the Enemy started cheating and using them again after we'd all dumped ours that things got unpleasant and we had to use the Brooch. That was the biggest counter-spell of them all, you see.'

'I see.' Danny rubbed his head. There was another story here, but one he had no wish to get involved in.

136

'Of course,' went on Angantyr, 'the Enemy's probably still got all his, and they don't make you invulnerable against conventional weapons. Still, it does even things up a bit.'

'Even so,' Danny said, 'I'm still a non-combatant. I don't know how to use swords and things.'

Angantyr shrugged his shoulders. 'Have it your own way,' he said. 'You'd better have the armour, all the same.'

Danny decided it would be easier to agree. 'I'll put it on later,' he said.

At that moment, Starkad, who had been left on watch, came running down the narrow spiral stairway. He was shouting something about a huge metal seagull with wings that went round and round. A moment later, Danny could hear the sound of rotor-blades passing close overhead and dying away in the distance.

'Dragons?' Angantyr asked. Danny told him about helicopters. 'It means they're looking for us,' he said. 'They might have those infra-red things that can trace you by your body-heat. Unless those count as magic.'

But Angantyr hadn't heard of anything like that. Danny felt vaguely proud that the twentieth century had at least one totally original invention to its credit.

'Don't like the sound of that,' Angantyr muttered.

'That's what I've been trying to tell you,' Danny said. 'This castle may have been impregnable once, but—'

Angantyr shook his head. 'Still is,' he replied. 'I don't mean that. It's just the noise that thing makes. It'll frighten off all the seagulls.'

'So now what do we do?' said Arvarodd.

'Speaking purely for myself,' said the King, 'I'll have the pancake with maple syrup. What is maple syrup?' he asked Hildy.

They were sitting in a deserted Little Chef in the middle of Buckinghamshire. How they had got there, Hildy had no idea; she had just kept on driving until the petrol-tank was nearly empty, then pulled in at the first service station for fuel and food. Her heroism of the previous night had thoroughly unnerved her, and she wanted to go home to Long Island.

'It's a sort of sweet sticky stuff you get from a tree,' she said absently. 'What *are* we going to do?'

'I haven't the faintest idea,' said the King. He was taking it all very calmly, Hildy thought. Why, if it hadn't been for her. . . .

'If it hadn't been for you,' said the King suddenly, 'Odin knows what would have happened back there. That was quick thinking.'

'Pure luck,' Hildy said.

'Yes,' agreed the King, 'but quick thinking all the same. Five pancakes, please,' he ordered. 'All with maple syrup.'

'Do you think they'll follow us?' Hildy asked.

'They'll try,' said the King, 'but not too hard. We must get rid of that van first. Isn't that number written on the back and front some sort of identification mark? They're bound to have seen that. We'll sell the van in the next town we come to and get something else.'

Hildy realised that she should have thought of that. She made an effort and pulled herself together. 'And after that?' she said.

'After that, we'll do what we should have done in the first place.'

'What's that?'

'We'll get hold of that bloody wizard,' said the King grimly, 'and hold his head underwater until he thinks of something.' The wizard made a soft grinding noise, but they ignored him. 'After all, he got us into this mess.'

They stared aggressively at the wizard, who took a profound interest in his pancake. He seemed to have lost his appetite, however, and put his spoon down.

'Get on with it,' said the King. The wizard snarled and draped his paper napkin over his head. There was an anxious silence; then from under the napkin came a noise like a coffee-mill which went on for a very long time.

'Are you sure?' said the King. The coffee-mill noise started up again.

'Positive?'

The napkin nodded.

'What did he say?' Hildy demanded.

'Well,' said the King, leaning forward, 'he reckons that there's a brooch with a spell-circuit – you know, like the dragon-brooch – that might be able to cut off the magic inside the tower, and it should be possible to run it off a much weaker source of power, like a car battery.'

'How does he know about car batteries?' Hildy asked.

'Worked it out from first principles,' said the King. 'Anyway, if we get hold of this brooch, we might have a chance. According to Kotkel, it was made by Sitrygg Sow, who had the design from Odin himself. But he's only seen it once, and he's never tried it out for himself. It's a very long shot.'

'But God knows where it's got to,' said Hildy. 'Even if it still exists, it's still probably buried somewhere.'

'In that case,' said the King, 'all we'll need is a shovel and a map. You see, it belonged to a king of the Saxons down in East Anglia, and it was buried with him. One of the Wuffing kings, can't remember which one. But he was the only one buried in a ship, that I can tell you. In a minute, I'll remember the name of the place.'

'Sutton Hoo,' Hildy murmured.

'That's it,' said the King. 'How did you know that?'

'Is this brooch', Hildy asked, 'also in the shape of a dragon?' There was a bright light in her eyes, and her hands were shaking.

'That's right,' the King said. 'More of a fire-drake, actually. Never had any taste, Sitrygg.'

'Gold inlaid with garnets?'

'Yes.'

'Then,' said Hildy, 'I know where it is. It's in London. In fact, it's in the British Museum.' She rummaged about in her organiser bag for her copy of the latest *Journal of Scandinavian Studies*. 'Is this it?' she said, thrusting the open book under the wizard's nose. The wizard pointed to plate 7*a* and nodded.

'Is that good or bad?' asked the King.

# 9

'ORIGINALLY,' said the lecturer, 'this was believed to have been the king's standard, to which his troops rallied in time of war. It has now been reidentified as a hat-stand.'

He looked round his audience. For once, he noticed, there were a couple of intelligent faces among them. One of them, a big man with a beard, was nodding approvingly. He decided to tell them about the quotation from *Beowulf* after all.

'He's wrong, of course,' whispered Brynjolf to Hildy, 'but he wasn't to know that. Only idiots like the East Saxons would use a hat-stand for a battle-standard.'

Hildy sighed. The neatly argued little paper intended for the October edition of *Heimdall* in which she proved conclusively that the Chelmsford Standard was in fact a toast-rack would have to be shelved.

'These', said the lecturer, pointing at a glass case, 'are among the earliest finds from the period of Scandinavian settlement in Sutherland and Caithness. The Melvich Arm-Ring....'

Arvarodd was staring. Hildy prodded him in the ribs, but he didn't seem to notice. 'That's mine,' he whispered.

'Are you sure?' asked Hildy.

'Course I'm sure. Given to me when I killed my first wolf. Sure, it's only bronze, but it has great sentimental value.'

'Keep your voice down,' Hildy hissed.

'Bergthora said if I didn't chuck it out and get a new one

she'd give it to a museum,' went on the hero of Permia. 'I never thought she'd do it.'

'Who was Bergthora?' Hildy asked. Arvarodd blushed.

'Although the workmanship is crude and poorly executed,' continued the lecturer, 'and not at all representative of the high Urnes style that was shortly to. . . .'

'He's getting on my nerves,' Arvarodd said. Hildy glowered at him.

The lecturer moved on and started to tell his audience about a set of drinking-horns. The King and his party hung back.

'Remember,' he said, 'we're just here to have a look, so don't get carried away. We'll come back later when it's not so crowded.'

'And here we have the crowning glory of our Early Medieval collection,' the lecturer said proudly, 'the Sutton Hoo treasure. Until recently, this was the richest find ever made on the British mainland. Now, however, the recently discovered Rolfsness treasure. . . .'

Arvarodd muttered something under his breath, but the wizard was pointing. So was the lecturer.

'The dragon-brooch', he was saying, 'is one of the most interesting pieces in the entire hoard.'

When the lecture was over, and Hildy had managed to distract Arvarodd's attention when the lecturer asked if there were any questions, the King and his company went for a drink. They felt that they had earned one.

'Simple theft is what I call it,' Arvarodd complained. 'How would he like it if I took his watch and put it in a glass case and made funny remarks about it?'

'Shut up about your arm-ring,' said the King. 'They've got all my treasure down in their basement, and I'm not complaining. Well, almost all. That reminds me.'

From his finger he drew a heavy gold ring. Hildy had often admired it out of the corner of her eye.

'While we're here,' he said, 'we'd better sell this. I don't suppose there's much money left by now.'

Hildy, as treasurer, nodded sadly. She hated the

thought of such a masterpiece going to some unscrupulous collector, but buying the new car had more or less cleaned them out, and even then they'd only been able to afford a horrible old wreck, held together by body putty and, after the wizard had been at it, witchcraft. She took the ring and put it in her purse.

'Back to business,' said the King. 'After we've got this brooch, we'll have to move quickly. I'm still worried about the others. . . .'

At that moment the television above the bar announced the one o'clock news.

'There have been dramatic new developments', said the newsreader, 'in the manhunt in the north of Scotland, in which the police are seeking the eight armed men who are believed to have abducted a female archaeologist and a BBC producer. Helicopters equipped with infra-red sensors. . . .'

Picture of the Castle of Borve.

'Don't worry,' said Angantyr Asmundarson.

But Danny was very worried. He'd seen the police marksmen getting into position all morning, and the way Angantyr was testing his bowstring had made him shiver.

'How many do you reckon there are?' asked Hjort over his shoulder, as he plied a whetstone across his axe-blade.

'About ten each,' Angantyr replied. 'Still, if we wait a bit longer some more may turn up.'

'Cheapskate, that's what I call it,' Hjort grumbled. 'Hardly worth sharpening up for.'

'Anyway,' said Bothvar Bjarki, 'I'm having the one with the trumpet.'

'No, you're not.'

'We drew lots,' Bothvar whined.

'You cheated,' said Hjort. 'You always cheat.'

'I did not,' replied Bothvar angrily, surreptitiously slipping his double-headed coin into Danny's jacket pocket. 'Anyway, look who's talking.'

Danny wasn't listening. He was calculating whether it

142

would be possible to slip out unobserved while the heroes were squabbling. But, if he did, the police might shoot him. And if he were to put on one of the mail shirts the police would take him for one of the heroes and would undoubtedly shoot him.

'This is Superintendent Mackay,' came a voice from outside. 'We have you completely surrounded by armed police officers. Throw out your weapons and come out.'

That, Danny realised, could have been better phrased, given that the heroes were armed with javelins and throwing-hammers. He ducked under the parapet and put his hands over his head.

'You missed!' jeered Bothvar, as Hjort picked up another javelin.

'Of course I missed,' said Hjort, standing up to throw again. A bullet sang harmlessly off his helmet and landed at Danny's feet. 'There's few enough of them as it is without frittering them away with javelins.'

'I don't think they meant it like that,' Danny shouted. 'I think they want you to surrender.' A CS-gas canister whizzed over the parapet, spluttered and went out.

'Surrender?' Hjort's face fell under his jewel-encrusted visor. 'Are you sure?'

'Doesn't look like it to me,' said Angantyr cheerfully, as he caught a stun-grenade in his left hand. He looked at it, threw himself a catch from left to right, and hurled it back. It exploded. 'If they want us to surrender, they shouldn't be shooting at us.'

'They've stopped,' said Hjort wistfully. 'Call this a siege?'

'Here, Danny,' Angantyr said, 'what's the form these days?'

But Danny wasn't there. As soon as the shooting had stopped, he had slipped away and crawled back into the hall. Frantically he unbuttoned his shirt, which was white enough if you didn't mind the stewed seagull down the front of it, and tied the sleeves to the shaft of a javelin. He looked around, but all the heroes were at the parapet. Very cautiously, he started to climb the spiral stair.

*

'Reports are just coming in', said the newsreader, 'that the police have made an attempt to storm the ruined castle where the ten men have barricaded themselves in. According to the reports, the attempt was unsuccessful. It is not yet known whether there were any casualties. A spokesman for the Historic Buildings Commission. . . .'

The King clenched his right fist and pressed it into the palm of his left hand. His face was expressionless. 'I hate this job,' he said.

Hildy had taken out the seer-stone, but the King told her to put it away. 'I don't want to know,' he said. 'They'll have to look after themselves.'

'If I know them,' said Brynjolf, 'they'll be having the time of their lives.'


'Remember,' said the superintendent, 'the last thing we want is a bloodbath.'

The man in the black pullover grinned at him, his white teeth flashing out from the black greasepaint that covered his face. 'Sure,' he said, and stuck another grenade in his belt for luck. He hadn't been jolted about in a helicopter all the way from Hereford just to ask a lot of terrorists if they fancied coming quietly. 'How many of them are there?'

'Ten, according to our intelligence,' said the superintendent.

'One each,' said the man in the black pullover. He sounded disappointed.

Just then, there was a rattling of rifle-bolts. A solitary figure with a white flag had appeared on the side of the cliff. 'Hell,' said the man in the black pullover.

'Put your hands on your head,' boomed the megaphone, 'and walk slowly over here.' The man dropped the white flag and did as he was told.

'Be careful,' said the man in the black pullover, 'it could be a trap.' But his heart wasn't in it. He started to take the grenades out of his belt.

'It's that perishing sorcerer of yours,' muttered Hjort, staring out over the parapet. 'He's gone over to the enemy.'

'Has he indeed?' said Angantyr grimly. 'We'll soon see

about that.' He bent his great ibex-horn bow and sighted along the arrow.

'Don't do that,' said Hjort. 'You'll frighten them away. And there's some more just arrived. In black,' he added, with approval.

'What's going on?' said Bothvar, dropping down beside them. He had been searching everywhere for the magic halberd of Gunnar, which he'd put away safely before going into the mound at Rolfsness. Eventually he'd found it down behind the back of the treasure-chests. 'I do wish people wouldn't move my things.'

'We've just been betrayed by a traitor,' said Angantyr.

'That's more like it,' said Bothvar.


'And we're now going over live to the armed siege in Scotland,' said the newsreader. 'Our reporter there is Moira Urquhart.'

The sorcerer-king leant forward and turned up the volume. 'Are you taping this?' he asked.

Thorgeir nodded. 'I'm having to use the "Yes, Minister" tape, but it's worth it.'

'They'll repeat it again soon, I expect,' said the sorcerer-king. 'Look, isn't that Bothvar Bjarki?' The camera had zoomed in on a helmeted head poking out above the parapet. 'I'd know that helmet anywhere.'

'I've just thought of something,' said Thorgeir. 'That armour of theirs. . . .'

'One of the terrorists seems to be shouting something,' said the reporter's voice over the close-up of the helmeted head. 'We're trying to catch what he's saying. . . . Something about a seagull. . . . It could be that they're demanding that food is sent in.'

'I never could be doing with seagull,' said the sorcerer-king, spearing an olive. 'Except maybe in a casserole with plenty of coriander.'

'Fried in breadcrumbs, it's not too bad,' said Thorgeir. 'Isn't that Angantyr Asmundarson beside him?'

'It seems that the terrorists are in fact assuring us that they have plenty of food,' said the reporter. 'In fact they're telling us that they're capable of withstanding a long siege and inviting us to storm the castle. In fact', said the reporter, 'they've started slow hand-clapping.'

'Childish,' said the sorcerer-king.

'And since not much seems to be happening at the moment', said the reporter, 'I'm now going to have a few words with the BBC producer, Danny Bennett, who was held hostage by the terrorists and managed to escape a few minutes ago. Tell me, Danny. . . .'

'Who's he?' asked Thorgeir.

'Search me,' said the sorcerer-king.

'They aren't terrorists at all,' Danny Bennett was saying. 'More like . . . well, it's a long story. Big, but long.' He mopped his brow with the corner of the blanket they had insisted on putting round his shoulders. 'And they didn't kidnap me.'

'You mean you went with them voluntarily?'

'Sort of,' Danny said. 'That is, they rescued me when I was wandering about lost in the mountains. I'd got separated from the rest of the crew, you see. And then they told me all about it, and it was such a big story that I decided I'd stay with them. Until the shooting started, of course.'

'I see.' The reporter was trying to get a good look at the back of Danny's head, to see if there were any signs of a recent sharp blow. Still, she reflected, it was good television.

'I can't say much about the story just now,' Danny went on, 'because it's all pretty incredible stuff and, anyway, I told Derek all about it over the phone from the police station at Bettyhill. . . .'

'You mean you were in contact with the BBC at the time of the breakout?' The reporter was clearly interested. 'Are you trying to say there's been a cover-up?'

'How the hell do I know?' Danny said. 'There isn't a telly in that bloody cave.'

'What were you saying about their armour?' said the sorcerer-king.

'Oh, yes,' said Thorgeir Storm-Shepherd. 'It'll be enchanted, won't it?'

'Sod it,' said the sorcerer-king. 'Hang on, something's happening.'

'The hell with this,' said Bothvar. He was hoarse from shouting. 'If they're just going to sit there, when they know about the secret passage and everything. . . .'

'Maybe they don't,' said Angantyr. 'Maybe he hasn't told them.'

Bothvar laughed, but Angantyr wasn't so sure. Danny hadn't seemed the treacherous type to him. 'Maybe he went to negotiate,' he suggested.

'Without telling us?'

'We wouldn't have let him go if he'd told us,' said Angantyr. Bothvar considered this.

'True,' said Ohtar, testing the edge of his sword with his thumb. 'And he did say he liked my cooking. Can't be all bad.'

'And what does that prove?' said Bothvar. 'The man's either a liar or an idiot. How are we for javelins, by the way?'

'Running a bit low,' said the hero Hring, who was quartermaster. 'They don't throw them back, you see.'

'That's cheating,' said Bothvar. 'If they go on like that, we'll have to stop throwing them. Still, there's rocks.'

'I think he went out there to try to negotiate,' repeated Angantyr Asmundarson. 'Otherwise they'd have made an assault on the hidden passage by now.'

'Could be,' said Hjort. He could see no other possible explanation for the enemy's lack of activity. 'After all, they outnumber us at least eight to one.' He said this very loudly, in the hope that the enemy might overhear him. They obviously needed to be encouraged.

'And he did try to warn us about the big metal seagulls they used to find us. And about the Special Effects,' Angantyr continued. 'I think he got frightened and went out to try to negotiate.'

147

'Frightened?' said Bothvar incredulously. 'What by?' He picked a spent bullet out of his beard and threw it away.

'In which case,' said Hring, 'they've detained a herald.'

'That's true,' said Bothvar. 'We must do something about that.'

'The King did say we were only to defend ourselves,' said the hero Egil Kjartansson, called the Dancer, or more usually the Wet Blanket. 'No attacking, those were his orders.'

'But this is different,' said Angantyr. 'Detaining a herald is just like attacking, really. You've got to rescue your heralds, or where would you be?'

There was, of course, no answer to that. 'All right then,' said Egil Kjartansson, 'but don't blame me if we get into trouble.'

'Hoo-bloody-ray, we're going to do something at last.' Hjort rubbed his hands together and put his left arm through the straps of his shield. 'Starkad! Hroar! Come over here, we're going to attack.'

The remaining heroes rushed to the parapet, while Hring distributed the javelins. Starkad Storvirksson, who was the King's berserk, lifted his great double-handed sword and began the chant to Odin.

'Can it,' Bothvar interrupted him. 'We've wasted enough time as it is.'

With one movement, like a wolf leaping, Starkad Storvirksson sprang up on to the parapet and brandished his sword. Then he hopped down again.

'Bothvar,' he said plaintively, 'I've forgotten my battle-cry.'

'It's "Starkad!", Starkad,' said Bothvar. 'Can we get on, please?'

With a deafening roar of 'Starkad!' the berserk vaulted over the parapet and led the charge. After him came Bothvar, wielding the halberd of Gunnar, with Angantyr Asmundsson close behind and Hroar almost treading on his heels. Then came Egil Kjartansson, his shield crashing against his mail shirt as he ran; Hring and Hjort, running like hounds on a tantalising scent, and finally Ohtar, who had finished up the seagull flan because nobody else wanted any more, and had raging indigestion as a result. In their hands their swords flashed, like the foam on the crests of the great waves that pounded the rocks below them, and as they ran the earth shook. A man with a megaphone stood up as they charged, thought better of it, and ducked down; a moment later, Bothvar's javelin transfixed the spot where he had been standing, its blade driven down almost to the shaft in the dense springy peat.

'That'll do me,' said the man in the black pullover, as the spear-shaft quivered beside him. 'Let 'em have it.' His men shouldered their automatic rifles and started to fire.

'Don't bother with shooting over their heads,' said the man in the black pullover.

'We're not,' said one of his men. He looked worried.

'Told you,' said Thorgeir, pointing at the screen. The picture was wobbling fearfully, as if the cameraman was running: a close-up of one of the heroes, dribbling an unexploded grenade in front of him as he charged.

'Can't think of everything, can I?' grumbled the sorcerer-king. 'Anyway, we can fix that later.'

'It's unbelievable,' panted the reporter. 'All the bullets and bombs and things seem to be having no effect on them at all. They're just charging. . . . And the police are running away. . . . For Christ's sake, will you get me out of here? This is Moira Urquhart, BBC News, Borve Castle.'

The picture shook violently and the screen went blank. Someone had dropped the camera.

'Pity,' said the sorcerer-king. 'I was enjoying that.'

Bothvar Bjarki leant on his halberd and tried to get his breath back. 'Swizzle,' he gasped.

'You're out of condition, you are,' said Hjort, mopping his forehead with the hem of his cloak.

Overhead, the helicopters were receding into the distance, their fuselages riddled with javelins and arrows, flying as fast as they could in the general direction of Hereford. 'Chicken!' Hjort roared after them. He tied a knot in the barrel of an abandoned rifle and sat down in disgust.

'I nearly got the leader of those men in black,' said Starkad Storvirksson. 'I thought for a moment he was going to stand, but in the end he jumped on to the metal seagull along with all the others.' He dropped the piece of helicopter undercarriage he had been carrying and went off to help Hring pick up the arrows.

'Never mind,' said Angantyr. 'It was a victory, wasn't it?'

'I suppose so.' Bothvar yawned. 'Anyway, they might come back.' He chopped up a television camera to relieve his feelings. 'Oh, look,' he said, 'there's glass in these things.'

Angantyr sheathed his sword. 'You know what we haven't done?'

'What?'

'We haven't rescued the herald,' Angantyr said. 'That's no good, is it?'

'Maybe he wasn't a herald after all, only a traitor,' said Ohtar. He had found a lunch-box dropped in the rout and was investigating the contents. 'Anyway, we did our best.' But Angantyr jumped up and started to search. He did not have to look far. Danny, with a disappointing lack of imagination, had climbed a tree, only discovering when he reached the top that it was a thorn-tree and uninhabitable.

'Hello,' Angantyr said, 'what are you doing up there?'

'Help!' Danny explained. 'I'm stuck.'

With a few blows of his sword, Angantyr chopped through the tree and pushed it over. Danny crawled out and collapsed on the ground. 'What happened?' he said.

'We came to rescue you,' said Angantyr. 'You did go to try to negotiate, didn't you?' he asked as an afterthought. Danny assured him that he had. 'And you didn't tell them about the secret passage?'

'Of course not,' Danny replied. He had tried to, but no one would listen.

'That's all right, then,' Angantyr said cheerfully.

'You've got thorns sticking in you.' Danny followed Angantyr back to where the other heroes were sitting and thanked them for rescuing him. He didn't feel in the least grateful, but having seen the heroes in action he reckoned that tact was probably called for.

'No trouble,' said Ohtar. He bit into a chocolate roll he'd found in the lunch-box and spat it out again. 'Don't like that,' he said.

'You're supposed to take the foil off first,' Danny said.

'Gold-plated food,' said Ohtar admiringly. 'Stylish.'

The spokesman from Highlands and Islands Development Board was refusing to comment, and Thorgeir switched the set off. The sorcerer-king was counting on his fingers.

'So that leaves four unaccounted for,' he said. 'The King, the wizard, Arvarodd of Permia and Brynjolf the Shape-Shifter.'

'Plus that lady archaeologist makes five,' said Thorgeir. 'Trouble is we haven't the faintest idea where they are.'

'You're worrying again,' said the sorcerer-king. He turned to his desk and tapped a code into his desktop terminal.

'Trying the Hendon computer again?' Thorgeir asked. The sorcerer-king shook his head, and pointed to the screen. On a green background, little Viking figures were rushing backwards and forwards, vainly trying to avoid the two ravening wolves that were chasing them through a stylised maze.

'I had young Fortescue run it up for me this morning,' said the sorcerer-king. 'He's good with computers, that boy.'

Thorgeir shook his head sadly, but said nothing. There had been a word in one of the Old Norse dialects that exactly described the sorcerer-king. 'Yuppje,' he murmured under his breath, and went away to get on with some work.

The new car, despite being a useless old wreck, had a radio in it, and the King's company were listening to the news.

151

'The search is continuing', said the newsreader, 'for the ten men who routed police and SAS units in a pitched battle in the north of Scotland yesterday. They are believed still to be in the Strathnaver district. Two companies of Royal Marines have reinforced the police, and Harriers from RAF Lossiemouth are on standby. In the House of Commons, the Defence Minister has refused to reply to Opposition questions until the conclusion of the operation.'

The King shrugged his shoulders. 'Might as well leave them to it,' he said. 'They seem to be coping.'

'You should have told me about the armour,' Hildy said.

'You should have told me about the Special Effects,' replied the King. 'Now you see what I mean about the decline of civilisation. But we can't leave things too long. It depends on what he's doing. If he's gone up there or sent someone to put a counter-spell on the lads, it'll all be over in a matter of minutes. Of course, he'll have to find them first. But with luck. . . .'

Hildy parked the car, praying that it wouldn't be clamped while they were inside the Museum, for that would interfere quite horribly with their well-planned escape. Still, she reflected, so many things could go wrong with this lunatic enterprise that it was pointless to worry about any one of them.

The King, the wizard, Arvarodd and Brynjolf had put their mail shirts on under large raincoats bought that afternoon with part of the proceeds of the King's ring and hung short swords by their sides. For her part, Hildy had been given a small flat pebble with a rune scratched on it which was supposed to have roughly the same effect as an enchanted mail shirt, and she had put it in her pocket wrapped up in two handkerchieves and a scarf, to protect her against the side-effect (incessant sneezing). She had also found the magic charms that Arvarodd had lent her on her first trip to London; she offered to return them, but Arvarodd had smiled and told her to hang on to them for the time being.

Past the guards at the big revolving door without any trouble. Up the main staircase and through the Egyptian galleries, then out along a room full of Greek vases and they were there.

The lecturer was giving the afternoon lecture. This time his audience consisted of five Germans, three schoolboys, a middle-aged woman and her small and disruptive nephew. No point in even considering the *Beowulf* quotation.

'Well,' said Brynjolf, as they stood in front of the big glass case that contained the shield, harp and helmet, 'what's the plan?'

'Who needs a plan?' replied the King. 'But we'll just wait till these people go away again.'

'That's all wrong, of course,' said Arvarodd, contemplating the helmet, which teams of scholars had pieced together from a handful of twisted and rusty fragments. 'You imagine wearing that.'

Unfortunately the lecturer, who was just approaching the Sutton Hoo exhibit, took that as a question. After all, it was a comment he had often been faced with, and by now he had worked out a short and well-phrased answer. He gave it. Arvarodd listened impatiently.

'Here,' he said when the lecturer had finished, 'give me a pencil and a bit of paper.' Resting the paper on the side of the glass case, he drew a quick sketch of what the helmet should have looked like. 'Try that,' he said.

'But that ... that's brilliant,' said the lecturer, his audience quite forgotten. 'So that's what that little bobble thing was for.'

'Stands to reason,' said Arvarodd.

The lecturer beamed. 'Tell me, Mr. ...'

'Arvarodd,' said Arvarodd.

The lecturer stared. Perhaps it was something in the man's eyes, but there was something about him that made the hair on the back of the lecturer's head start to rise. The palms of his clenched hands were wet now, and he found it difficult to breathe. He narrowed his eyebrows.

'Arvarodd?'

'That's right,' said Arvarodd.

The lecturer took a deep breath. 'Aren't you the Arvarodd who went to Permia?' he asked.

Arvarodd hit him.

'That', he said, 'is for stealing my arm-ring.' He strode across to the glass case, drew his short sword, and smashed the glass. Alarms went off all over the building.

'Quick,' said the King. With his own short sword, he smashed open the case containing the brooch, grabbed it, and stuffed it into his pocket. The middle-aged woman shrieked, and the small nephew kicked him. 'Right,' said the King, 'move!'

But Arvarodd was gazing at his arm-ring, running his fingers over the beloved metal, his mind full only of the image of his first wolf, at bay on the hillside above Crackaig. The lecturer wiped the blood from his nose and staggered to his feet.

'*Your* arm-ring?' he said in wonder.

'Yes,' snapped Arvarodd, wheeling round. His hand tightened on his sword-hilt. 'Want to make something of it?'

'But it's eighth-century,' said the lecturer. 'And you're seventh.'

'Who are you calling seventh-century?'

'But your saga. . . .' Heedless of personal danger, the lecturer grabbed his sleeve. 'Definitely set in seventh-century Norway.'

'I know,' said Arvarodd sadly. 'Bloody editors,' he explained.

Suddenly, the gallery was filled with large men in blue uniforms. Before Hildy could warn them, they ran towards the King. Glass cases crashed to the ground.

'Oh, no,' Hildy wailed, as a case of silver dishes was crushed beneath a stunned guard, 'not here.' Suddenly she remembered Arvarodd's magic charms. She fished in her pocket and pulled out the fragment of bone that made you irresistibly persuasive. Quickly she seized hold of the nearest guard.

'Not theft,' she said, 'fire.'

154

The guard looked at her. She tightened her hand round the fragment of bone. 'Fire,' she repeated. 'It's a fire alarm.'

'Oh,' said the guard. 'Right you are, miss.' He hurried off to tell the others. The battle stopped.

'Then, why did he break that glass case?' asked the chief guard.

'You know what it says on the notices,' replied Hildy desperately. 'In case of fire, break glass.'

The guards dashed away to evacuate the galleries.

Just as Hildy had feared, they had clamped the car. But the King was in no mood to be worried by a little thing like that. With a single blow of his sword, he sliced through the yellow metal and flicked away the wreckage. There were several cheers from passing motorists. The King and his company jumped into the car and drove away.

'That was quick thinking,' said the King, as Hildy accelerated over Waterloo Bridge.

'What was?'

'The way you got rid of those guards.'

'It was nothing,' Hildy said quietly. 'It was all down to that jawbone thing of Arvarodd's.'

'Nevertheless,' the King smiled 'I think you've definitely done enough to deserve a Name.'

'A Name?' Hildy gasped. 'You mean a proper Heroic Name?' She flushed with pleasure.

'Yes,' replied the King. 'Like Harald Bluetooth or Sigurd the Fat, or', he added maliciously, 'Arvarodd of Permia. Doesn't she, lads?'

From the back seat, the heroes and the wizard expressed their approval. In fact Arvarodd had been addressing himself to the problem of a suitable Name for Hildy for quite some time; but even the best he had come up with, Swan-Hildy, was clearly inappropriate.

'So from now on', said the King, 'our sister Hildy Frederik's-daughter shall be known by the name of Vel-Hilda.'

'Vel-Hilda?' Hildy frowned. 'I don't get it,' she said at last.

The King grinned. 'The Norse word *vel*,' he said, 'as you

know better than I, is short and means "well". The same, Hildy Frederik's-daughter, may be said of you. Therefore. . . .'

'Oh,' said Hildy. 'I see.'

# 10

'CHECKMATE.'

Anyone looking through binoculars at the darkened windows of Gerrards Garth House would have thought that someone was signalling with a torch. In fact the little points of flickering light were Prexz, blinking in disbelief.

'Ninety-nine thousand, nine hundred and ninety-nine sets and nine games to you,' said Zxerp, almost beside himself with malicious pleasure, 'and *nine* games to me. All the nines,' he added, and sniggered.

'You're cheating,' Prexz muttered. But Zxerp only smiled.

'Impossible to cheat at Goblin's Teeth,' he said benignly. 'God knows, I've tried often enough. No, old chum, you've just got to face the fact that I'm on a winning streak. Mugs away.'

'Let's play Snapdragon, for a change.'

'Your move.'

'Or Dungeons and Dragons. You used to like Dungeons and Dragons.'

'Or would you rather I moved first?' Zxerp grinned broadly. 'For once.'

Angrily, Prexz slammed down the dice and moved his knight six spaces.

'"Go directly to Jotunheim,"' Zxerp read aloud. 'Hard luck, what a shame, never mind. Six,' he noted, as he examined the dice he had thrown. 'Getting to be quite a habit. I think I'll take your rook.'

'I think it's something to do with that thing over there,' grumbled Prexz. He pointed at the computer banks.

'Could be,' said Zxerp. 'But. . . .' He quoted rule 138. Prexz muttered something about gamesmanship and tried to get his knight out of Jotunheim. He failed.

'And now your other rook,' chuckled Zxerp. 'That's bad, losing both your rooks. Remember how I always used to do that?'

Suddenly, the room was flooded with light. From somewhere down the corridor came the noise of confused shouting and the ring of metal. Zxerp looked up, and Prexz nudged his queen on to a black square.

'I'll see you,' he said.

But Zxerp wasn't listening. 'Something's happening,' he whispered.

'I know,' replied Prexz, 'I'm seeing you.'

'Shut up a minute,' hissed Zxerp. 'There's someone coming.'

The door to the office flew open. Five men in boiler-suits staggered into the room, beating vainly at an enormous bear with bunches of marigolds and tulips. With a swipe of his huge paw, the bear sent them flying into the computer bank, which was smashed to pieces. The bear stopped, nibbled at the tulips for a moment, then advanced on its terrified assailants, who took cover behind the spirits' tank. At that moment, the King, Hildy and the wizard came running in.

'Here they are,' shouted Hildy. The bear vanished, and was replaced by Brynjolf the shape-changer, spitting out tulip petals. 'What kept you?' asked Brynjolf.

The King looked down at the front of his coat, to make sure the Sutton Hoo brooch was still there, and drew his short sword. The men in boiler-suits covered their eyes and whimpered as he strode up to the tank, but the King paid no attention to them. With a wristy blow, he shattered the glass.

'Quick,' he said to the wizard. In the doorway Arvarodd appeared. He had a boiler-suited guard in each hand, and there was pollen all over his sleeves. 'All clear,' he said.

'The rest of them have bolted, but I don't think they're going to bother us.'

The wizard had disconnected the wires around the spirits' throats, and replaced them with wires of his own. Prexz struggled for a moment, but Zxerp was too busy bundling the pieces into their box to offer any resistance. All over the building, sirens were blaring.

'Right,' said the King, 'that's that done. Time we were on our way.'

At the end of the corridor, Thorgeir Storm-Shepherd crouched behind a fire-door and listened. He had been working late, trying to catch up on the Japanese deal. He had realised immediately what was happening, and had hurried down to see the King and his bunch of idiots being blasted back into the realms of folk-tale by the automatic weapons of Vouchers. From his hiding-place he had seen the guns turn into bunches of flowers, and Arvarodd and Brynjolf scattering the bemused guards. He had seen the Sutton Hoo brooch on King Hrolf's chest. It had reminded him that he never had tracked down the prototype of the Luck of Caithness.

He should have had two options, he reflected. One would have been to stand and fight, the other to run away. The latter option would have had a great deal to be said for it, but sadly it was no longer available to him. He sighed, and glanced down at his crocodile shoes, his all-wool Savile Row suit, and the backs of his hands, which were now covered in shaggy grey fur. His nails had become claws again, and his dental plate was being forced out of his mouth by the vulpine fangs that were sprouting from his upper jaw. He pricked up his ears, growled softly, and wriggled out of his human clothes. Wolf in sheep's clothing, he thought ruefully. He lifted his head and howled.

'Jesus!' said Hildy. 'What was that?'

'Just a wolf, that's all,' said Arvarodd, tightening his grip on the two squirming guards. 'Hang on, though,' he said and frowned. 'I knew there was something odd going on, ever since I woke up in the ship, but I couldn't quite put my finger on it. No wolves.'

'There aren't any more wolves,' said Hildy, shuddering. 'They're extinct in the British Isles.' She had never actually seen a wolf, not even in a zoo; but she remembered enough biology to know that wolves are related to dogs, and she was terrified of all dogs, especially Airedales.

'No, you're wrong there,' said Arvarodd firmly. There was a hopeful light in his eyes, and he was fingering his newly recovered arm-ring. 'For a start, there's one just down the corridor. Here, hold these for me.' He thrust the two guards at Hildy and ran off down the corridor. Without thinking, Hildy grabbed the guards by the collar. They made no attempt to escape.

'Where's he gone?' asked the King. 'We haven't got time to fool about.'

'He heard a wolf,' said Hildy faintly.

'Him and his dratted wolves,' said the King impatiently. 'All he thinks about.'

'But there aren't any wolves,' Hildy insisted, 'not any more.'

'Oh.' The King turned his head sharply. 'Aren't there now?' He looked at the wizard, who nodded. 'That's awkward,' he said.

'Awkward?'

'Awkward. You see, our enemy had a henchman, Thorgeir Storm-Shepherd. Originally, Thorgeir was not a human being but a timber-wolf of immense size and ferocity, whom the enemy transformed into a human being by the power of his magic. . . .' He fell silent.

'And the magic's been cancelled out by the brooch we took from the Museum,' said Brynjolf. He was looking decidedly nervous. 'So if Thorgeir's anywhere in the building he'll have changed back into a wolf.'

'Who is this person?' Hildy asked, but the King made no reply. 'Someone ought to go and tell Arvarodd that that isn't an ordinary wolf,' he said quietly. 'Otherwise he might get a nasty shock.'

As it happened, Arvarodd was on the point of finding out for himself. The excitement of the wolf-hunt had chased all

160

other thoughts from his mind: the quest, the need to get out quickly, even his duty to his King. It did not occur to him that office-blocks are not a normal habitat for normal wolves until he rounded a corner and came face to face with his quarry. He drew his short sword and braced himself for the onset of the animal; as he did so, he noticed that this was a particularly large wolf, bigger than any he could recall having seen in all his seasons with the Caithness and Sutherland. The fact that its coat was so dark as almost to be black was not that unusual – melanistic wolves had not been so uncommon, even in his day – but the way that its eyes blazed with unearthly fire and the foam from its slavering jaws burnt holes in the carpet tiles marked it out as distinctly unusual. A collector's item, he muttered to himself, as he tightened his grip on his sword-hilt.

The wolf was in no hurry to attack. It stood and pawed at the carpet, growling menacingly and lashing its tail back and forth. In fact it was trying to remember exactly how a wolf springs, and regretting the second helping of cheesecake it had had with its dinner at the Wine Vaults that evening. It is difficult for a wolf to feel particularly bellicose on a full stomach, unless its whelps are being threatened; and Thorgeir's whelps, to the best of his knowledge, were quite safe in their dormitory at Harrow. He growled again, and showed his enormous fangs. Arvarodd stood still, just like the picture in the coaching manual: weight on the back foot, head steady, left shoulder well forward.

'Get on with it,' growled the wolf.

Arvarodd raised an eyebrow. Wolves that talked were a novelty to him, and he didn't think it was strictly ethical. 'Did you say something?' he said coldly.

'I said get on with it,' replied the wolf. 'Or are you scared?'

'If I was scared, I wouldn't be standing here,' said Arvarodd indignantly. 'I'd be running back down the passage, wouldn't I?'

'Not if you were too terrified to move,' said the wolf. 'Then you'd just be standing there mesmerised, waiting for me to spring. Rabbits do that.'

'But I'm not a rabbit,' Arvarodd pointed out. 'And I'm not mesmerised. Neither am I stupid. It's your job to attack.'

'Says you,' retorted the wolf. 'So let's have less chat and more action, shall we? Unless', he added, trying to sound unconcerned, 'you'd rather scratch the whole fixture.'

'You what?'

'I mean,' said the wolf, relaxing slightly, 'you're not going to attack, and I'm buggered if I am. So we can wait here all night, until the sorcerer-king turns up and zaps you into a cinder, or we can go our separate ways and say no more about it. Up to you, really.'

'You're not really a wolf, are you?' said Arvarodd.

'Don't be daft,' said the wolf, and growled convincingly. But Arvarodd had remembered something.

'Our enemy had a sidekick called Thorgeir,' he said. 'Nasty piece of work. Used to be a wolf, by all accounts. Not a pure-bred wolf, of course.' The wolf snarled and lashed its tail. Arvarodd pretended not to notice. 'I seem to remember there was a story about his mother and a large brindled Alsatian—'

The wolf sprang, but Arvarodd was ready for it. He stepped out of the way and struck two-handed at the beast's neck (plenty of bottom hand and remember to *roll those wrists!*). But the wolf must have sensed that he was about to strike, or perhaps instinct made him twist his shoulders round; Arvarodd's blow overreached, so that his forearms struck on the wolf's back and the sword was jarred out of his hands. The wolf landed, turned and prepared to spring again. Arvarodd shot a glance at the sword, lying on the other side of the corridor, then clenched his fists. As he prepared to meet the animal's onslaught, he thought of what his coach had told him about facing an angry wolf when disarmed. 'Stand well forward and brace your feet,' he had said. 'That way, the wolf might break your neck before he has a chance to get his teeth into you.'

'Never believed that story myself,' he said. 'I hate malicious gossip, don't you?'

'No,' snapped the wolf, and leapt at his throat.

'Hell,' said the King. 'A wire's come loose on the brooch. Look.'

When the wolf turned back into a middle-aged stark-naked businessman in mid-air, Arvarodd was surprised but pleased. He made a fine instinctive tackle, and threw his assailant through a plate-glass door. Then he made a grab for the sword. But Thorgeir had the advantage of local knowledge. He picked himself up and ran. After a short chase through a labyrinth of offices, Arvarodd gave up. After all, his enemy might change back into a wolf again at any minute, and he was clearly out of practice. He retraced his steps, and met the King and his company by the lift-shaft.

'Where the hell have you been?' said the King.

'There was this wolf,' said Arvarodd, 'only he wasn't. I think it was Thorgeir.'

The King seemed to regard this as a reasonable explanation. 'We've got to go now. This brooch got unconnected from its batteries for a couple of minutes, and I'm not going to take any chances.'

'Good idea,' said Arvarodd. He was feeling slightly foolish. But not as foolish as Thorgeir. No sooner had he escaped from Arvarodd than he changed back into a wolf; and then, as he had gone bounding down the corridor to see if he could continue the fight where he had left it, he had turned back into a human being again, at the very moment when the King (and the Sutton Hoo brooch) had left the building. He gave the whole thing up as a bad job and went to look for his clothes.

As soon as he saw the smashed tank and the cowering guards, he guessed what had happened. He sat down on a wrecked photocopier and thought hard. He ought to go at once to the sorcerer-king and warn him, to give him time to prepare his defences. But something seemed to tell him

163

that this would be a bad idea. What if the sorcerer-king should lose and be overthrown? Thorgeir bit his lip and forced himself to consider the possible consequences. On the one hand, the boss's magic had preserved him, in human form, for twelve hundred years – without it, he would go back to being a twelve-hundred-year-old wolf, and wolves do not, even in captivity, usually live more than sixteen years. If the sorcerer-king's spell was broken, he would become, in quick succession, an extremely elderly wolf and a dead wolf; and if that had been the pinnacle of his ambition he would never have left the Kola Peninsula. On the other hand, King Hrolf's wizard was presumably competent in all grades of anthropomorphic and life-prolonging magic, and his employer might just be persuaded to do a little deal. On the third hand, if the sorcerer-king won, which was not unlikely, and he found out that his trusty aide had betrayed him, being a dead wolf would be a positive pleasure compared to the penalty the boss would be likely to impose. Tricky, Thorgeir thought. He took a small slice of marrowbone from his pocket and chewed on it to clear his head.

Of course, in order for the sorcerer-king to win or lose, there would have to be a battle; if he could make sure that that battle took place, quickly and on relatively even terms, he could then have a claim on the eventual winner, whoever he turned out to be. Looked at from all sides, that was the safest course, but there was one deadly drawback; he didn't have the faintest idea where King Hrolf was. He sighed, spat out the marrowbone, and put his socks back on. Just then, the telephone rang. He picked it up without thinking.

'Olafsen here,' he said. Who could it be at this time of night?

'Mr Olafsen?' It was the governor-presumptive of China. Thorgeir groaned; he was not in the mood for young Mr Fortescue.

'I thought I should tell someone at once,' said young Mr Fortescue. 'I've just heard that the car that Our Enemies are using', and he mentioned the type and registration

164

number, 'has been traced and seen by a police patrol in Holland Park. I'm there now, in fact. I'm talking to you' – there was a hint of pride in the young man's voice – 'over my carphone. What should I do now?'

Thorgeir muttered a quick prayer to Loki, god of villains, and said: 'Follow them. For crying out loud, don't lose them. And keep me posted on my personal number, will you?'

'Will do, Mr Olafsen. Do you think', asked Mr Fortescue diffidently, 'I could have Korea as well?'

'Of course you can,' replied Thorgeir indulgently. 'So long as you don't lose that car, you can have Korea and Mongolia as well.'

'Thanks, Mr Olafsen.'

Thorgeir put the receiver down, and found an unbroken computer terminal. Within a few minutes, he had withdrawn the car from the police computer – the last thing anyone wanted was a cloud of bluebottles getting in the way. Then he sprinted down to the underground carpark and got out his car. Almost before he had closed the door, the phone buzzed.

'They're just moving,' said Mr Fortescue. 'Going up towards Ladbroke Grove.'

'Stay with them,' urged Thorgeir. 'I'll be with you shortly. And Tibet,' he added.

Just as the dial reached £11.65, petrol started to overflow from the tank, and Hildy put the filler nozzle back in its holder and went to pay. Just her luck, she reflected; another thirty-five pence worth of petrol, and she would have got two Esso tokens, which would have been enough for the trailing flex.

Had she been a true Viking, of course, she would have gone on filling, and to hell with the spilt petrol and the fire risk. Reckless courage was the hallmark of the warrior. She looked at her reflection in the plate-glass window of the filling station and, not for the first time, wished that there was rather less of her face and rather more of the rest of her. Short and means well. True. Very true.

As she waited her turn in the queue, it occurred to her that if she bought a couple of Mars bars, she could knock the grand total up over twelve pounds. Shrewdness and cunning are the hallmark of the counsellor, and you don't have to look like one of those creatures on the magazine covers to be clever. The cashier took her money and handed her one token.

'Excuse me,' she said assertively, 'my purchases were over twelve pounds. I should get two tokens.'

'Only applies to petrol,' said the cashier. 'Can't you read?'

Someone in the queue behind her sniggered. She scooped up her token and fled.

'What's up?' said the King. 'You look upset.'

For a split second, she toyed with the idea of asking the King to go and split the cashier's skull for her, but she decided against it. That would be over-reacting, and the wise man knows when to do nothing, as the Edda says. 'No, I'm not,' she replied. 'Where to now?'

'Somewhere nice and quiet,' said the King, 'where we won't be disturbed.'

Hildy nodded and started the engine. She drove for nearly an hour in silence, heading for no great reason for the Chilterns. The heroes were asleep, and the wizard was reading a spell from a vellum scroll by the faint light of Zxerp and Prexz.

'This'll do,' said the King.

Hildy stopped the car beside a small spinney of beech-trees and switched off the lights. The car which had been behind her all the way from London drove on past and disappeared round a corner. Hildy breathed a faint sigh of relief; she had been slightly worried about that.

'I don't suppose anyone's considered anything so prosaic as food lately,' said Brynjolf, stretching his arms and yawning. 'I had this marvellous dream about roast venison.' Hildy frowned and offered him a Mars bar.

'What's this?' he asked.

'You eat it,' Hildy said.

Brynjolf shrugged, and did as she suggested. Then he

166

spat. 'No, but really,' he said. 'A joke's a joke, but—'

'Go turn yourself into a sandwich, then,' Hildy snapped. 'I'm exhausted, and I can't be doing—'

'All right,' said Arvarodd wearily, 'leave it to me. Only it'll have to be rabbit again.'

'If I have any more rabbit,' said Brynjolf, 'I'll start to look like one.'

'That's a thought,' replied Arvarodd. 'Decoy,' he explained. The two heroes got out of the car and wandered away.

'That, Vel-Hilda,' said the King, 'is heroic life for you. Rabbit seven times a week, and that's if you're lucky. Just be grateful you're not on a longship. Let's get some air.' He opened his door and climbed out, stretching his cramped limbs.

'Will the wizard be all right on his own?' whispered Hildy. 'I mean. . . .'

'We won't go far,' said the King. 'You'll be all right, won't you, Kotkel?'

The wizard looked up from his scroll, nodded absently, and muttered a spell. On the seat beside him a giant hound appeared.

'Just a hallucination,' explained the King, 'but who's to know?'

Hildy shrugged, and strolled out into the spinney. It was a still night, slightly cold, and the wind was moving the leaves on the tops of the trees. The King spread his cloak over a stump and sat down. Across his knees he laid his broadsword in its jewelled scabbard.

'This sword', he said, 'is called Tyrving. You're interested in the old days. Would you like to hear about it?'

Hildy nodded, and sat down beside him.

'One day', said the King, in a practised storyteller's voice, 'the gods Odin and Loki were out walking far from home. Why, I cannot tell you. I always thought it was a strange thing for them to be doing, since by all accounts they hated each other like poison. However, they were out walking, and there was a sudden thunderstorm. Again, it

167

seems strange that Thor should inflict a sudden thunder-storm on his liege-lord and best friend Odin for no reason, but perhaps it was his idea of a joke. Odin and Loki sought shelter in a little house, where they were greeted by a little old woman. She did not know that they were gods, so the story goes – and if you believe that, you'll believe anything; but she offered them some broth, although she had little enough for herself, and put the last of the peat on the fire so that they might be warm. All clear so far?'

'Yes,' said Hildy. 'Go on.'

'When the two gods had finished their broth and dried their clothes, they lay down to sleep. The old woman gave them all her blankets, and the pelts of otters for pillows. In the morning the gods woke up and it had stopped raining. "Old woman," said Odin, "you have treated us kindly." I don't know if Odin was given to understatement, but that's what the story says. "Learn that the guests you have sheltered are in fact the gods Odin and Loki. In return for your hospitality, I shall give you a great gift." And he drew from his belt his own sword, which the dwarfs had forged for him in the caverns of Niflheim, and gave it to the old woman, who thanked him politely, no doubt through clenched teeth. Odin then put a blessing on the sword, saying that whoever wielded it in battle should have victory. But Loki, who is a malevolent god, put a curse on it, saying that the first man to draw it in battle should eventually die from a blow from it. The old woman put the sword away safely, and in due course she gave it to her grandson Skjold, who went on to become the greatest of the Joms-vikings. When Skjold was an old man, and had long since given up fighting, he used to laugh at Loki's curse. But one day he was teaching his little son Thjostolf how to fight, and Thjostolf parried a blow rather too vigorously. Skjold's sword flew from his hand and struck him above the eye, killing him instantly. Thjostolf went on to lead the Joms-vikings as his father had done, and when he died his son Yngvar succeeded him, and the sword brought him victory. But one day he lost the sword when out hunting, and in the next battle he fought he was killed, and all his men with him. Eventually, the sword came into the hands of my grandfather, Eyjolf, who was Odin's grandson. That story is supposed to prove something or other, but I forget what.'

Hildy sat still and said nothing. The moon, coming out from behind a cloud, cast a shaft of light through the trees which fell on the hilt of the sword, making it sparkle. The King smiled, and with an easy movement of his arm drew the sword from its scabbard. For some reason, Hildy started to shiver. In the moonlight the blade glowed eerily, and the runes engraved on its hilt stood out firm and clear.

'Of the sword itself,' continued the King, 'this is said. The blade is the true dwarf-steel, but the hilt and furniture was replaced by Yngvar with the hilt of the sword Gram, which Sigurd the Dragon-Slayer bore. The blade of that sword was lost, but the hilt was preserved as an heirloom by the children of Atli of Hungary. In turn, my grandfather Eyjolf had a new quillon added; that came from the sword Helvegr, which once belonged to the Frost-Giants of Permia. My father Ketil added the scabbard, which once housed the sword of the god Frey, and fitted to the pommel the great white jewel called the Earthstar, which fell from the sky on the day I was born, and after which I am named.' He smiled, and laid his hand gently on the hilt. 'It's not a bad sword, at that. A bit on the light side for me, but nicely balanced. Here.' And he passed the sword to Hildy. For a moment she dared not take it; then she grasped it firmly and lifted it up. She was amazed by how light it seemed, like a living thing in her hands.

'It's wonderful,' she said. As she gazed at it, blazing coldly in the moonlight, her eyes were suddenly opened, and she saw, as in a dream, the faces of many kings and warriors, and blood red on the blue steel. She saw the dwarfs busy over their forge in a great cave, vivid in the orange light of the forge, and heard the sound of their hammers, the hiss as the hot metal was tempered, and the scrape of whetstones as the edge was laid. She saw a tall dark figure muffled in a cloak, who watched the work and added to the skill of the smiths the power of wind, tide and

169

lightning. She saw him take the blade in his hands, as she was doing now, and look down it to make sure that it was straight and true. Then, suddenly as it had come, the vision departed, leaving only the moonlight, still flickering on the runes cut into the langet of the hilt. As she spelt out the letters one by one, her heart was beating like a blacksmith's hammer.

*Product of more than one country.*

The moon went back behind its cloud.

'Very nice,' she said, and gave it back to the King, who grinned and slid it back into the scabbard.

'For all I know,' he said, 'the legends are all perfectly true. True but largely unimportant. Like I said, that's heroic life for you. Like all heroes have magnificent bushy beards because it's difficult to shave on a storm-tossed longship without cutting yourself to the bone.'

'I see,' said Hildy.

'And this particular adventure', said the King, 'is all heroic life, too; and you are a heroine just as much as we are heroes. It's incredibly dangerous, but you haven't been thinking about that. Just a game, a little reprise of childhood – or why do you think that in the end all the legends of heroes and warriors end up as children's stories? When I was a little boy, I wanted to be a fisherman.'

'When I was a little girl,' said Hildy, 'I wanted to be a Viking.' She laughed suddenly. 'It's been fun,' she said, 'but not in the way I thought it would be. If we do get killed, will we go to Valhalla, across the Rainbow Bridge?'

'The Rainbow Bridge', said the King, 'is something to be crossed when you come to it. If we fail, then we leave the world in the hands of its natural enemy. But, for all I know, nobody would notice except a few of the leading statesmen. Still, that's not a risk worth taking. Not only is our enemy very cruel and very evil, he is also very, very stupid. A good magician – the best ever – but I wouldn't trust him with running a dog-show, let alone the world. And I don't think, for all his magic, that he could ever become ruler of the world; if he can't catch us, then he hasn't got the resources, and anyway I think the world has changed too much, though I don't suppose he's realised. But what he would almost certainly do is start enough wars to finish off the human race, one way or another, which would be rather worse. And he's certainly a good enough magician to manage that.'

'Don't let's talk about it,' said Hildy. 'We'd better go see how Kotkel's getting on.'

Just then, Arvarodd came hurrying up. Brynjolf was with him, dragging along a man by the lapels of his jacket.

'Guess who's just turned up,' said Arvarodd.

'My liege,' said the man, bowing low to the King. 'I have come. . . .'

'Hello, Thorgeir,' said the King. 'I was expecting you.'

'Thorgeir?' Hildy stared. 'You said he was a wolf or something.'

'Only sometimes,' said the man. 'It's a long story.'

'Shaggy-wolf story,' muttered Arvarodd. 'I found him snooping about in the woods back there. By the way, we couldn't find any rabbits, so it'll have to be squirrel.'

'I wasn't snooping,' said Thorgeir. 'I came here to tell you something that you might like to hear.'

'How did you find us?' The King's face was expressionless.

'Oh, that was easy,' said Thorgeir. He smoothed out the lapels of his jacket and sat down, his manner suggesting that he wouldn't mind at all if they all did the same. 'You don't suppose I haven't known all along, do you?'

'Of course you didn't know,' said the King. 'Otherwise we'd all be dead.'

'You'd have been dead if my lord and master knew where you were,' said Thorgeir patronisingly. 'I knew all along. He leaves things like that to me, you see, and a lot of trouble I've had keeping it from him.'

'And why should you want to do that?' asked the King.

'Guess.' Thorgeir smiled.

'For some reason, envy or fear or hatred, you want to betray him to us. Or you wanted to see which of us was more likely to win before you chose sides.' The King raised an eyebrow. 'Something like that?'

'More or less.' Thorgeir scratched his ear, where for some reason a little grey fur still remained. But the King's eyes were on him.

'I was born', said the King, 'in the seventh year of the reign of Ketil Trout. In other words, not yesterday. What you meant to say was that owing to your extreme negligence we were able not only to escape the notice of your lord and master, but also to recapture the two earth-spirits we need to overthrow his power. As soon as you realised that we had an even chance of winning, you decided to hedge your bets. By a stroke of good luck – I can't say what, but I expect I'm right – you found us. You decided to come to me and persuade me to attack at a certain time and place. If I win, you claim to have given me victory. If he wins, you can claim to have brought me to him. Correct?'

'Absolutely.' Thorgeir widened his smile slightly. 'Isn't that what I said?'

'More or less.' The King leant back and thought for a moment. 'What you will do is this. You will get in touch with your master and tell him that you have found us, that we are weak and unprepared, and that something has gone wrong with our magic. You will do this gladly,' said the King, 'because for all I know it may very well be true and, if I lose, you can take the credit, as you originally planned. While we are waiting for our enemy to arrive, you will tell me everything you know about his strength and, more important, his weaknesses. You will do this truthfully, firstly because if you do not my champion Arvarodd will cut you in half, secondly because it probably won't have any effect on the outcome, one way or another. Is that clear?'

'As crystal.' Thorgeir nodded approvingly. 'But what if he won't come?'

'He'll come,' said the King. 'Sooner or later there must be a fight, and I expect your master is as impatient as I am.'

'But he doesn't want to come out to you. He wants you to go to him.'

'Then, why', said the King gently, 'did you imagine that

you could save yourself by tempting him to come and fight on even terms? Be consistent, please.'

Thorgeir shrugged his shoulders. 'And if I do what you ask,' he said, 'and if you do win, what will happen to me?'

'I have no idea,' said the King. 'It'll be interesting finding out, won't it? I could promise to spare you, or even give you a kingdom in Serkland, but you wouldn't trust me, now would you?'

'Of course not,' said Thorgeir. 'So that's settled, then, is it?'

'Settled.' The King clapped him on the shoulder. 'And to make sure Arvarodd will stand one step behind you all the time with his sword drawn. Arvarodd is bigger than you, at least so long as you are in human shape, and I fancy he doesn't like you after your confrontation earlier this evening. Now, tell me all about it.'

So Thorgeir told him.

'But why there?' said the sorcerer-king for the fifth time. 'I thought we agreed. . . .'

Thorgeir glanced over his shoulder at Arvarodd. 'Because it may be your last chance at anything like decent odds,' he said. 'It's worth the risk, believe me. Listen, Hrolf and his men have got those two spirits back. They broke into the office and rescued them.' He held the receiver away from his ear. Judging by the noises that come out of it, this was a wise move. When they had subsided, he said: 'I know, I'm sorry, it's not my fault. But I followed them here, and it'll be a couple of hours before they get the brooch wired up. There's still time.'

'Hold your water, will you?' Thorgeir waited breathlessly, and behind him Arvarodd patted the flat of his sword on the palm of his hand and made clucking noises. 'Even if you're right,' said the sorcerer-king, 'there won't be time to muster any force. It'd be suicide.'

'Balls,' said Thorgeir. 'I'm looking at them now. There's the King and that female, the wizard, Brynjolf and Arvarodd. You know,' he couldn't resist adding, 'the one who went to—'

'I know, I know. Shut up a minute. I'm thinking. Look, I could get together a portable set and some Special Effects, and there's the Emergency Kit all charged up, of course, and you could be a wolf. With that and the lads from Vouchers—'

'It'd be a doddle,' Thorgeir urged. Arvarodd was pressing his sword-point against the back of his neck. 'Get a move on, though, or they'll see me. God knows how I followed them so far without them spotting me.'

'If this goes wrong, I'll have your skull for an eggcup,' muttered the sorcerer-king. Thorgeir shut his eyes and offered a prayer of thanksgiving to his patron deity. 'Don't worry,' he said, 'it'll be no problem. Promise.'

'How long will it take me to get there?'

'The way you drive, forty minutes tops. It's just past the turning to Radnage. You got that?'

'The trouble with you, Thorgeir,' said the sorcerer-king, 'is that you combine stupidity with fecklessness. Be seeing you.'

There was a click and the dialling tone. 'Well,' said Arvarodd, 'is he coming or do I chop you?'

'He's coming,' said Thorgeir, straight-faced. 'Exactly like you wanted it. And he hasn't got any time to get his forces together; it'll be him and a couple of extras. You'll walk it, you'll see.'

Arvarodd shook his head and marched Thorgeir away. As he went, Thorgeir congratulated himself on his rotten memory. He had honestly forgotten all about the Emergency Kit.

# 11

'I STILL THINK this is a bad idea,' whispered Danny Bennett. Angantyr nudged him in the ribs, expelling all the air from his body, and told him to be quiet. Utterly wretched, he lay still in the heather and turned the matter over in his mind.

On the credit side, he had persuaded them not to declare war. That had taken some doing, after such a conclusive victory. Hjort had already prepared the Red Arrow, to shoot over the battlements of Edinburgh Castle, and Angantyr was talking glibly of annexing Sunderland as well. It was the thought that they might conceivably win that had spurred Danny on to unimagined heights of eloquence, and in the end he had succeeded. But in order to do so he had had to make certain concessions, the main one being that they should all go to London and help the King. Although they would not admit it, some of the heroes were beginning to worry, and all of them hated the thought of missing the final excitement. So here they all were, lying in wait for the first suitable vehicle, and it was Danny's turn to be seriously anxious, although he had no qualms at all about admitting it. There was bound to be violence. There might well be bloodshed. If they did manage to get a van or a bus, he was going to have to drive it.

Round the bend in the road came a large red thing, with the number 87 displayed in a little glass frame above its nose. Danny closed his eyes and hoped that his companions wouldn't notice it; but they did.

'Here, Danny,' hissed Angantyr, 'how about that one?'

'Oh, no, I don't really think so,' Danny gabbled. 'I mean, it's probably too small.'

'Doesn't look it,' said Hjort on his other side.

'They're much smaller inside than out,' said Danny. 'Really.'

Hjort shook his head. 'No harm in trying,' he said cheerfully. 'What do you think, lads?'

Several heads nodded, the boar-shaped crests of their helmets visible above the heather like a covey of skimming larks. 'When you're ready, Starkad,' said Hjort.

'Hold it, hold it,' snarled Angantyr. 'And since when were you in charge of this, Hjort Herjolfsson?'

'Someone's got to do it, haven't they?' Hjort raised his head to glower at Angantyr.

Danny saw a gleam of hope. If he could start them quarrelling. . . . 'I'm with you, Angantyr,' he said, and looked expectantly at Hjort.

But the hero simply shrugged and said, 'See if I care.'

'Here,' said Starkad, 'do I go, or what?'

'Yes,' said Hjort and Angantyr simultaneously. They glared at each other.

Starkad was on his feet. He could run like the wind if he didn't trip over something, and soon he had overtaken the bus. With a spring like a wild cat, he leapt at the driver's door, grabbed the handle and, bracing his feet against the frame, wrenched it open. The bus swerved drastically, mowed down a row of snow-poles and stopped dead.

The driver, his head spinning, pushed himself up from the steering-wheel and stared helplessly at the group of maniacs who had come running up out of nowhere. All save one of them were waving antiquated but terrifying weapons: swords, spears and axes. It could conceivably be a group of archaeology students staging a reconstruction of Culloden, but he wasn't hopeful. The one who was unarmed leant forward into the cab and cleared his throat.

'Excuse me,' he said, 'does this bus go to London?'

The driver dragged breath into the vacuum of his lungs. 'If it's the money you're after,' he gasped, 'there's three pound forty-two pence. Take it all.'

'Actually,' said the unarmed man, 'would you mind if we borrowed your bus? It's just for a day or a week or so.'

'Are you hijacking my bus, then?' asked the driver.

'Yes,' said the unarmed man unhappily. The driver went white, and Danny felt panic coming on. What if the man tried to resist and defend his passengers? Bothvar Bjarki would like that.

'It's all right, really,' he said, as reassuringly as possible, 'I'm with the BBC.'

'Is that right?' said the driver. He did not look reassured. 'Would you be the blokes who beat up all those coppers and soldiers at Farr the other day?'

'Yes,' said Angantyr. He stuck out his bearded chin impatiently and tapped his sword-blade with his fingers.

'The Army's looking for you,' said an old lady from the second row of seats. 'They're all over Strathnaver with armoured cars.'

'Really?' Angantyr's eyes lit up. 'Hey, lads,' he called out, 'did you hear that? They've come back.' The heroes began to chatter excitedly.

It was, Danny decided, a moment for action, not words. He grabbed the driver by the sleeve and pulled him out of his seat. 'Right,' he tried to shout (but the words came out as an urgent sort of shriek), 'I want everybody off the bus.'

'You must be kidding, son,' said the old lady. 'There's not another bus till Wednesday, and I've the week's shopping to do.'

Bothvar Bjarki climbed inside. 'You heard him,' he growled. 'Off you get, now.'

'Are we being taken hostage?' asked an old man in the fourth row.

'No,' said Danny. 'You're free to go.'

'Pity,' said the old man. 'That would have been one in the eye for George Macleod and his pigeons.' He shrugged his shoulders wearily and picked up his shopping-bag.

The passengers shuffled off the bus, all of them taking a good look at Danny as they went, and the heroes scrambled in. Danny took a deep breath and sat in the driver's seat. The driver raised an eyebrow.

'Do you know how to drive a bus then, mister?' he asked.

'I haven't the faintest idea,' Danny confessed. 'Is it difficult?'

'Yes,' said the driver. 'Very. Are you going far?'

'London,' Danny said.

The driver shook his head sadly, and deep inside Danny's soul something snapped. Perhaps he had Viking blood in his veins, or perhaps he was just fed up. 'All right,' he said quietly, 'you drive.'

'Me?' The driver stared. 'All the way to London?'

'Yes,' said Danny.

'Now, look here,' said the driver. 'The Ministry regulations say—'

'Stuff the Ministry regulations.' Danny wished he had accepted Angantyr's offer of a sword. 'Drive this bus to London or you'll be sorry.' Behind him, Angantyr nodded approvingly and clapped Danny on the shoulder.

'That's right,' he said, 'you tell him.' For some reason which he could never fathom, Danny glowed with pleasure.

'Right,' he said, giving the driver a shove. 'Let's get this show on the road.'

'What show?' asked Hjort, but Danny ignored him, for he had had a sudden inspiration. He leant forward and pointed to the roller above the driver's seat that changed the number on the front of the bus. 'Change that,' he ordered.

'What to?' asked the driver.

'"Special", of course,' Danny replied. 'Come on, move it.'

The driver did as he was told, and then started the engine. Danny stuck his head out of the window and waved to the ex-passengers.

'Never mind,' he shouted, 'there'll be another one along in a minute.'

The bus moved off, and Danny sat down in the front row of seats, feeling very surprised at himself but not at all repentant. He was, he realised, starting to enjoy all this.

'You realise', said the driver over his shoulder, 'we'll run out of fuel before we're past Inverness.'

'Then, we'll get some more, won't we?' Danny replied. 'Now, shut up and drive.'

Angantyr came forward and sat down beside him. 'Have some cold seagull,' he said. 'I saved some for you.'

'Thanks.' Danny bit off a large chunk. It tasted good.

'You did all right back there,' said Angantyr Asmundson. 'In fact, you're coming along fine.'

'It was nothing,' said Danny with his mouth full. .

'I know,' said Angantyr. 'But you handled it pretty well, all the same.'

'Thanks.' Danny chewed for a moment, then scratched his head. 'Angantyr,' he said, 'I've thought of something.'

'What?'

'When we get to London, how will we find them?'

'Don't ask me,' said Angantyr. 'Is it a big place?'

'Quite big.' Danny frowned. 'So you don't know where they're likely to be?'

'It was your idea we go,' Angantyr replied.

'Was it?'

'Yes,' said Angantyr. 'Don't you remember?'

Danny leant back in his seat. After all, it was a long way to London. He would have plenty of time to think of a plan.

'So it was,' he said, and yawned. 'You leave everything to me.'

Angantyr grinned. 'You've changed your tune a bit, haven't you?' he said. Danny shook his head.

'It just takes some getting used to, that's all,' he said. 'And you've got to start somewhere, haven't you?'

'That's very true,' said Angantyr.

'It was the same when I shot my first feature,' Danny went on. Angantyr nodded.

'Did you miss?' he said sympathetically.

Danny remembered the reviews. 'Yes,' he said.

'Same with me and my first wild boar,' said Angantyr. 'Nerves, principally. They all laughed.'

Danny sighed; he knew the feeling. 'The main thing is', he said, 'not to let it get to you.'

'That's especially true of wild boar,' Angantyr agreed.

'Tusks like razors, some of them. I remember one time in Radsey—'

He stopped short and stared. A great black cloud had appeared out of nowhere and was covering the sky. In a few moments it was as dark as night. From where the sun should have been there came a piercing cry; but whether it was pain or triumph no one could tell. A great wind rose up all around, and the air was filled with rushing shapes, like bats or small black birds. Then a great bolt of lightning split the sky, and hailstones crashed against the windows of the bus. The driver pulled over and hid under the seat, whimpering.

'Oh, well,' said Angantyr, 'looks like we're going to miss all the fun.'

King Hrolf staggered, tripped, fell and lay still. For a moment he could do nothing except listen to the beating of his own heart and the howling of the storm. Then he became aware of the blaring of the horns and the cries of the huntsmen and forced himself to rise. The savage music was too close. He commanded his knees to bear his weight, leant forward and ran.

Something had gone wrong, many hours ago now. A man whose face was familiar had driven up in a small black car. He had climbed out and walked forward, as if to surrender. Arvarodd had turned to look, and then Thorgeir had broken free from his grip. Before anyone could stop him, he had wrenched away the wires from the brooch, and then the storm had begun. However brave and strong he may be, a man cannot fight against lightning, or waves of air that strike him like a hammer. He had clung on to his sword and ran, and the storm had followed him.

That was all a long time ago, and he had not stopped running. He had passed through towns and villages, frozen and lifeless in the total darkness, across open fields and through woods, whose trees were torn up by the roots as he passed. Lightning had scorched his heels, flying rocks had grazed him, and the hailstones whipped and punched him as he ran. Sometimes his path had been blocked by strange shapes, sometimes human, sometimes animal; sometimes the ground had opened up before him, or burst into flames under his feet; sometimes the hail gave way to boiling rain that scalded his face and hands, or black fog that filled his lungs like mud. All these, and other things, too, he had run through or past, while all the time his pursuers were gaining on him; slowly, a yard or so each hour, but perceptibly closer all the time. So must the hour hand feel when the minute hand pursues it.

He stumbled again, and crashed to the ground. This time, his knees refused to obey, and the earth he lay on shook with the sound of many feet. King Hrolf raised his head and wiped the blood away from his eyes. In front of him the ground had fallen away on all sides. He was on a plateau, with a sheer drop all around him. Suddenly the wind dropped. Absolute silence.

King Hrolf drove his sword into the ground and used it to lever himself up to his feet. He filled his lungs with air and held it there.

'So.' The voice was all around him. 'This is where it must end.'

'This is as good a place as any,' said the King. The voice laughed.

'It is indeed. Was it worth it, Hrolf Earthstar?'

The King jerked his sword out of the turf and held it in front of him. 'That depends on the outcome,' he said.

'The voice laughed again, and the skin of the earth vibrated like the surface of a drum. 'Well said, Hrolf Ketilson. If you wish, I will let you run a little further.'

'I am getting too old to run,' replied the King. 'I have lived long enough.'

'Too long.' The voice laughed a third time.

'I have only one favour to ask you,' said King Hrolf, raising his head and smiling. 'It is a small thing, but it would please me to know your name.'

'My name? That is no small thing. But because you have run well, and because when you are dead no one will ever be born again who would dare ask it, I shall tell you. Listen carefully, Earthstar.'

King Hrolf lowered his sword and leant on it. 'I am listening,' he said.

'Well, then,' said the voice, 'I am called Vindsval and Vasad, Bestla and Beyla, Jalk and Jafnhar. In Finnmark my name is Geirrod, in Gotland Helblindi, in Markland Bolverk, in Permia Skirnir, in Serkland Eikenskjaldi. Among Danes I was called Warfather, among Saxons Master; to the Goths I was Gravemaker, and in Scythia Emperor. The gods called me Hunferth, the elves named me Freki, to the dwarfs my name was Ganglati and to men. . . .'

King Hrolf put his hands over his ears.

Hildy rolled over on to her side and opened her eyes. That meant she was still alive, for what it was worth. Through the gloom she could see Brynjolf lying on his face where the first gust of wind had blown him, and the wizard Kotkel, where Thorgeir had struck him down. Painfully she lifted herself up on one elbow and looked round. There was Arvarodd, or his dead body, and over it stood a great grey wolf. She remembered how they had fought until Arvarodd's sword had shattered into splinters in his hand, and his shield had crumpled like a flower under the impact of the wolf's assault. Then something had flown up into her face, and she had seen no more. Of the King there was no sign.

The wolf turned its head and growled at her, and licked blood off its long jaws. But Hildy was no longer afraid. She had reached the point where fear can no longer help, and anger offers the only hope of survival. She hated that wolf and she was going to kill it. She looked around for a weapon, but could see none, except the hilt of Arvarodd's sword. The wolf was trotting towards her, like a dog who has heard its plate scraping on the kitchen tiles; she watched it for a moment, suddenly fascinated by the delicacy of its movement. Then, inexplicably, her hand was in her pocket. The little roll of cloth that Arvarodd had given her all that time ago had came loose, and her fingers touched and recognised the contents of it; the stone that gave mastery of languages; the splinter of bone that gave eloquence; the pebble that brought understanding; the pebble from the shores of Asgard. . . .

*If you throw it at something, it turns into a boulder and flattens pretty well anything. Then it turns back into a pebble and returns to your hand.*

She threw it. She missed.

The wolf gave a startled yelp and galloped away. The pebble came whistling back through the air, stinging Hildy's palm as it landed, so that she nearly dropped it. She swore loudly and threw again. A loud crash told her that this time she had hit the car. By the time the pebble was between her fingers once more, the wolf was nowhere to be seen. She started to run after it, but stopped in mid-stride.

'Aren't you forgetting something?' said a voice.

She turned unsteadily on her heel and peered through the darkness. There were two tiny points of light. . . .

'Instead of throwing things at us,' said the voice, 'you might get this contraption wired up.'

'Shine brighter,' said Hildy. 'I can't see.'

The lights flared up, and Hildy could make out the outline of the car.

'You could see well enough to throw that rock at us,' said the light. 'What harm did we ever do you?'

'I wasn't throwing it at you,' said Hildy. 'There was this wolf. . . .'

'Pull the other one, it's got bells on it,' said the light. 'The brooch is just over there.'

The light flashed brilliantly on a garnet, and Hildy picked up the brooch. 'What do I do?' she said.

'Twist the ends of the wires round our necks,' said the light.

'Have you two got necks?' said Hildy doubtfully. All she could see was a pool of light. The pool of light flickered irritably.

'Of course we've got necks,' said the pool of light. 'You'll find them between our heads and our shoulders.'

Hildy grabbed at the light. 'Ouch,' it said, 'do you mind?'

'Sorry.' She grabbed again.

'Getting warmer,' said the light. 'Up a bit. That's it.'

With her other hand, Hildy took the end of one of the wires. 'Stay still,' she begged.

'Difficult,' said the light. 'It tickles.'

Hildy drew a loop in the wire and tied it. There was a spluttering noise and she apologised. She did the same with the other wire.

'Idiot,' said the light. 'That's my ankle.'

'Oh, for Chrissakes.' Fumbling desperately, she untied the wire and lunged. 'That's right,' gasped the light, 'throttle me.' She tied the second knot.

Suddenly, the sun came out.

The sorcerer-king froze. Something had gone wrong. He stared wildly at the sun, riding high in the clear blue sky, and the ground, inexplicably beneath his feet. He swallowed hard.

'But you', he said, 'can call me Eric.'

'Right,' said the King, 'Eric. Shall we get on with it?' He lifted his sword and whirled it around his head.

'I'm in no hurry,' said the sorcerer-king, backing away. 'As you know, I'm firmly opposed to needless violence.'

'What about necessary violence?' asked the King unpleasantly.

'That, too,' said the sorcerer-king. 'Besides, I seem to have come out without my sword.'

'What's that hanging from your belt, then?'

'Oh,' said the sorcerer-king, 'that.' Very unwillingly, he drew the great sword Ifing from its scabbard. The sun flashed on its well-tended blade.

'Ready?'

'No,' said the sorcerer-king.

'Tough.' Hrolf took a step forward.

'Toss you for it?' suggested the sorcerer-king. 'Heads I go away for ever, tails I disappear completely.'

'No,' said Hrolf. 'Ready now?'

'Best of three?'

'No.'

'Oh, have at you, then,' said the sorcerer-king wretchedly, and launched a mighty blow at the King's head. Hrolf parried, and the two swords rang together like a great bell. Hrolf struck his blow, first feinting to draw his adversary over to the left, then turning his wrist and striking right; but he was wounded and exhausted, and the sorcerer-king, who had always been his match as a swordsman, was fresh and unhurt. The blow went wide as the sorcerer-king side-stepped nimbly, and Hrolf fell forward. Quickly, the sorcerer-king lifted Ifing above his head and brought it down with all his strength, hitting Hrolf on the shoulder. The blade cut through the steel rings of the mail shirt and grazed the flesh, but that was all. The armourers of Castle Borve made good armour. In an instant, Hrolf was on his feet again, breathing hard but with Tyrving firm in both hands.

'Cheat,' said the sorcerer-king.

'Cheat yourself,' replied Hrolf, and lunged. The sorcerer-king raised his guard and parried the blow with the foible of his blade. Hrolf leant back, and the sorcerer-king swept a powerful blow at his feet. But Hrolf had anticipated that, and jumped over the blade. The sorcerer-king only just managed to avoid his counter-attack.

'Sure you wouldn't rather toss for it?' panted the sorcerer-king. 'Use your own coin if you like.'

Hrolf shook his head and struck a blow to the neck. His opponent stopped it with the cross-guard, and threw his weight forward, sliding his sword down Hrolf's blade until the hilts locked. For a moment, Hrolf was taken off balance, but just in time he moved his feet and drew his sword away sharply. The sorcerer-king staggered, lost his footing and fell, his sword flying from his hand as he hit the ground. Before he could get up, Hrolf was standing over him, and the point of Tyrving was touching his throat.

'Now we'll toss for it,' Hrolf said.

'Why now?' said the sorcerer-king bitterly. 'You could have done me an injury.'

'Heads,' said Hrolf, 'I let you have your sword back.' The

sorcerer-king started to protest violently, but Hrolf smiled. 'What's up?' he said. 'Lost your sense of humour?' He lifted the sword and rested it against his shoulder.

'All right, Cleverclogs,' said the sorcerer-king, struggling to his feet, 'you've made your point. Can we call a halt to all this fooling-about now?'

Hrolf grinned and put his foot on the sorcerer-king's sword. 'Is your name really Eric?' he asked.

'There's no need to go on about it,' muttered the sorcerer-king. 'I tried spelling it with a K, but people still laughed.'

'I think it's a nice name,' said King Hrolf.

'You would.'

'Seriously, though,' said King Hrolf, leaning on his sword, 'I've got to kill you sooner or later, and I'd much rather you defended yourself.' He kicked Ifing over to the sorcerer-king, who scowled at it distastefully.

'I'm not really evil, you know,' said the sorcerer-king.

'You do a pretty good imitation.'

'Where I went wrong was fooling about with magic,' the sorcerer-king went on. 'Dammit, I don't even enjoy it. I'd far rather slop around in old clothes and play a few games of Goblin's Teeth.'

'Goblin's Teeth?'

'It's a sort of a game, with dice and—'

'I know,' said the King, with a strange expression on his face. 'So you play Goblin's Teeth, do you?'

'Yes,' said the sorcerer-king. 'Why, do you?'

The King inspected his fingernails. 'I used to dabble a bit,' he mumbled.

'Really?'

'Actually,' the King admitted, 'I was Baltic Champion one year. Pure fluke, of course.'

'I won the Swedish Open two years running,' said the sorcerer-king with immense pride. 'I cheated,' he admitted.

'You can't cheat at Goblin's Teeth,' said the King. 'It's impossible.'

The sorcerer-king smirked. 'No, it's not,' he said.

'Go on, then,' said King Hrolf, 'how's it done?'

'I can't explain just like that,' said the sorcerer-king. 'I need the board and the pieces.' He stopped, and gazed at Hrolf hopefully. 'You haven't got a set, by any chance? I lost mine back in the fifteenth century.'

'No,' said King Hrolf, his eyes shining, 'but I know someone who has.'

Brynjolf sat up and rubbed his head. It hurt.

'What happened?' he asked.

'No idea.' Brynjolf looked up and saw Arvarodd leaning against the car. 'But it's not looking too bad at the moment. Is it, Kotkel?' But the wizard shook his head, and made a sound like a worried cement-mixer.

'Pessimist,' said Arvarodd. 'Me, I always look on the bright side. Even when that perishing wolf was standing over me making snarling noises, I said to myself: Arvarodd, you've been in worse scrapes than this one.'

'Where?' muttered Brynjolf. 'In Permia?'

'I'll ignore that remark,' said Arvarodd coldly. 'And, sure enough, I just pretended to be dead and it went away. Saw a rabbit, I think. Then, I grant you, I passed out. But I'm still alive, aren't I?'

'Where's Vel-Hilda?' said Brynjolf.

'Here,' said Hildy as she came out from the spinney. 'I've been wolf-hunting. Look.'

On the end of the piece of rope she held in her hand was a sullen-looking wolf. 'Sit,' she said. The wolf glared at her, and sat.

'I'm going to call you Spot, aren't I, boy?' she said. The wolf growled, but she took a pebble from her pocket and showed it to him. He wagged his tail furiously and rolled on his back, waving his paws in the air.

'What are you so cheerful about?' said Brynjolf resentfully.

'I've just seen the King through the seer-stone,' she said. 'He's all right and I think he's captured the Enemy. In fact, they seemed to be getting on fine.' She leant forward and tickled the wolf's stomach. 'Who's got four *feet* then?' she asked. The wolf scowled at her.

187

'By the way,' said Arvarodd, 'in case you were worried, we're all alive.'

'I know,' said Hildy, apparently oblivious to all irony. 'I made sure of that before I went after the wolf. Lucky.'

'I dunno,' moaned Brynjolf. 'Women.' He turned himself into a statue of himself. Statues, especially stone ones, do not have headaches. Hildy tied the wolf's lead to his arm and sat down.

'I'm glad it's all worked out so well,' she said.

# 12

'THIS', Hildy said, 'is for you.'

'Are you sure?' said the King gravely. Hildy nodded.

'Yes,' she said, and handed the decanter to him. She had finally traded in all her Esso tokens. 'Think of me when you use it in Valhalla,' she said.

'I shall, Vel-Hilda,' replied the King. 'What's it for?'

'You could put mead in it,' she said. 'But be careful. It's fragile.'

The King nodded, and with scrupulous care wrapped it up in his beaver-fur mantle. 'It is a kingly gift,' he lied.

The last rays of the setting sun shone in through the skylights of the Castle of Borve. It had not been easy getting there through the cordon of armoured cars, and in the end the wizard had had to make them all invisible. This had caused difficulties; in particular, Arvarodd kept treading on Hildy's feet, which he could not see, and it took the wizard several hours and three or four embarrassingly unsuccessful attempts to make them all visible again. Eventually, however, they had reached the castle, where the other heroes, located by Hildy through the seer-stone and warned by Brynjolf in corvid form to expect them, had prepared a triumphant banquet of barbecued seagull and seaweed mousse.

'Time to switch on the lights,' said the King. He nodded to Kotkel, who connected some wires up to the two chthonic spirits, who were sulking. They had just been playing a three-handed game of Goblin's Teeth with the sorcerer-king, and they suspected him of cheating.

'Don't ask me how,' whispered Zxerp to his companion. 'I just know it, that's all.'

Two great golden cauldrons, filled from the enchanted beer-can, were passed round the table, and Danny Bennett replenished his horn. It had been made by Weyland himself from the horns of a prize oryx, and the spell cast on it protected the user from even the faintest ill-effects the next morning. That was probably just as well. Nevertheless, he had reason to celebrate, for his career and his BAFTA award were now both secure; his interview with King Hrolf, complete with an utterly convincing display of magical effects by the wizard to lend credibility to the story, was safely in the can, thanks to a video-camera he had recovered from the spoils of the Vikings' most recent encounter with the forces sent to subdue them. Angantyr had been the cameraman; he had shown a remarkable aptitude for the job, which did not surprise Danny in the least. 'You're a born cameraman,' Danny had said to him, as they had played the tape back on the monitor. Fortunately, Angantyr was ignorant enough to take this as a compliment.

'I'll make sure you get your credit,' Danny assured him. 'Camera – A. Asmundarson, and the EETPU can go play with themselves.' He drained his horn and refilled it.

'Pity I won't see it,' said Angantyr.

'If only you were staying on,' Danny said. 'I could get you a job, no trouble at all.'

'Wish I were,' said Angantyr. 'The way you describe it, sounds like the life would suit me fine. But there it is.'

'Tell you what,' said Danny, putting his arm round his friend's shoulders, 'why don't you take the camera and the monitor with you to Valhalla? There's plenty of spare tapes. It'd be something to do if you got tired of fighting and feasting.'

'Good idea,' said Angantyr. He filled up his friend's horn. 'In return, I must give you a gift.'

'A gift?' Danny beamed.

'A gift,' said Angantyr, wishing he hadn't.

'Really?' Danny slapped him on the back, making him spill his horn. 'That's . . . well, I'm touched, I am really.'

'Oh, it's just heroic tradition,' said Angantyr, wiping beer off his mailshirt. He felt slightly ashamed of his previous reluctance, and considered what Danny might find most useful. An enchanted helmet? An arrow that never missed its mark, in case he ever went feature-hunting again? Somehow, such a gift seemed meagre. He braced himself for the ultimate act of generosity.

'I shall give you', he said tight-lipped, 'my own recipe for cream of seagull soup.'

'Oh,' said Danny. 'How nice. Hold on while I find a pencil. Right.'

'First,' Angantyr dictated, 'catch your seagull. . . .'

'Count yourself lucky,' said Arvarodd. 'It's a damn sight better than "Arvarodd of Permia".'

'I suppose so,' said Hildy sadly. 'Even so. . . .'

'Even so nothing.' Arvarodd sighed. 'I had dreams, you know, once. Poet-Arvarodd, or Arvarodd the Phrase-Maker, was what I wanted to be called. And, instead, what am I remembered for? Bloody Permia. At least', he said, brightening slightly, 'my saga survived. That's one in the eye for King Gautrek. I told him when he showed me his manuscript. Illiterate rubbish for people who move their lips when they read.'

Hildy nodded. She did not have the heart to tell him that *Gautrek's Saga* had made it through the centuries as well, and was regarded as the masterpiece of the genre. Men die, cattle die, only the glories of heroes live for ever, as the Edda says.

'But I was never satisfied with it,' Arvarodd continued. 'Needed cutting.' He fell silent and blushed.

'What is it, Arvarodd?' Hildy asked. He looked away.

'I don't suppose,' he said suddenly. 'No, it's a lot to ask, and I don't want to be a nuisance.'

'What?' Hildy leant forward.

'Well,' Arvarodd said, and from inside his mail shirt he

drew a thick scroll of vellum manuscript. 'Perhaps, if you've got a moment, you might. . . .'

Hildy smiled. 'I'd be delighted,' she said. She glanced at the scrawl of runes at the top of the first page. "Arvarodd's Saga 2," it read, "The Final Battle." Out of the bundle of sheets floated a scrap of fading papyrus. Hildy caught hold of it and ran her scholar's eye over it. 'Dear Mr Arvarodd, although I greatly enjoyed your work, I regret to say that at this time. . . .' Hildy felt a tear escaping from the corner of her eye; then a sudden inspiration struck her.

'When did you write this?' she asked.

'Just before the battle of Melvich,' said Arvarodd. 'I was greatly influenced at the time by. . . .'

Hildy thought fast. The manuscript was twelve hundred years old; carbon dating would verify that. No one would be able to doubt its authenticity. And if she was quick she would just be in time for the next edition of the *Journal of Scandinavian Studies*.

'What you need', she said, 'is a good agent.'

'Checkmate,' said the sorcerer-king.

'Sod it,' said Prexz.

'That's nine games to us,' said King Hrolf, 'and none to you. Mugs away.'

'You're cheating,' said Zxerp angrily.

'Prove it,' said the sorcerer-king.

'What I still don't understand', said Starkad Storvirksson, 'is how it manages to move without oars.'

Hildy scratched her head. 'Well,' she said desperately, 'it's magic.'

'Oh,' said Starkad. 'Why didn't you say so?'

'Starkad,' said Brynjolf, 'why don't you go and get Vel-Hilda some more seagull?'

'Actually,' Hildy started to say, but Brynjolf kicked her under the table. Starkad got up and went to the great copper cauldron that was simmering quietly on the hearth.

'I'm very fond of Starkad,' said Brynjolf, 'but there are times. . . .'

At the other end of the table, Danny was telling the sleeping Angantyr all about his President Kennedy theory. Hildy sighed.

'I wish you all didn't have to go,' she said. 'There's so much you haven't seen, so much you could do. We need you in the twentieth century.'

'I doubt it,' said Arvarodd. 'There aren't any more wolves to kill or sorcerers to be overthrown, and I think we'd just cause a lot of confusion.'

'Let's face it,' said Brynjolf, 'if it hadn't been for you, Vel-Hilda, I don't know what would have happened.'

Hildy blushed. 'I didn't do much,' she said.

'No one ever does,' said Arvarodd, smiling. 'What are the deeds of heroes, except a few frightened people doing the best they can in the circumstances? Sigurd had no trouble at all killing the dragon; it was a very old dragon, and its eyesight was starting to go. If he'd waited another couple of weeks it would have died of old age.'

'Or take Beowulf,' said Brynjolf. 'Weedy little bloke, got sand kicked in his face on the beach as often as not. But he just happened to be in the right place at the right time. It's not who you are that matters, it's what you do.'

'No,' said Arvarodd, 'you're wrong there. It's not what you do, it's who you are.'

'Whichever.' Brynjolf frowned. 'Or both. Anyway, Vel-Hilda, what I'm trying to say is that we couldn't have managed without you. Well, that's not strictly true,' he added. 'But you helped.'

'That's right.' Arvarodd nodded vigorously. 'You helped a lot.'

'Any time,' said Hildy. 'I'll miss you. It won't be the same, somehow.'

'Sorry, Vel-Hilda,' said Starkad Storvirksson, returning with an empty plate, 'but Bothvar Bjarki had the last of the seagull. There are still a few baked mice, if you'd like some.'

193

'No, thanks,' said Hildy, 'really. I couldn't eat another thing.'

Starkad breathed a sigh of relief and went off to eat them himself.

'I'm quite partial to a bit of baked mouse,' said Arvarodd, leaning back in his seat and pouring himself a hornful of beer. 'I remember when I was in Permia. . . .'

'Checkmate.'

Zxerp glared at King Hrolf with deep hatred. 'You two', he said at last, 'deserve each other.'

King Hrolf rose to his feet and banged on the table for silence. He poured a horn of beer from the decanter and drank it, then cleared his throat. Even Angantyr woke up. The company turned their heads and listened.

'Friends,' said the King, 'our work is done. Despite the perils that threatened us, we have overthrown the power of darkness and saved the world from evil.'

'Steady on,' said the sorcerer-king.

'Now our time in this world, which has been unnaturally long, is over, and it is time for us to go to feast for ever in Odin's golden hall. Roast pork,' he added before Angantyr could interrupt, 'and all the mead you can drink. At the head of the table sits Odin himself; at his right hand Thor, at his left Frey. With her own hands Freyja pours the mead, and the greatest of heroes are the company. There we will meet many we have known, many of whom we have sent there, in the old wars which are forgotten. They say that in Valhalla the men go out to fight in the morning, and at night all those who have fallen rise up again to go to the feast, and fight again the next day. There is also, I am assured, a swimming-pool and a sauna. Personally, I think it all sounds very boring being cooped up with a lot of dead warriors all day, but don't let me put you off. I intend to take a good book with me. Anyway, tomorrow we sail across the great sea. Long will be our journey, past Iceland and Greenland and into the region of everlasting cold, until we pass over the edge of the world and see before us Bifrost, the rainbow bridge.'

Hildy scratched her head. If they followed the route the King had described, it sounded to her as if they would end up at Baffin Island. But she had stopped doing geography in fourth grade, and only recently found out where Hungary is.

'Sorcerer-Eric and I have settled our differences,' continued the King, 'and he will be coming with us to Valhalla.' A murmur ran round the table, but the King held up his hand. 'That is settled,' he said firmly. 'He has been an evil man and our and the world's enemy, but in Valhalla all earthly enmities are put aside, for all who go there, so it is said, are soon united in common hatred of the catering staff. Besides, there is always a place at Odin's table for men who are brave and have fought well, however misguided their cause, and who can play a good game of Goblin's Teeth.'

The murmur subsided. That, after all, was fair enough.

'Behind us', went on the King, 'we leave one who has deserved a place in the company of heroes, our sister Vel-Hilda Frederik's-daughter. But for her.... Well, she helped, and it is not by blows or good policies alone that battles are won.'

That didn't leave much, Hildy reflected, but presumably he meant it kindly. She blushed.

'In our day, the skalds would have sung of her deeds; but now, it seems, the skalds sing no more at the feasts of kings. In our day, her story would have been told by the fireside, when the shadows are long and children hear ghosts when the sheep climb on to the roof to eat the houseleeks. But of our last fight no songs will be made; no one will ever know that we have been here or done what we have done. So it will be for all of us at the world's end, we who thought to cheat death by living for ever in the words of men. Nevertheless.' The King smiled and made a sign with his hand. Arvarodd rose to his feet, and drew a harp out from under the table. 'I wrote it in the car coming up,' he whispered, as Hildy's eyes started to fill with tears. 'Hope you like it.'

'Vel-Hilda,' said the King, 'you have deserved a song,

195

and one song you shall have. Arvarodd of Permia,' he commanded, 'sing us your song.'

'The name of this song is Hildarkvitha,' proclaimed Arvarodd. 'Any unauthorised use of this material may render the user liable to civil and criminal prosecution.' He drew his fingers across the strings, took a deep breath and sang:

> 'Attend!
> We have heard the glories
> Of god-like kings,
> Heard the praise
> And the passion of princes. . . .'

Hildy stifled a sob and reached for her notebook.

The young lieutenant was excited. He had never been in this sort of situation before.

'We've found them,' he said. 'They're back in that fortified position on the cliffs above Farr. God knows why we didn't leave a unit there; they were bound to come back. Anyway, that's where they are. Do we go in, or what?'

The man in the black pullover scowled at him.

'Oh, go away,' he said.

Young Mr Fortescue stared in disbelief at the While-You-Were-Out message on his desk.

Message from Eric Swenson, Chairman and Managing Director, Gerrards Garth group of companies.

Expansion programme scratched owing to unforeseen difficulties, so no China for you. Consolation prize chair, managing directorship of entire shooting match, try not to cock it up too much, why am I saying this, that's why we've chosen you. Written confirmation follows, good luck, you'll need it, suggest you get out of electronics entirely.

Message at 10.34.

It would, of course, be a challenge, and it was nice to think that the boss had such confidence in him ('that's why we've chosen you'). Nevertheless, it would have been better if he had known he was being groomed for greatness rather earlier. He could have taken notes.

'All aboard,' said Danny Bennett cheerfully. 'Move right down inside please.'

The entire company was embarking. They were going on a long tour of the kingdom of Caithness and Sutherland, just for old times' sake and to fill in the hours before it was time to set sail; down Strathnaver to Kinbrace and Helmsdale, then up the coast to Wick and across to Thurso, and on to Rolfsness. The tank was full of petrol, magically produced by the wizard from peat.

'Danny's in no fit state to drive, you know,' Hildy whispered. The King smiled.

'For some reason he wanted to,' he said. 'Insisted that it was his bus, he'd captured it single-handed, so he was going to drive. The wizard's put a spell on him, so we should be all right.'

Hildy shrugged. 'Oh, well,' she said, 'if you're sure. I've done enough driving these last few weeks to last me, anyway.'

These last few weeks. . . . How long had it been since her adventure started? She could not remember. It had been the same with holidays when she was a girl; week merged seamlessly with week, and soon she had not known which day of the week it was, or what month, or what season of the year, except that the sun always seemed to shine. It was, of course, shining now; strong orange evening light that made even the scraggy brown sheep look somehow enchanted.

'Hrolf,' she asked, 'what am I going to do once you've all gone?'

'As little as possible for at least a month,' replied the King. 'First, you're going to have to help Danny Bennett explain all this to the rest of the world – only for God's sake don't let him tell them the whole truth. Have you still got that bit of jawbone Arvarodd gave you? That ought to do the trick.'

'Shouldn't I give it back?'

'Certainly not,' said the King. 'It makes him insufferable. We'll see just how long his reputation as a wise counsellor lasts without it. Anyway, after you've done

197

that, I advise you to go away for a while and persuade yourself that none of this ever happened. It'll be for the best, in the long run.'

'Oh, no,' Hildy said, 'I couldn't do that. Even if I wanted to.'

'And you don't.'

'No. I've had' – Hildy searched for the right words – 'the time of my life,' she said.

'Funny,' said the King. 'Oh, well, it takes all sorts. I'm not exactly overjoyed at the prospect of going to Valhalla myself, but I haven't got much of a choice.'

'Shall I see you there?' Hildy asked suddenly. 'Eventually, I mean?'

'I haven't the faintest idea,' said the King. 'But don't be in any hurry to find out.'

'I won't, don't you worry,' said Hildy, grinning. 'I guess I've had my adventure. And I know what I'm going to do. I'm going to publish the saga that Arvarodd gave me, and become the world's leading authority on the heroic age of Scandinavia. They'll make me a full professor before I'm thirty.'

'Is that a good thing?'

'Probably. Anyway, it's what I want to do, and I reckon I'll do it rather better now that I know what it was really like.'

'What was it really like, Vel-Hilda?'

'Just like everything else,' said Hildy, 'only there were less people, so what they did mattered more at the time.'

'You could put it like that.'

'I will,' Hildy assured him, 'only with plenty of footnotes. Of course, I won't be able to tell them about the magic, so most of what I say will be totally untrue. You won't mind that, will you?'

'Nothing to do with me,' said King Hrolf.

'It'll be strange, of course. When I'm giving a lecture on Bothvar Bjarki and speculating on whether he was really just a sun-god motif imported from early Indo-European myth.'

'Is he?'

198

'Undoubtedly,' Hildy said. 'The parallels are conclusive.'

'I'll tell him that,' said the King. 'He'll be livid.'

'So are you,' she said, 'probably. Or you're an amalgamation of several pseudo-historical early dynasties, conflated by oral tradition and rationalised by the chroniclers. Your deeds are a fictionalised account of tribal disturbances during the Age of Migrations, and you have no real basis in historical fact.'

'Thank you, Vel-Hilda,' said the King. 'That's the nicest thing anyone's ever said about me.'

'What about me, then?' said the sorcerer-king, leaning over from the row in front.

'Oh, you're just a personification of bad harvests and various diseases of livestock,' said Hildy. 'No one's ever going to believe in you.'

'I believe in me,' said the sorcerer-king.

'And look where it's got you,' said King Hrolf.

'True,' said the sorcerer-king. 'But aren't I in Arvarodd's saga?'

'Like he said himself, it's heavily influenced by the *fornaldarsögur* tradition. You're symbolic.'

'Allegorical?'

'Very.'

'Oh. Fancy a quick game, then?'

'Later,' said the King. The sorcerer-king leant forward again and scratched the wolf behind the ear. It growled resignedly.

'That's sad, in a way,' said King Hrolf. 'I wouldn't have minded being forgotten, but I'm not so keen on being debunked.'

'Men die,' Hildy quoted, 'cattle die, but the glory of heroes lives for ever. It's just that these days people hate leaving well alone. They can't bear anything to be noble and splendid any more. But who knows? In a couple of hundred years or so, they may start believing in the old stories again. That'd be nice, wouldn't it?'

'Like I said,' replied the King, 'nothing to do with me. There was a man at my father's court who had been a very great hero in his youth. He'd been with King Athils, and he'd killed frost-giants, and he'd wrestled with Thor himself. Unfortunately, he made the mistake of surviving all his adventures and becoming old. Nobody believed he was still alive any more, and when he used to tell stories of his youthful feats, people used to think he was wandering in his wits and either pretending or believing that he was one of the heroes out of the fairy-tales he'd heard as a boy. So he stopped telling his own stories, and had to sit still in the evenings when the poet sang songs about him, which were always inaccurate and sometimes downright slander. In the end he did go mad and started telling everyone that he'd created the world. Nobody took any notice, of course. It's a terrible thing to be a legend in your own lifetime.'

'What was his name?' Hildy asked. 'Maybe. . . .'

'Can't remember,' said the King. 'It was a long time ago.'

Suddenly the King and the entire bus disappeared, and Hildy could see the ground moving below her at about forty miles an hour. She started to shriek, then realised that the wizard had made the bus invisible to get them past the soldiers. She started to laugh; she would never get used to magic, but she would miss it when it wasn't there any more. She said as much to where the King had been. He agreed.

'I've never given it much thought,' he said. 'It's like winter, or all these new machines of yours. You don't know how they work, but you accept them as part of life. We used to enjoy our magic rather more than you do. In fact, we enjoyed everything rather more than you do, probably because the conditions of life were rather more horrible then than now. I'm starting to sound my age, aren't I?'

'You don't look it,' said Hildy.

'That', said the King, 'is because I'm invisible.'

The surveyor opened the door of his car.

'Hold on,' he said, 'I'm just going to take a leak.'

A still night on the Ord of Caithness, with only the pounding of the sea on the rocks below to disturb the

200

silence. God, how he hated this place!

Suddenly, round the bend of the road came a number 87 bus. That was strange enough at half-past one in the morning, but what was stranger still was the fact that it appeared to be full of Viking warriors, plainly visible in the pale ghostly glow of two points of light that shone from inside. The warriors were singing, although he could not hear them, and passing a drinking-horn from hand to hand; and there, sitting on the back seat, was that female archaeologist he had taken up to Rolfsness just before she disappeared so mysteriously. The surveyor stared. The archaeologist – or her spectre – was waving to him. He shuddered, and remembered the old tales of the phantom coach taking the souls of the dead to Hell that he had always been so scornful of as a boy. The bus moved silently, eerily on, and suddenly vanished from sight.

Trembling, the surveyor returned to the car.

'I've just seen a phantom bus,' he said. 'An eighty-seven, with Rolfsness on the front.'

'Time you got a new joke, Donald,' said his companions, who hadn't been watching. 'That one wasn't even funny the first time.'

Past the new wind-generator high above the road ('Look, Prexz, electricity on draught!'). Past the turf-roofed houses of Ulbster and Thrumster, looking exactly as their prede-cessors had done when Hrolf's subjects had built them as Ideal Homes twelve hundred years ago. Past Gills Bay and Scarfskerry, where Bothvar Bjarki had watched the circ-ling cormorants and given the place its name. Past Dunnet Head and Castletown, the slate fences with broom twigs tucked into them to frighten away the deer. Past Scrabster ('I could tell you a thing or two about Scrabster,' muttered Hring Herjolfsson), and the strange complex of buildings that Hildy said was a power station and which made Zxerp and Prexz suddenly feel thirsty. The flat coastal strip dwindled away into moorland and rock, and Ben Ratha was visible against the night sky. Across the little burn called Achadh na Greighe ('I never could cope with those damnfool Gaelic names,' said Angantyr. 'Why not call it something straightforward, like Sauthajarmrsfjall?'). Ben Ruadh. Rolfsness.

'It was nice to see it all again,' said King Hrolf. 'Godforsaken place, Caithness, but what the hell, it was my kingdom.'

'I like it,' said Hildy faintly. 'It's sort of—'

'You would,' said the King. 'Come to Caithness, they said to my grandfather, the Soft South. Agreed, it's a bit less bleak than Norway or Iceland, and there are bits of Sweden I wouldn't give you a dead vole for. It's all right, I suppose. In its way.'

The moon mirrored in the waters of Loch Hollistan. A rabbit scurrying for cover as the company approached. The sea.

'Well,' said Angantyr, 'here we all are again.' He slapped Danny Bennett violently on the back. 'It's been fun. Thanks for your help, and remember – you don't add the fennel until the meat is almost brown.'

'I'll remember,' said Danny. He suspected a bone was broken.'Remember, if in doubt, stop down. Better to be a stop over than a stop under.'

The great mound, covered over and wired off, a slice cut out of it by the archaeologists. The King shook his head. 'I don't know what they're all so excited about,' he said, as he saw the signs of their scrupulous and scientific work. 'It's just a mound of earth, that's all.'

The ship. The moon flashed on the gilded prow, the gilded shields along its sides. As they stood and gazed at it, the west wind started to blow.

'I hate to mention this,' said the King, 'but how the hell are we going to get it down to the beach?'

'Same way we got it up, I suppose,' said Hjort cheerfully. 'Starkad, get the ropes.'

'Couldn't we all go in the bus instead?' pleaded Starkad. 'It's so nice and comfy.'

Patiently, Brynjolf explained that the bus wouldn't go over water.

'Why?' asked Starkad.

Brynjolf thought for a moment. 'Because it hasn't got any oars, Starkad,' he said.

'Oh,' said Starkad Storvirksson. 'Pity, that.' He disappeared into the hold of the ship and emerged with several huge coils of rope. 'They're all sticky,' he said.

'That's the preservative they've put on them,' said Hildy. 'Lucky they didn't take them back to the labs.'

Starkad passed ropes underneath the keel and called to the heroes, who took their axes and set about demolishing the mound and the trellis of oak-trunks. In a remarkably short time, the work was finished, and the heroes took their places at the ropes.

'Better get a move on,' said the King, looking at the sky. 'It'll be dawn soon, and I want to catch the tide.'

With a shout, the heroes pulled on the ropes and the ship rose up out of the ground. Starkad tied a line round the figurehead and, exerting all his extraordinary strength, dragged the ship off the cradle of ropes on to the grass. The other champions joined him, and, with a superhuman effort and a great deal of bad language, hauled Naglfar down the long slope to the beach. As the keel slid into the water, Starkad gave a great shout.

'Is that his battle-cry?' Hildy asked.

'No,' said Arvarodd, 'the keel went over his foot.'

The first streaks of light glimmered in the East, and the heroes saluted the coming dawn with drawn swords. The wizard stepped forward and, sounding like a hierophantic lawn-mower engine, blessed the longship for its final voyage. Bothvar Bjarki hauled on the yards, and the sail rose to the masthead and filled as the west wind grew stronger. On the sail was King Hrolf's own device, a great dragon curled round a five-pointed star.

'I told the sailmakers Earthstar,' he explained, 'but they had to know best. That or they couldn't read my writing.'

'So this is goodbye,' said Hildy.

'About my manuscript,' said Arvarodd. 'The middle section needs cutting.'

'I'm sure it doesn't,' said Hildy. There were tears in her eyes, but her voice was steady.

'I'm appointing you my literary executor,' Arvarodd went on. 'I know you'll do a good job. And I want you to keep those things I gave you – you know, the jawbone and the pebbles and things. I won't need them again, and. . . .'

He turned away and went down to join the other heroes.

'Right, Vel-Hilda,' said the King, 'it's time we were going. Kotkel wants you to keep the seer-stone, and we both think you should hang on to these.'

He handed her a bundle wrapped in a sable cloak. She took it.

'That's the Luck of Caithness,' he said. 'After all, you never know. There may be new sorcerers one day. And we're letting Zxerp and Prexz stay behind; they've earned their freedom, and they've promised to be good.'

'We're going to go and live at the hydro-electric plant on Loch Shin,' said a faint light at Hildy's feet.

'But the condition of their freedom is that, if ever you need them, they'll be ready and waiting. Won't you?' said the King menacingly. 'Because if you don't Kotkel has put a spell on you, and you'll end up in the National Grid so fast you won't know what's hit you.' The lights flickered nervously. 'Oh, and by the way,' added the King, 'thanks for the Goblin's Teeth set.'

'You're welcome,' snarled Zxerp. 'We were bored with it anyway.'

'Also in the bundle', said the King, 'is the sorcerer-king's sword, Ifing. It's lighter in the blade than Tyrving, and easier to handle. That's also just in case, and he won't be needing it. He's a reformed character, I think. And this, Vel-Hilda Frederik's-daughter, is for you, in return for that lovely glass thing and all your help.'

From round his neck he took a pendant on a fine gold chain. 'The kings of Caithness never had a crown,' he said. 'This passed from my grandfather to my father to me. Once it hung round the neck of Lord Odin himself. To wear it is to accept responsibility.' He hung the chain around Hildy's neck. 'I appoint you steward of the kingdom of Caithness and Sutherland, this office to be yours and your children's until the true king comes again to reclaim his own. Which', he added, 'I hope will never happen. Look after it for me, Vel-Hilda.'

Hildy bowed her head and knelt before him. 'Until then,' she said.

'And now I must go, or they'll all start complaining,' said the King, and there were tears in his eyes, too. 'Think of us all, but not too often.'

He put his arms around her and hugged her. Before she could get her breath back, he was gone.

'There he goes,' muttered Zxerp, 'taking the game with him.'

'Cheer up,' said Prexz, softly. 'It could be worse.'

'How?' asked Zxerp.

'I could have forgotten to swipe their chess-set,' chuckled Prexz.

Hildy ran down to the beach. Already the ship was far out to sea, the oars slicing through the black-and-red water. As a dream slips away in the first few moments of waking, it was slipping away towards the edge of the world, going to a place that had never been on any map. Yet as she stood and waved her scarf, she thought she could still hear the groaning of the timbers, the creaking of the oars in their rowlocks, the gurgle of the slipstream as the sharp prow cut the waves, the voices of the oarsmen as they strained at their work.

'I don't suppose anybody thought to pack any food.' Could it be Angantyr's voice, blown back by some freak of the wind? Or was it just the murmuring of the sea?

'You said you were going to pack the food.'

'I didn't.'

'You did.'

'I bloody didn't.'

And perhaps it was the cry of the gulls as they rose to greet the new day, or perhaps it was the voice of the King, just audible over the rim of the sky, telling the sorcerer-king about rule 48. Hildy stood and listened, and the sun rose over the sea in glory. Then she turned, shook her head, and walked away.

About six months later, Hildy sat in her office at the Faculty of Scandinavian Studies at Stony Brook University. It was good to be home again on Long Island, thousands of miles away from her adventure, and she had her new appointment as professor to look forward to and the proofs of *Arvarodd's Saga* to correct. Around her neck was an exquisite gold and amber pendant; a reproduction, she assured all her colleagues, but she knew they had their suspicions. Still, she would continue to wear it a little longer.

She leafed through the day's mail. Three circulars with details of conferences, two letters from universities in Norway asking her to go over and give lectures, yet another flattering offer from Harvard, and a postcard with a stamp she had never seen before. She stared at it.

It had been readdressed from St Andrews and was written in Old Norse. She turned it over; there was a picture of a tall castle. Her heart started beating violently. She screwed up her eyes to read the spidery handwriting.

'Food awful, company worse,' it read. 'My window marked with X (see photo). Arvarodd sends his regards. Hope this reaches you OK. See you in about sixty years, all the best, Hrolf R.'

She lifted her head and looked out of the window. 'Until then,' she said.

Futura now offers an exciting range of quality fiction and non-fiction by both established and new authors. All of the books in this series are available from good bookshops, or can be ordered from the following address:

Futura Books
Cash Sales Department
P.O. Box 11
Falmouth
Cornwall TR10 9EN.

Please send cheque or postal order (no currency), and allow 60p for postage and packing for the first book plus 25p for the second book and 15p for each additional book ordered up to a maximum charge of £1.50 in U.K.

B.F.P.O. customers please allow 60p for the first book, 25p for the second book plus 15p per copy for the next 7 books, thereafter 9p per book.

Overseas customers including Eire please allow £1.25 for postage and packing for the first book, 75p for the second book and 28p for each subsequent title ordered.

# interzone

## SCIENCE FICTION AND FANTASY

Bimonthly          £1.95

- *Interzone* is the leading British magazine which specializes in SF and new fantastic writing. We have published:

| | |
|---|---|
| BRIAN ALDISS | GARRY KILWORTH |
| J.G. BALLARD | DAVID LANGFORD |
| IAIN BANKS | MICHAEL MOORCOCK |
| BARRINGTON BAYLEY | RACHEL POLLACK |
| GREGORY BENFORD | KEITH ROBERTS |
| MICHAEL BISHOP | GEOFF RYMAN |
| DAVID BRIN | JOSEPHINE SAXTON |
| RAMSEY CAMPBELL | BOB SHAW |
| ANGELA CARTER | JOHN SHIRLEY |
| RICHARD COWPER | JOHN SLADEK |
| JOHN CROWLEY | BRIAN STABLEFORD |
| PHILIP K. DICK | BRUCE STERLING |
| THOMAS M. DISCH | LISA TUTTLE |
| MARY GENTLE | IAN WATSON |
| WILLIAM GIBSON | CHERRY WILDER |
| M. JOHN HARRISON | GENE WOLFE |

- *Interzone* has also published many excellent new writers; graphics by **JIM BURNS, ROGER DEAN, IAN MILLER** and others; book reviews, news, etc.

- *Interzone* is available from good bookshops, or by subscription. For six issues, send £11 (outside UK, £12.50) to: **124 Osborne Road, Brighton BN1 6LU, UK** Single copies: £1.95 inc p&p (outside UK, £2.50).

- American subscribers may send $22 ($26 if you want delivery by air mail) to our British address, above. All cheques should be made payable to *Interzone*.

- - - - - - - - - - - - - - - - - - - - - - - - - - - - - - - - - - - - -

To: **interzone** 124 Osborne Road, Brighton, BN1 6LU, UK.

Please send me six issues of *Interzone*, beginning with the current issue. I enclose a cheque/p.o. for £11 (outside UK, £12.50; US subscribers, $22 or $26 air), made payable to *Interzone*.

*Name* _____

*Address* _____

_____